PRAISE FOR
YESTERDAY RISING

"An authentic police voice. It's like going on a ride-along."
—Colin Campbell, author of the
Jim Grant Thrillers

"For fans of TV crime shows, Stephen Burdick's *Yesterday Rising* is one part *Bones*, one part *Cold Case Files*, and one part *Criminal Minds*."
—Tim O'Mara, author of the
Raymond Donne series

"With *Yesterday Rising*, Stephen Burdick delivers a riveting read full of colorful characters. Homicide detective Joe Hampton's retirement to Crimson Conch Condominiums has not gone according to plan. The old detective can't resist the pull of being back on the job. And it turns out that sunny Clearwater Beach can be nearly as gritty as the streets of Philadelphia where he once worked."
—Joel W. Barrows, author of the
Deep Cover thriller series

"*Yesterday Rising*, Stephen Burdick's second set of three novellas featuring retired homicide detective Joe Hampton, is an engaging blend of murder, beautiful Florida settings, well-drawn characters, and challenging whodunits."
—Debra H. Goldstein, author of the
Sarah Blair mystery series

YESTERDAY RISING

BOOKS BY STEPHEN BURDICK

Deemer's Inlet
The Gray Detective
Yesterday Rising

STEPHEN BURDICK

YESTERDAY RISING

Three Crime Novellas

Down & Out Books
3959 Van Dyke Road, Suite 265
Lutz, FL 33558
DownAndOutBooks.com

Cover design by Margo Nauert

ISBN: 1-64396-301-5
ISBN-13: 978-1-64396-301-3

TABLE OF CONTENTS

For Lynn,
My mentor, My friend

MEMORIES
FORGOTTEN

CHAPTER 1

Joe Hampton shifted from one foot to the other and tugged at his tie. Being the focal point of the assembled group of detectives was to blame for his uneasiness, a feeling he hadn't experienced since his days as a rookie patrolman.

He'd been to the Homicide office of the Clearwater Police Department once before and felt like he'd come home. The detectives' desks with computers atop them were neatly arranged, each defining the personality of its owner with paperwork, files, and personal items lying about. The air smelled of various colognes and perfumes blended with strong coffee, a staple of humankind in every office. Gone was the odor of stale cigarette smoke.

Besides being difficult, today was different. Today he was joining the team.

"All right, everyone, listen up!" Detective Sergeant Carly Truffant began. "A suggestion to hire a consultant was passed along to the brass, and they have okayed it."

"Kissing up to the captain again, Carly?" Detective Cliff Parton said.

The group laughed—all but one.

Carly gave Parton a disgusted smile. "Looking to get back into uniform, Cliff?"

"Oooh!" the group sang.

Parton chuckled.

Joe nodded to him then shifted his eyes to the female detective who found no humor in the banter.

"As I was about to say," Carly continued, "our choice for the position is Joe Hampton, although I almost didn't recognize him all dressed up."

The group laughed again—except for the woman.

"Joe is a retired homicide detective from Philadelphia P.D., or Philly, as they like to say, and has assisted us in the past. I feel he will be a tremendous asset. He is with us on an as-needed basis, so let's not work him too hard. Any questions?"

The group murmured while exchanging glances.

Joe made eye contact with each detective before settling on the humorless woman. Her expression never changed.

"Joe, would you like to add anything?"

"Well, it's good to be here, and feel free to call on me at any time, day or night." He turned to Carly. "That's it."

"All right, let's get back to work."

Joe focused on the woman again and watched her all the way to her desk. "Who is that?"

Carly did a quick scanning of the room. "Which one are you talking about?"

"The detective with the sandy blonde hair just sitting down."

"Oh, that's Danielle McMasters. We call her Dani. She's new to the department."

"Takes her job seriously, doesn't she?"

"Doesn't everyone in the beginning?"

Joe glanced at his friend and grinned. "Some still do."

"All right, that's enough out of you."

"I may be wrong, but it seems like she resents me."

"Don't be so sensitive. You're a charming man, but you're not going to win over everyone right away."

"I don't pretend to think that I can, it's just..."

"So how's life at the Crimson Conch?"

"Couldn't be better. Things are running smoothly, residents are happy for the most part, and occupancy, even the rentals, is at capacity."

Carly twisted her mouth into a crooked smile. "Someone told me there's a new love interest in your life."

Joe furrowed his brow. "Who?"

"Who told me, or who's your new friend?"

"Do you mean Leslie?"

Carly's eyes danced skyward. "So now it's *Leslie*."

"Will you stop it! She happens to be from Pennsylvania and we...connected."

"She's from Philadelphia, *and* she has designs on you."

"Who told you that?"

"Hoo! Hoo!" Carly mocked, and laughed. "Ask me no questions, I'll tell you no lies."

Joe growled and shook his head. "Have you seen David lately?"

"Not since last week. I was planning on stopping by his apartment after I was finished here."

"Tell him I said hello, and I'll see him in the next couple of days."

Joe nodded. "The mobility in his shoulder is getting better."

"And I, for one, am glad. I'm hoping to get him back in a week or two."

"He's quite a young man."

"I know. It's not the same without him. I feel like I'm missing my right arm."

"He's a better man than I am."

Carly pinched up her face. She could see the hurt lingering in his eyes. "What're you talking about?"

"He forgave me for getting him shot. I don't think I could have done that."

"Of course you could, Joe. You know the risks of going out in the field every day."

"It should *never* have happened. You know it and I know it. I couldn't..."

"You couldn't what?"

"A couple of years after I made detective I was nearly killed because of a rookie's mistake. He was a patrolman just out of the academy. He mistook me for a killer we'd cornered. Lucky for me he was a bad shot. I was so mad they had to pull me off him. He tried to apologize a number of times. I didn't speak to him for almost a year."

"But you finally had a change of heart."

"Yeah, with a little help." Joe chuckled. "Joyce kept pushing and prodding me the way only she knew how."

"And it all worked out."

"Yeah. Good thing, too. Shortly before I retired that rookie became a captain."

Carly and Joe exchanged smiles as they had done so many times before.

"Well, I'd better get out of the way."

"Joe, let's do dinner sometime soon."

"Sounds good to me."

As he turned for the door, Joe looked over his shoulder.

McMasters's blue eyes were riveted on him, glaring in a most unpleasant manner.

David greeted Joe with a warm smile and a firm handshake at the front door of his apartment. His left arm was still in a sling, but his spirits had been lifted by being out of the hospital—that, and the sight of the old detective.

"Come in, come in. Can I get you some coffee?"

"No, I'm okay." Joe looked around, unsure as to where he should sit. "Is there any place in particular...?"

"No, no, anywhere is fine."

A brown, two-seater sofa shared a chocolate area rug with a gray vinyl recliner. Facing them was a forty-inch television, the only item on the four vanilla walls, except for two wood-framed, black-and-white photos mounted side-by-side on the rear wall.

I guess anywhere is here, Joe thought, and dropped down onto the sofa. "How's your shoulder? I'd have thought you would have tossed the sling by now."

David beamed as he took to the recliner. "I don't need it. I only keep it on because the doctor said I should. You know, keep the department and the insurance company happy."

"When are you planning to go back?"

"Next week, I hope. That's what I'm pushing for."

"Before I forget, Carly says hello, and she'll be coming to see you soon."

David's elation faded. "I sure do miss being at work. I never thought I would. It's funny how you don't think you'll miss something until it's gone. Know what I mean?"

Joe stared at him a second then smiled.

"Of course you know what I mean. How could I be so stupid? You're the new consultant, right?"

Joe fiddled with his tie. "Indoctrinated this morning. I think I'm overdressed."

"I almost didn't recognize you."

"Well, take a good look because you won't see me duded up like this very often."

"Did you meet the gang today?"

"Yes. Not individually, though."

"We have a good team. You'll enjoy working with them."

The thought of inquiring about Danielle McMasters crossed Joe's mind. "I hope so. I'm still not convinced I should have accepted the position."

"Are you kidding? Once you get to know them and they get to know you, you'll be glad you did."

"What can you tell me about Detective McMasters?"

"Dani? She's the newest member of the team. Been with us five or six months, I believe. Why?"

"She didn't seem too thrilled with my being there. Maybe something else was bothering her."

"Really? That's not like her. She's always been very friendly around me."

"Is she having a hard time adjusting to Homicide?"

"Not that I can tell. She's made a few mistakes. New kid stuff, but nothing major."

"Is she married?"

"Why, Joe, I'm surprised at you. She's young enough to be your granddaughter."

"I can tell you're feeling better."

David laughed. "No, she's not married. I don't think there's anyone in her life right now. She hasn't mentioned it, anyway."

Joe nodded.

"Maybe her day didn't start off right. Don't let it worry you."

"Okay. Well, I'd better be going. Time to get back to my other job."

"You keeping all the residents in line?"

"As best I can.

"Carly tells me you've got a new girlfriend."

"Oh, she did, did she? I can see there won't be any secrets with you two around."

David's bursting into laughter made him feel better.

"She just moved in. She's from Pennsylvania. We enjoy talking about home."

"You out-of-towners, I swear."

"What?"

"You move to Florida, but all you talk about is home. Home is where you *are*, Joe, not where you *were*."

"I'll try to remember that."

David walked Joe to the door, and they shook hands. "Don't be a stranger," David said.

"I won't."

As Joe walked to his car, he began to think about Dani McMasters. Something was definitely bothering the rookie detective. And he was sure that something had to do with him.

CHAPTER 2

Memorial Causeway stretched from the edge of downtown Clearwater to Clearwater Beach, flanked on both sides by water. Joe had traveled the road many times, not as many as some of the natives liked to remind him, but as much as any other transplant. Born and raised Floridians always enjoyed poking fun at the newcomers and winter visitors—snowbirds they called them—and their inability to cope with the real Florida weather that arrived in July and August.

Joe had dismissed the events of the morning except for the lingering agitation as to why Dani McMasters had given him the stink-eye. He wasn't a threat to her job. He wasn't taking over the department. To his way of thinking, his knowledge and expertise would seldom be called upon. When it was, she would benefit the most. What she found objectionable about his presence was a mystery to him.

"I guess I remind her of someone she doesn't like," he muttered to himself. "Hope it's not a relative...or her father."

He steered his car onto Island Way and negotiated his way through the parking lot of the Crimson Conch Condominiums a short distance later. Easing to a halt in his designated parking space, he removed his tie, picked up his coat from the passenger seat, and got out.

The mid-morning sun was close to a full burn and baking the asphalt, releasing an all-too-familiar odor as he strolled past the long line of cars. A bead of sweat streamed down the left side of his face, dropping onto his white dress shirt when he mounted the sidewalk under the concrete overhang. Summer was just around the corner and he could feel it already.

The glass doors to the lobby slid open and a blast of cold air rushed out to greet him. A drastic change in temperature that always took some getting used to—the hotter the day, the stronger the shock.

Joe headed straight for the building manager's office. He draped his coat over the back of the padded office chair and sat down, then wheeled himself up to the desk. A flashing light on the telephone indicated that someone had left a message. He punched the button and waited.

"Joe, this is Tessie Birnbaum, number five-fifty-one. The kitchen sink is drooling. Would you, please, arrange for a plumber to come by? Thank you."

Smiling, he picked up the receiver, checked the caller I.D., and rang the woman.

"Oh, Joe, thank goodness. I was getting worried."

"What seems to be the problem, Tessie?"

"The sink is drooling...I mean, water is drooling into the sink from the spout."

"The water won't shut off?"

"The water *is* shut off. It's running into the sink from where the spout goes into the base."

"Sounds like a bad seal. Is the water coming out fast?"

"No, it's just...drooling."

"Okay, I'll get a plumber out here right away."

"It won't burst, will it, Joe? The seal I mean?"

"Don't worry, Tessie. It'll be fine."

Joe let go a sharp exhale through his nose as he hung up the receiver. "At least I hope it'll be fine." He picked up the receiver, pressed the button for the Contacts List then punched the Speed Dial button for Stop-Leak Plumbing.

A soft knocking pulled his eyes to the door. The door slowly opened, and a small, stocky woman stepped into the room. Her smile was as bright as her brown eyes, and the silver streaks in her wavy black hair perfectly framed her soft, round face. The years had forgotten her age, one of the first things he'd noticed when she'd come to inquire about a vacancy. He held up one finger.

"This is Joe Hampton at the Crimson Conch Condominiums. I have a situation that needs attention."

He provided the woman who answered with the information, stressing the concern of the resident, and was assured the problem would be addressed as soon as possible.

Joe replaced the receiver and smiled at the five-foot-three woman standing beside the desk. "And how may I help *you*, Mrs. Symington?"

The woman's smile disappeared, her brow furrowed, and she pressed her lips together in thought.

"I'm looking for someone. He wasn't home, so I left a note on his door, but he hasn't come back yet."

"Have you tried calling him?"

"I did. He didn't answer. I think he forgot his phone."

"What does he look like?"

"He's about your height, has gray hair like yours, and is about the same weight, but he's much better looking."

"Hey!"

The woman laughed—an enjoyable sound that lifted his spirits higher.

Joe laughed with her.

"I'm sorry, Joe. I couldn't resist."

"You're in a good mood today, Leslie."

"So good that I'm thinking of going out for lunch. Care to join me?"

"I'd be delighted."

"Is one o'clock okay? The lunch crowd should start thinning out by then."

"Sure."

"And you'll wear something that won't make you look like an old stuffed shirt?"

"If you insist. Do you have some place special in mind?"

"I've been dying to try Wally's Weiner Wonderland on Pier 60."

"Wally's Weiner Wonderland?"

"They have a wide variety of hot dogs and Bratwurst. You don't care for hot dogs?"

"Well, *frankly* speaking, my dear, we could throw some dogs on the grill out back and *woof* them down by the pool."

Leslie laughed again. "Oh, Joe, you are *so* funny."

"Wally's will be fine."

"I was just joking. I'd really like to go to Frenchy's Rockaway Grill."

Joe's elation vanished.

Leslie noticed the change in him. "Would you rather go somewhere else?" Her voice was soft with concern.

"No, uh, Frenchy's is fine. The food is good."

"What is it, Joe?"

"I'll tell you about it sometime."

He did his best to smile, hoping to chase away the vision of Rusty Goodfellow. Rusty's wife, Nancy, had moved to Boca Raton, unable to remain at the Crimson Conch after Rusty was murdered.

"I don't want to force you if it makes you feel uncomfortable."

Joe shook his head. "You'll like it. I can already taste my favorite, the Mahi Mahi sandwich."

"Are you sure you're okay with going there?"

"Certainly. They have a wonderful view of the Gulf."

Leslie was still tentative as she lingered by door. "I'll meet you in the lobby at one o'clock, okay?"

"See you then."

After she was gone, Joe leaned back in the chair and folded his hands over his stomach. He had had nothing to do with Rusty's death. Tony Dunham or Martha and Lionel Berkshire, either. He had to get over this feeling of guilt.

Of course you didn't, he heard Joyce say.

Then why do I feel so bad?

You can't save everyone, Joe. I know you don't like hearing that.

I can try.

You have tried. And you did your best. Now let it go. You deserve to be happy.

I don't know if I can. I keep thinking about David.

He forgave you. Now forgive yourself.

The phone rang and shattered his thoughts. After a deep breath he picked up the receiver.

"Joe, it's Carly. You don't have your cell phone, do you?"

"I guess I left it in the condo. You need me already?"

"Yep, a slice and dice at the end of Pierce Street and Ewing Avenue on the east side of Prospect Lake Park. I need you to help us put the pieces together."

"That's a terrible pun. Pierce Street? Close to the station?"

"Yeah, it's two blocks west of the park. Get here as soon as you can, okay?"

"Give me ten minutes."

Joe cradled the receiver and sat back. An odd sense of relief flowed through him. Now he wouldn't have to confront his demons by going to Frenchy's. The reason was not the best, but a viable reason, nonetheless. And Joyce was right. He needed to forgive himself. That would come in time. For now he would change clothes, grab his phone, and call Leslie. He paused. She deserved better than a phone call. He'd apologize to her face-to-face on his way out.

CHAPTER 3

On Chestnut Street, followed by a turn onto Ewing Avenue, Joe was battling additional guilt. The disappointment he saw on Leslie's face when he told her he couldn't make their lunch date only compounded his uneasiness. He entertained thoughts of bowing out of the consultant position, envisioning disruption after disruption of his personal life. Especially since Leslie had entered the picture. Eighteen years as a detective had produced enough turmoil for one person to bear. Only Joyce's patience and understanding had saved their marriage. At this point in his life, the last thing he needed was the phone calls at all hours and seeing more dead people. Joyce was right. He'd done his best. He shouldn't offer to give anymore of himself.

Approaching the dead end where Ewing Avenue and Pierce Street met, he was welcomed to Prospect Lake Park by a familiar sight: Patrol vehicles, uniformed officers, and Criminal Analysis technicians populated the northeast quadrant. Joe slowed his car to a halt when he saw a young patrolman heading in his direction.

Here we go again, he thought. *I wish they'd given me a badge.*

The officer stopped by the driver's-side door and leaned down as Joe lowered the window.

"May I see some identification, please?" the officer said.

"Oh, of course." Joe reached into his right rear pocket, pulled out his wallet, and removed his driver's license. "I'm Joe Hampton."

The young man eyed his license. "Thank you. Mr. Hampton. Sergeant Truffant is expecting you."

"Thank you, Officer, uh...Officer Smith." He stared at the officer's name plate a second time.

"It's okay, Mr. Hampton, I get that a lot."

Joe smiled and nodded then eased the door open. He proceeded to make his way to the sidewalk, bordered on both sides with acorn-bulb lamps, that encircled the lake.

Carly and a Criminal Analysis technician were huddled near a small stand of palm trees, their attention drawn to an object lying at their feet. Joe glanced to his right and noticed a woman stepping away from the pair. Now she was leaning against a chain link fence that marked the boundary line to a tract of private property.

"Here's the first one," Carly said.

Joe looked down at a bare human arm, jagged and severed at the shoulder, lying atop a scattering of brown mulch. The slender wrist and size of the hand suggested it had belonged to a woman.

"You said the first one?"

The technician moved to one side.

A second arm, also chopped off at the shoulder, lay five yards away. A plastic evidence marker sat beside it.

"There are two legs a little farther down by the water."

"Did you find the torso?"

"We're still looking." Carly nodded to the technician. "Desiree Morton, this is Joe Hampton, our new consultant. Tell him what we know so far."

"We found two human arms and two human legs, ethnicity to be determined. One arm and leg appear to be female, the others, male. There's a large amount of discoloration on all the limbs."

"Do the other limbs look as ragged as this one, where it was severed?"

"Yes, Mr. Hampton. In my opinion none of them was surgically removed."

"The legs are closer to the lake?"

"Yes, sir."

"Are there alligators in the lake?"

Morton looked at Carly.

Carly shrugged. "We haven't seen any."

"I don't believe an alligator did this," Morton said.

"I don't, either. Besides, a gator would have stowed it somewhere to eat later."

"It's possible that another animal might have found them," Joe said, "but it's unlikely that an animal or animals would discriminate between male and female body parts." He looked in the direction of the woman standing beside the fence. She hadn't moved. "I'd like to take a look at the legs."

"Thank you, Desiree," Carly said.

As he and Carly strode along the sidewalk, Joe took a long look at the second arm. "Definitely belongs to a man."

Carly didn't speak.

"Are you working this one alone?"

"No, I brought Dani McMasters with me. Her partner is on vacation, and since David is still out, I figured she could use the experience."

"Is that her, leaning against the fence?"

"She lost it the second she saw the first arm. At least she made it to the fence before she tossed her breakfast."

"Glad that never happened to me."

"Me, too."

The veterans exchanged knowing smiles and continued their trek.

The sidewalk began to angle to the left, following the green St. Augustine shoreline. Palm trees were the dominant theme in the park with very little supporting foliage to accompany them. The objects of their curiosity were easy to discover.

Joe took a moment to study one leg then shifted his attention to the other. Similar to the arms, approximately five yards separated the appendages. He turned his gaze to the stand of palm trees before resettling on the limbs in the grass.

"I'm sure you've already determined that whoever did this took great care in their placement," he said.

Carly looked around to make certain they were far enough away from the others. "We've got a psycho on our hands, Joe. I know it and you know it."

"No doubt in my mind."

"And I don't want to think about how many victims there might be."

"We know for certain there are two. What bothers me is the discoloration of the limbs. We could be looking at someone who's been doing this for years."

"I'd hate to think that these have been on ice for any length of time."

"I agree, but it wouldn't be the first time."

"I'll contact the other agencies in the area to see if they've had cases similar to this one."

Nothing else needed to be said. Both of them hoped she was wrong. A serial killer, especially a mutilator, was the last thing they wanted or needed.

Joe spied McMasters as she trudged toward them, more embarrassed than pale. The young detective hung her head when she reached them.

"I'm sorry, Sergeant. It won't happen again."

"It's okay, Dani," Carly said. "And it's okay if it happens again. I threw up on my partner the first time."

McMasters looked up and gave her a weak smile.

"Dani, this is Joe Hampton. You were introduced to him earlier this morning."

"Nice to meet you, Dani."

"Mr. Hampton." The detective's face held no expression.

"Carly, in my opinion, I don't think you're going to find anything else around here. Hate to say it, but we'll just have to wait."

"Why are you giving up?" McMasters asked.

Joe locked eyes with her. "I'm not giving up, Detective. It's just my opinion. This is just the beginning. Whoever did this is..." He stopped, wondering if she would believe him.

"Go ahead, Joe," Carly urged. "She needs to know."

"Whoever did this is issuing a challenge."

"Daring us to catch him?" McMasters asked.

"Right. We don't have enough evidence to even know where to begin to look for this person. And if we don't find any clues, then we'll have to wait until—"

"We find more evidence," McMasters interrupted. "We're dealing with a psycho, aren't we?"

"Let's not jump to conclusions," Carly said. "For now, I want you to scour the lake and see what you can find. Check with Criminal Analysis before you get back to me."

"Do you want me to start a search of runaways and missing persons when we return to the office?"

Smart girl, Joe thought.

"Yes, but let me set some parameters first. Is there anything else, Joe?"

"Let me give everything a good going over, and I'll touch base with you before I leave."

"Okay."

McMasters turned to begin her search of the lake.

"Say, Joe, have you talked to David?" Carly asked.

"Saw him this morning."

McMasters stopped and spun around. "How's he doing?"

"He's looking like his old self again. Says he only wears the sling to keep the doctor and the insurance company happy."

"I'm relieved to hear that. When I first heard what happened, I..." She noticed Carly staring. "I'd better get to work."

Joe watched her hurry down the sidewalk.

"Are you thinking what I'm thinking?" Carly asked.

"If you're thinking that she has designs on David, then yes, I am."

"I wonder if he knows."

"I doubt it. You didn't—until just now."
"All right, smart guy, I think it's time that *you* got to work."
A grin covered Joe's face. "Yes, ma'am."

CHAPTER 4

Joe felt a little better as he drove home. The reason for the animosity being directed at him by Dani McMasters had come to light. She held a secret attraction to Detective David Sizemore. And she blamed Joe for Sizemore's getting shot. As if he weren't already buried in enough guilt of his own.

When the opportunity presented itself, he would square things with McMasters. Show her how badly he felt for a grievous mistake. Prove to her that he wasn't prone to acts of recklessness. Satisfied with his decision, Joe began to ponder his next problem. How would he make up with Leslie?

The fellow Pennsylvanian had garnered his attention the first time he'd seen her. Initially reluctant to act since his instant attraction to Victoria Combes had proved nearly fatal, he'd remained detached. Whether obvious to her or not, she showed no signs of ceasing her efforts to make a connection, appearing more and more often to go out of her way to be around him. After a time, he had relented. Feeling he'd probably overreacted in the beginning. Spurred on by increasing loneliness, he welcomed seeing her more and more. A decision she relished.

He was blessed with the perfect idea as he entered the condo parking lot and parked in his designated space. The remedy was simple: he'd invite Leslie to supper. He shook his head, wondering why he'd agonized so long to come up with such a simple solution.

"I hate being old," he muttered.

Getting out of his car, he headed for the entrance. He noticed dark clouds forming over the Gulf and figured that rain was on the way. Or they might be empties from Cuba on their way to the Panhandle. Once inside, he glanced around the lobby. "I've got to remember to thank the maintenance crew," he whispered. "They always do such a fine job keeping the place so neat and clean."

He breezed around the corner, ignoring his own office, and headed straight for the elevator.

Leslie resided on the top floor of the eight-story building, the "top of the world," she called it. Another condo on a lower floor had been available when she'd come searching, but she'd preferred the highest roost.

"I can see clear to the Gulf of Mexico," she'd told him. "It's so beautiful."

Joe's excitement mounted as he stood in front of her door. He took a deep breath and cleared his throat before knocking.

A few seconds passed. Time enough for her to look through the peephole.

He heard the chain lock rattle and the deadbolt slide before the door opened. Seeing her, he offered his best smile.

"Oh, Joe, I'm so glad you're back. Please come inside." Her expression suggested concern more than unhappiness.

"Is anything wrong?"

Leslie closed the door behind him.

"About an hour after you stopped by this morning, I went downstairs. I was going to take a walk to get some exercise and then sit by the pool for a while. It's such a lovely day." Her brown eyes widened. "Just as I came out of the elevator a man was walking toward me from the lobby. I'd never seen him before."

"Leslie, you haven't lived here very long. I'm certain there are a number of people you haven't seen before. This is a very large building."

"Joe, he acted confused, like he didn't know where he was going. He smiled when he walked past me and went out the rear door."

"Did you see him again?"

"I went to the door in time to see him heading for the recreation room. Then I went back upstairs."

"What did he look like?"

"He was tall...and young. In his thirties, maybe. He had dark red hair and green eyes."

The face of Rogan Cavanaugh appeared in Joe's mind. "Was he wearing a uniform, like for pest control or appliance repair?"

"No, he had on a dress shirt and slacks."

"I wouldn't worry, Leslie. It was probably some salesman looking for me."

"Oh. I didn't think of that."

"He probably slid his business card under the office door before he left."

"I'm sorry, Joe. After you told me about that dreadful man vandalizing your car, I guess I let my imagination run wild."

"It's nice to know that someone is keeping an eye on the place."

"Did everything go well with your, uh, *commitment?*"

Joe hadn't explained his new position at the Clearwater Police Department to her yet. "Yes, all went well. I'm sorry about lunch."

"That's okay. I had a bologna with cheese and pickle sandwich."

"You didn't go out to eat?"

"No."

"In that case, I'd like to make up for it by buying you supper."

"Really? Tonight?" Leslie was radiant.

"Wherever you like."

"Oh, my gracious, let me think. Oh, what's the name of that place in Tampa I've heard so much about?"

"Do you mean—?"

"I know, Vern's Steak House! I've heard the food is exceptional."

Joe felt a pain in his wallet. Vern's was an expensive restaurant and one of the finest in the Tampa Bay area. He swallowed hard.

"Well, I'll have to call and make a reservation. Otherwise, we probably won't be able to get in."

The smile he had come to adore brightened her face. She laughed a wonderful sound. "I'm just teasing you, Joe."

"I guess I deserved that."

"I'd still like to go to Frenchy's. What time were you thinking?"

"Maybe seven o'clock? I'll try to wangle a table on the beach side so we can watch the sunset."

"Oh, that sounds wonderful."

The dark clouds Joe had assumed were drifting to the north were actually building on a sea breeze offshore and moved onto land an hour later, bringing a solid curtain of rain. With no chance of ending soon, the downpour soaked the region as well as Joe and Leslie, leaving them damp and chilled inside the air-conditioned restaurant.

"I'm glad I brought my sweater," Leslie said.

Wish I'd brought mine, Joe thought, trying hard not to let on that he was cold.

They studied their menus, she unable to decide on one of the many delicious offerings, while he struggled to ignore the bead of water trailing down the back of his neck.

"What are you going to have, Joe?"

"I'm leaning toward the baked stuffed grouper tonight."

"That does sound tempting. Have you had the North Beach scallops before?"

"No, but I've never been disappointed by anything I've ordered here."

Their server arrived, and Leslie suggested that Joe go first. He obliged by ordering the grouper. She held off for another minute then decided on coconut shrimp.

Joe collected the menus and passed them to the server, directing a smile to Leslie after she'd gone.

"I'm sorry we won't be able to see the sunset. I find it to be therapeutic when I'm on the beach."

"Really? Are you sure you know what that word means?"

Joe knew what the word meant. What Leslie didn't know was how much he abhorred going to the beach after the murder of the Berkshires and David's shooting. Only recently had he forced himself to face one of several on his list of demons.

"What I mean is that I enjoy the serenity it brings me."

"I was teasing you. This is so different from what we have in Pennsylvania."

A number of idle seconds lingered between them.

"Do you miss home, Joe? What I mean is, would you ever consider going back?"

The streets, alleys, and neighborhoods he once frequented, as well as his many friends and his best friend, Joyce, came to mind.

"I don't think so, Leslie. What few relatives I had are gone. Most of my friends are gone or have moved away. And I can't imagine facing those winters again. I guess I've gotten spoiled since I moved here."

"You miss Joyce very much, don't you?"

"No sense denying it."

"I miss Paul, too. We had a wonderful life together. Not perfect, what marriage is? One of the reasons I left Philly was because there were so many memories. That and..." She lowered her brown eyes to the glass of water in front of her and slowly turned it with her left hand.

Seeing that she was choking on emotion, Joe didn't push her to answer.

"My brother passed away a number of years ago," she said. "It was difficult for him toward the end. Difficult for me as well."

"I take it you were close."

"We had a typical brother-sister relationship, I suppose. We couldn't stand each other when we were children, taunted each other as teenagers, and loved one another unconditionally as we grew older."

"Sounds pretty normal to me. We're at an interesting point in our lives, aren't we? On the one hand we've worked hard to get here, and we're supposed to relax and enjoy doing whatever we want in the time we have left. On the other hand, we have to stand by and watch our family and friends leave us without having a say in the matter."

The server appeared and placed with their meals.

Leslie waited until she was gone. "You surprise me, Joe Hampton. I never would have guessed that you were a philosopher."

"Well, Leslie Symington, I knew the minute I laid eyes on you that you had good taste."

The stocky, well-rounded woman burst into laughter.

"You are *so* funny."

CHAPTER 5

Drizzling rain was the first sound Joe heard as he woke. No surprise, really. At certain times of the year the rain was commonplace. A subtropical climate invited precipitation more often than not.

Languishing under the covers, he was glad he'd taken a hot shower after returning from his supper with Leslie, needing to rid himself of the chill in his bones. He'd enjoyed their time together, and he hoped the same was true for her. At this point in her life, she appeared to be in a place he knew very well: positive and upbeat on the outside, lonely and longing for companionship on the inside. The upbeat façade only carried a person so far. After a while the wall of self-protection would crumble, stone by stone, the bare truth exposed in the light. Then he would know whether the moment was right to open his heart. Until that time, he would wait.

Joe rolled over on his left side and pulled the covers up to his chin.

I have to get up, he thought. *But I don't want to get up. I don't have anything to do.* He released a long, slow sigh. *Yes, I do. I need to tend to condo business.*

Yesterday had held one distraction after another, although unlike Leslie, his new position with the police department could hardly be considered a distraction. He grinned at the thought of his new friend. She was a pleasant distraction.

Throwing off the covers, he swung his bare feet to the floor, taking a second to yawn, and stood up. The traces of morning glowing around the edges of the drapes provided enough light for him to get dressed, but he lacked the will to do so.

Down the hall and into the bathroom was a path he'd sleep-walked many times before. Feeling better today than most days, he negotiated a pair of simple right turns out of the hallway and into the kitchen. The small window above the sink revealed a gray day looming, giving him reason to pause. Television served as his escape from rainy days if the networks provided programs worth watching.

The coffeemaker sat idle, a silent reminder that planning and preparation were required to produce the desired results. Today, his forgetfulness didn't matter. Opening the cabinet door under-neath the sink, he tossed the old filter full of damp grounds into the beige trash can, still marveling at how a simple evening out could bring about a much-needed attitude adjustment.

With a new filter and fresh coffee grounds in place, he filled the reservoir with water, closed the lid, and pressed the button that would begin the creation of positive reinforcement.

"Glad I don't have anywhere to be," he whispered. "Last night's soaking was enough to last for me the next few days."

The coffeemaker belched its final note, pulling Joe from the miserable display framed by the kitchen window. His favorite mug, stained brown from years of use, served as the perfect vessel to hold the liquid rejuvenator.

Joe raised the mug to his lips and blew over the top, relishing the aroma emanating from the elixir. Patience rewarded, he drank a good amount and savored the warmth flowing through his body. Nothing could beat the first cup of the day.

In the middle of pouring a second cup, he decided to go to the office and catch up on unfinished condo business. He replaced the carafe, turned off the coffeemaker, and carried his mug to the bedroom.

Setting his mug on the dresser, he took a moment to consider what he should wear. Seeing he was staying close to home, he yanked open the second drawer, grabbed a faded gray t-shirt with *Phillies* emblazoned in red on the front and the faded jeans he'd left draped over a nearby chair. His favorite black running shoes completed the ensemble.

With his coffee mug in hand, and his keys and cell phone stuffed into his pockets, he headed out the front door and into the despised pink walls and maroon carpet of the hallway.

A solo ride on the elevator, coupled with a cordial greeting to residents whose names he couldn't remember, led him to the office.

He almost missed seeing the envelope at his feet when he opened the door. Pausing, he wondered about its contents and took a sip of coffee before bending down to pick it up. A second later he grinned, noticing the absence of a name or address, believing the sender to be someone he knew—someone who'd recently shared supper with him.

Settling into the office chair, he set down his mug and tore open the envelope. Confusion wiped the grin from his face when he saw the yellowed newspaper clipping.

Removing and unfolding it, he stared at a headline from the past. His past.

—Thewlis Found Guilty—

Aaron Thewlis had been a financial advisor employed by a reputable firm in Philadelphia, who was caught embezzling from the firm by a co-worker. When his attempt to bribe the co-worker failed, Thewlis killed him. He was convicted but spared the death penalty and given a life sentence. The detectives responsible for his apprehension and conviction had been Joe and his partner, Bill Foster.

Mesmerized by the article, Joe struggled to recall when it had happened. No date was mentioned or appeared at the top of the ragged-edged clipping. A simple solution sat in front of him: a computer. He laid down the article and was about to begin a search when a melody unlike the one that had emanated from the coffeemaker found his ears. This one was far from delightful. He sighed and removed his phone from his pocket.

"Joe, if you were sleeping, I'm sorry I woke you," Carly said.

"I was working on my second cup of coffee. What's got you out on a day like this?"

"A repeat performance from yesterday. Better break out your rain gear."

"Where are you this time?"

"Cooper's Bayou Park."

"That's a new one on me."

"It sits on Old Tampa Bay, close to being in Safety Harbor."

"What's your suggestion on how to get there?"

"Head east on Drew Street to the end. That'll be North Bayshore Drive. Turn left and start looking for San Bernadino Street. The entrance and parking are on the right."

Joe laid his phone on the desk. He had known it was only a matter of time before the mutilations surfaced again. Sooner than later, was not good. Usually a number of days, weeks, and sometimes months, passed between incidents.

"Unless they're already dead," he mumbled to himself.

An ugly image took shape in his mind—body parts stored in a refrigerator or a freezer.

"We're dealing with a psycho," he remembered Dani McMasters saying.

Or worse, they could be dealing with a cannibal the likes of Jeffrey Dahmer.

Joe shifted his attention to the article on Aaron Thewlis. No one in the condo complex knew that much about his past. Or did they? He stared at the computer. Anyone could have run a search. Then he remembered Leslie telling him about the stranger she saw poking around the lobby yesterday.

"That's got to be it."

He pulled open the desk drawer, scooped up the article and

envelope, and dropped them inside. He would talk more with Leslie about the man when he got back.

Finding Cooper's Bayou Park wasn't difficult once Joe turned onto North Bayshore Drive. Even the officer guarding the entrance stepped aside and pointed to the parking lot. The uniforms were starting to recognize him.

Leaving his car, he picked up the brown paper bag and cup carrier holding three coffees. After so many years, he'd become oblivious to the sight of Criminal Analysis technicians milling about.

The bag was getting damper by the second, being pelted by the rain, so he unsnapped his dark blue rain jacket and shoved it inside, thankful that the narrow, winding path by the small body of water wasn't very long.

Carly and Dani McMasters stood beside a bench near a sharp bend in the path. Carly's raven pixie-cut hair was shiny and plastered against her head. Dani's sandy blonde locks hung scraggily beneath her ears.

"I like a man who comes bearing gifts," Carly said.

Joe produced the bag.

"And food, too. I think I'm in love." She relieved him of the bag and carrier, offering the coffee to Dani.

The young detective plucked out a cup and peeled off the lid.

"There are cream and sugar packets," Joe said to her. "I wasn't sure how you liked your coffee."

Dani said nothing before taking a sip. "Thanks."

Carly was busy eyeing the contents of the bag. "There are only two donuts in here, Joe."

"I ate mine on the way."

In truth he'd only bought two donuts, figuring Dani would be off somewhere throwing up.

Carly handed him the carrier, and held out the open bag. "What'll it be, Dani, Boston Cream or powdered raspberry filled?" As Dani leaned forward to look inside, Carly snatched it away. "Time's up! You lose!" Claiming the Boston Cream, she passed the soggy bag to the rookie.

"How did you know the powdered was raspberry?" Joe asked.

"I'm a detective," Carly mumbled through a mouthful, and lifted a coffee from the carrier.

Joe removed the last cup and tossed the carrier into a trash can by the bench.

"Over here," Carly said, motioning with her head.

The trio walked toward a wall of mangrove trees lining the shore of Old Tampa Bay. Ten feet from the trees, resting inside a cordoned-off area, were four body parts: two arms and two legs.

Joe glanced at Dani.

She'd finished the donut, crumpled up the bag, and was drinking her coffee. What she wasn't doing was staring at the limbs.

Carly smacked her lips after the last bite of donut and swallowed. "Now it's getting a little weird," she said.

Joe studied the assortment. "I've never seen anything like this."

The arms were bent at the elbow, and the legs were bent at the knee. If attached to a torso, the person would appear to be running. A noticeable difference lured him closer.

"They have fewer darker areas than the others."

"I noticed that, too."

"What, exactly, does that mean?" Dani asked.

"It could mean the victim was killed recently. We should get verification from Criminal Analysis."

"I don't care for the looks of this at all," Carly said.

Dani started to walk away.

"May I have a word with you?" Joe asked.

"I need to look for evidence."

"Detective, I think you should listen to what Mr. Hampton has to say," Carly said. "That's an order, not a request."

She left the pair alone.

"Dani, please let me explain something to you."

The brown eyes of the disgruntled woman were narrowed and hard.

"I've made quite a few mistakes in my life. Some I've come to regret. But, believe me when I tell you, the one mistake I regret the most is not telling David beforehand about squaring off against the man who shot him. What happened to him haunts me every day."

Wearing no expression, Dani appeared unmoved by Joe's confession. "Outside of trying to relieve yourself of guilt, why are you telling me this?"

"Because he's a fellow detective, your comrade-in-arms, someone like yourself who..." He could tell by her lack of emotion that his explanation was pointless. "I just...thought it was important for you to know."

"Are you finished?"

Joe nodded.

"Then you'll excuse me."

He watched her head toward the nearest Criminal Analysis technician, who was sifting through a clump of mangroves.

Carly walked up behind him. "All done?" she asked.

"Maybe for good."

"What?"

"Never mind. Our killer is moving fast. Too fast by my thinking. If he has more body parts stashed, he'll continue to play his game. If he doesn't, he may take off."

"I don't care for either scenario."

"How's your search of missing persons and runaways going?"

"Slowly."

"No new evidence?"

"None so far."

"I guess we'll just keep plugging along then."

A low buzzing sound distracted them. As it grew louder, they looked up, the rain playing havoc with their eyes.

"There!" Carly said, and pointed.

From across North Bayshore Drive, and about fifty feet

overhead, came a drone. It flew past them to the area bound by black and yellow barricade tape, hovered a few seconds, and then buzzed away in the direction from which it had come.

"What do you make of that?" Joe said.

"Probably some curious kid," Carly grumbled. "There are times when I hate technology."

CHAPTER 6

Two hours later found Joe returning home on Drew Street. The rain was coming down harder, and the slapping of the windshield wipers became an annoyance as his thoughts jumped between latest gruesome discovery and the Thewlis newspaper article he'd discovered earlier.

Scouring Cooper's Bayou Park for clues to bolster the investigation had been in vain, so he'd huddled with Carly before leaving, both of them damp and frustrated. They agreed that all patrols city-wide should be alerted to pay special attention to parks, stretches of beach, or any open tract of land for signs of unusual activity. Around-the-clock observation might be the catch-all necessary to end the butcher's unsavory acts. They knew it was a long shot, but with little evidence, it was better than doing nothing.

Before Joe left the park, Carly shared with him the results of the forensics report on the four limbs found yesterday at Prospect Lake Park. Later, Joe thought about what she'd told him as he stopped for the traffic light at Belcher Road. The news had been grim. None of the limbs matched, a disheartening fact meaning that four people had fallen under the knife—or whatever instrument had been used.

The only similarity was verification that the limbs had belonged to both genders.

Joe feared the same would be true of this latest group, as

well, adding to the list of victims. He wondered where the killer could hide so many bodies. He shook his head and tried not to think about the possible number of victims.

The light turned green and he accelerated, the annoying wipers continuing to slap-clean the windshield.

Anywhere. The bastard could be hiding his mutilated victims anywhere. A garage, a storage unit, a warehouse, anywhere with an area large enough to hold a freezer. Or two. Or three.

Joe furrowed his brow as a list of notorious mutilators filed through his mind: Jeffrey Dahmer, Edmund Kemper, Karen Lee Huster, Kelly Marie Cochran. He knew they had to catch this son of a bitch and catch him fast...or catch her fast.

He was still in the middle of processing when the russet Ford Focus pulled out from a driveway. Realizing too late that the car wasn't up to speed, Joe slammed on his brakes. The wheels locked up, but his Camry skated freely on the slippery track, propelled by the rain-soaked asphalt. The collision was sudden and loud. Joe stopped immediately, the airbag exploding in his face. The Focus fishtailed for a half-block, then jumped the curb and slammed into a metal sign at the entrance to a small strip mall of businesses.

Dazed and not quite able to comprehend what had just happened, Joe gripped the steering wheel and stared at the glowing taillights of the Focus. Seconds seemed to stretch into minutes before a tapping on the window pulled Joe out of his stupor. He eased his head around.

Concerned brown eyes belonging to the dripping wet face of a woman about Carly's age peered through a collection of droplets.

"Are you hurt?"

Barely hearing her, Joe didn't respond.

"Sir! Are you hurt? Your nose is bleeding!"

"No," he managed, and swiped his upper lip with the back of his right hand.

The woman dashed through the puddles on the shiny street, raising a phone to her ear. Another Samaritan was tending to the other driver.

Joe watched as several people converged on the Focus, one opening the passenger door and climbing part-way inside. In the time it took for him to fully comprehend the situation, a wailing siren invaded his ears. He looked in the rearview mirror and caught sight of an SUV's pulsating blue lights behind him. A patrolman rapped on his window a short time later.

Joe pressed the button to lower the window and was pelted with raindrops as he turned off the ignition.

"Are you injured, sir?" the patrolman asked.

"No, just shaken up a little."

Behind the patrolman, another SUV, blue lights flashing and siren loudly announcing its arrival, rolled by.

"You're certain you're not injured? I see blood on your upper lip."

"The airbag...I'm okay."

"Then may I see your license and registration?"

"In my right rear pocket," Joe said without thinking, leaving his left hand on the steering wheel and retrieving his wallet with his right.

Passing the articles to the patrolman, he glanced out of the windshield. Steam was pouring out from underneath the crumpled hood of his Toyota.

I'm not driving this baby home, he thought. *I'd better call someone.*

A miserable day had gotten worse. Now he must find someone to take him home, make arrangements to purchase another car if the damage to this one was too extensive, and still tend to his responsibilities. He released a sharp breath.

Leslie kept glancing at Joe as she steered her tan Buick Lacrosse along Memorial Causeway. He hadn't said much since extending his thanks for coming to his rescue. She wondered if there wasn't more than his simply worrying about his car. Maybe he was attempting to tough out an unseen injury.

"Joe?"

"Yes."

"Are you all right?"

"Yes."

"Are you sure your nose isn't broken?"

"The EMT assured me it wasn't."

"You're awfully quiet."

His stoic expression didn't change. "I guess I'm still shook up a bit. And I've got a lot on my mind."

"Concerning your car?"

"That's part of it."

"You can talk to me if you like."

Joe wasn't in the habit of discussing police work with those on the outside, though he'd spoken to Joyce about some cases at her urging. That was years ago, and he knew he could trust her. He was still getting to know Leslie Symington.

"I've got some decisions to make, and I want to be certain of the consequences before I do."

"You're not...you're not hurt more than you're letting on, are you?"

"I'm just a little sore." He paused, realized the error in his answer, and set his eyes on the boundless mountains of gray clouds in the distance. "I'm fine, really. I've just...taken on more responsibility, and now I'm not sure I should have."

"As in your being the building manager *and* your mysterious commitment yesterday?"

"I really don't need a job. I took it to stay busy...and active."

"You mean *jobs*, don't you? And that's what you're concerned about at a time like this?"

Joe figured he'd better shut up before she pried the truth out of him. "It's nothing serious, believe me. It wouldn't be a disaster if I were to leave."

Leslie slowed the Buick and eased around the corner onto Island Way.

"Joe, I think you should see a doctor just to be safe. I'll be glad to take you to the hospital or a clinic."

"No need, Leslie, I'll be fine once I lay down for a while."

He could tell by her expression that she wasn't convinced, but he admired her restraint in not starting an argument to persuade him to go. He wasn't in the mood to argue.

After pulling up to the entrance to the Crimson Conch Condominiums, Leslie got out and started around the rear of the car. Joe was pulling himself out of the front seat when she reached him.

"Let me help you," she said, and took hold of his right arm.

Echoes of voices who'd offered assistance in the past resounded in his head—some pleasant, some not.

"It's not necessary, Leslie. I'm a little stiff, that's all."

"And ten minutes ago, you were a little sore. I'm going to park the car. I want you to wait for me."

"You don't have to go to all that—"

"Wait for me, Joe!"

He knew it was pointless to continue to protest. Accepting her help to satisfy her maternal instinct was his only recourse—and it would put him in a better position to gather information. Once they were settled in his condo, he would probe her memory for details about the stranger she had seen in the lobby the day before. Then, if possible, he would search his past for a familiar face.

Joe entered the lobby, its cold air delivering a mild jolt. He gasped, trying hard not to shiver. His steps slowed as his whole body ached and stiffened from the chill.

He heard the "swoosh" of the automatic front doors as he stood in front of the elevator, figuring Leslie was on her way. When he leaned against the wall, he wished he'd given in to the insistence of his friend and waited by the front doors. He took a shallow breath and reached out to press the button.

Leslie walked up and took hold of his arm. Warmth began to steadily flow through his body.

"I told you to wait for me," she whispered.

Joe didn't answer.

The icy air no longer bothered him, so he straightened up when the elevator doors opened and stepped inside on cautious feet. He winced when the elevator stopped abruptly on his floor and made a mental note to discuss this problem later with the elevator maintenance company.

The stretch of hallway leading to his door seemed to go on forever, as did the amount of time it took to get there. He handed Leslie the keys, she opened the door, and together they tottered inside.

She helped him out of his rain jacket, draped it over the back of a dining-room chair, then led him to his green-and-blue-striped sofa. The plush cushions had never felt as good as they did now when Joe sank down into them. Leaning back, he sighed heavily.

Leslie sat down beside him. "Feeling better, Joe?"

"A little."

"Can I get you anything?"

"Yeah, go to the computer and find Amazon. Order me a new body, something in a sixty-eight-year-old, medium height with gray hair."

Leslie smiled.

"I'm fine, thank you."

She reached out and laid her hand on his shoulder.

Joe closed his eyes. The newspaper article on Aaron Thewlis appeared.

Apprehending the murderer had been difficult and wearisome given his intelligence, wealth, and social standing. The trail had been complicated, and the atmosphere a media circus of prominent witnesses. Thewlis' lawyer played every hand available to defend his client. In the end, a man with an unblemished reputation—his lawyer's words—was convicted. A majority of Philadelphia's population agreed with the verdict.

"Leslie?"

"Yes, Joe."

"The stranger you saw here yesterday. Can you tell me any more about him?"

"Not really. Not much more than I have."

Joe opened his eyes. "How did he look?"

"I told you. He had dark red hair and green eyes, and he was in his thirties."

"What I mean is you said he looked confused. And that he smiled when he saw you. Do you think it was an act?"

"An act?"

"Did he look genuinely confused, or do you think he was up to something else?"

"I don't know, Joe. He made me nervous."

"When he went out of the back door, to the rec room, was he moving with confidence or with hesitancy?"

"I...I have no idea what you mean. He looked confused. I didn't notice how he was walking."

"I'm sorry, Leslie, I didn't mean to put you on the spot."

She removed her hand from his shoulder. "I thought you said he was a salesman. Didn't he leave his calling card?"

Joe realized he'd pushed her too hard and hesitated. "He didn't leave a card. I...was thinking that he might be looking to move in here." He knew she didn't believe him.

"If you don't need anything else, I must be going. I have something in the oven."

Joe tried to stand up.

"Now you stay still. I'll see myself out."

His head as well as his body was aching when she closed the door.

I shouldn't have questioned her, dammit! I should have waited!

CHAPTER 7

The hollow knocking with a slight echo behind it sounded far off. Louder and nearer the second time, its unknown origin left Joe confused, unable to determine the possible existence of an entity in the surrounding darkness. The third series erupted right next to him and he jumped—an involuntary reflex. The pain ricocheting through his body ripped his eyes open. He'd fallen asleep on his sofa.

A broad ribbon of light stealing in through the window next to the dining table lay over the entire room—enough to guide him to the front door. He made an effort to stand and the pain intensified, a merciless hand holding him down. A string of shallow breaths was all he could manage.

The knocking stopped.

"I'm awake," he whispered. "I know I'm awake."

The next sound invaded the silence as a muffled melody, closer, easier to distinguish coming from his pants pocket. He was in no hurry to remove his phone.

"Joe, where are you?"

Carly's voice was soothing.

"On the sofa."

"Didn't you hear me knocking?"

"I'm having...I...couldn't..."

"Were you asleep?"

"Yes."

"Well, open the door."

She didn't wait for him to answer.

He gritted his teeth and pushed himself forward. A dizzying flash of pain wrenched his insides.

"Ohhh!"

Seconds passed. The pain was unending.

Joe reached out and grabbed the coffee table, leaned into it, and raised up. Again came the pain, merciless, but he managed to stay upright, then trudged with great effort to the door.

Carly was short on patience when the door opened. "What took you so long?" She breezed past him. "Why is it so dark in here?" She flipped on the overhead light, the first good look she'd had of him. "What's wrong? Why are you all hunched over?"

"I wrecked my car."

Carly's emerald eyes went wide. "Oh, my god!" She tried to steady him.

Joe winced, releasing short sharp breaths.

"I'm sorry. Let's get you back to the sofa."

After many stunted steps, she eased him down.

"Is anything broken?"

"No, I'm just stove up."

"Did you go to the hospital? What did the doctor tell you?"

"No," he huffed.

"Dammit, Joe! You should have gotten checked out!"

"Yes, dear."

"Damn you! Don't start that crap with me!"

Silence claimed the next few minutes.

Joe finally caught his breath. "I rear-ended a guy on the way home. I hit him pretty hard. I'm just stiff and sore."

"You've got a bruise on your face, and it looks swollen."

"The air bag nailed me."

"You should be in bed."

The look he gave her said *don't I know it.*

"You stopped by for a reason. What's on your mind?"

"It can wait. You should rest."

"Carly."

She tightened her lips and took a seat beside him on the sofa. "After you left, Dani knocked on some doors along San Bernadino Street. There are no kids living near the park, only adults."

"What does that mean?"

"Don't you remember? The drone. I said it probably belonged to some kid."

"Oh, right. Okay, so some kid passing by saw the activity, and when he got home, nowhere near where we were, he sent up the drone. Do you have any idea of the range they have?"

"It seems my rookie partner knows quite a bit about them. Dani says that some of the more sophisticated non-military models have a range of a little over four miles."

"Four miles is quite a distance. I would imagine the operator would have to be pretty good."

"Dani says they're not easy to pilot."

Joe grunted as he straightened a bit. "I'm thinking the weather conditions would have to be factored in somehow, you know, like with aircraft."

"A major consideration, I'm told. The high-end models have something called Waypoint. It's a program that coordinates the identity of points in physical space, like for taking photos.

It also can set the flight path, hover duration, and bring the drone back to the launch point."

"I think I'm going to be sick."

"Are you going to vomit? Let me get a waste basket."

"No, my head is spinning from all the technological data. I suppose there's more these contraptions can do?"

"Some have a flight time of twenty-five-plus minutes, and, by law, aren't supposed to fly higher than four hundred feet. I'll spare you the details on the Orbit, Follow, and Return to Home features."

"There is a God." Joe paused to think about Dani McMasters, still saddened by the insensitive way she'd treated him. "Why the sudden interest in this drone? I thought you decided it was just another tool to invade someone's privacy?"

"Dani brought up an interesting point. Suppose the drone was being piloted by the killer?"

Joe furrowed his brow, relieved by the absence of pain. "What purpose would that serve?"

"To make sure there were no clues left behind. Or to keep tabs on us…see how we're progressing."

"It was a little late to be following up by the time we saw that thing."

"Maybe the first fly over was done before we got there."

"Hmm. Did you happen to see one at Prospect Lake Park?"

"No, but I wasn't looking for one, either…and would we have seen it if it was four hundred feet in the air?"

"I still don't see the point of using this flying machine if it isn't meant to assist the killer in a way other than for reconnaissance—if it belongs to the killer at all." He grunted when he shifted again.

Carly's eyes glistened, serious. "Suppose the killer is taunting us?"

Joe started to respond, but quickly swallowed his words.

"Think about it, Joe. You told Dani that the killer was issuing a challenge by the positioning of the body parts at Prospect Lake Park. A handwritten letter, a typed letter, even a computer-generated letter printed out can be traced one way or another, but a drone buzzing overhead? How are we going to deal with being ridiculed like that?"

The many minutes of back and forth with her had dulled the pain in Joe's body, now close to non-existent as he pondered her questions.

"By using another drone," he said.

"Interesting you should say that. Dani came to the same conclusion."

"Does your prodigy know how to fly one of those things?"

"That's where we have a problem. She's only piloted one a couple of times."

Silence settled between them.

"Is it still raining?" Joe finally asked.

"I don't think it's ever going to stop."

"Is there anything else you feel I should know?"

"Not really." Carly's serious eyes grew soft. "Are you hungry?"

"No." He pushed himself forward and groaned. "I've got to get up."

"Why don't you sleep on the couch? You're already there."

"I'll feel better in bed." He paused and drew two short breaths. "God, I ache all over. I must have severe body trauma."

Carly stood up. She leaned over and took hold of his right arm. "This is going to hurt you more than me."

"I'm ready."

She lifted, and he rose.

"Oh my god that hurts!" he bellowed.

"Let me know when you're ready.

"We'd better go now. If I wait any longer, I'll stand here all night."

Slow and deliberate steps were taken, an excruciating reminder of the earlier incident. When they reached the bedroom door, Carly steered him to the side of his bed, and took care in turning him around. She started to lift his T-shirt.

"Carly, what are you doing?"

"I'm taking off your shirt. I know it's going to hurt, but raise your arms."

"You don't have to do that."

"Really? Then who's going to do it? You? Raise your arms, Joe."

He did as she ordered, failing to stifle a short grunt.

She laid his shirt on the bed then started to unbutton his jeans.

"I can manage from here, thank you."

"Just be quiet."

"Carly."

"Joe, you can hardly move. I'm surprised you can breathe without hurting. Now stop complaining."

He took a shallow breath as she slid his pants down to his ankles. She untied his running shoes, gently pulled them off his feet, and stood up, wrapping her hands around his forearms.

"Now step out of your pants."

"That's right, take advantage of an injured old man." He grunted as he freed each leg.

"Now stay still," she said, releasing his arms and pulling back the covers. She secured his arms again. "Ready? Easy does it, old man."

His cries of pain were louder, but the bed welcomed his body like a warm embrace.

"Thank you, Carly."

"I'm taking your keys, Joe. I'll stop by in the morning."

"You don't have to, but I'm too tired to argue."

Standing over him, she was barely able to make out his face in the pale illumination emanating from the hallway. Wishing she could do more, she bent down to pick up his jeans. She muffled her laughter as she stood up.

"What's so funny?"

"This is the second time I've seen you in your underwear." She tossed his clothes to the foot of the bed.

"Well, remember what you said the last time."

She pulled the covers over him and brushed his cheek with her hand.

"Don't worry. It'll be our little secret," she whispered.

CHAPTER 8

Aware that someone was standing beside his bed, but unaware that he was awake, Joe rolled over on his left side. A second later he wished he hadn't.

"Ohhh!"

"Joe, are you all right?"

"Fine, Joyce, I forgot about being in the wreck."

The pain subsided, and he opened his eyes.

Carly was looking down at him.

"You were dreaming."

"I guess I was. I thought you were leaving."

"I did. It's morning."

"Really? It seems like I just...did it stop raining?"

"For now. Another line of showers is due in an hour."

Joe eased onto his back. "Why don't you go make some coffee while I get dressed."

"Who are *you* trying to kid?"

"I can dress myself."

"Right, and I suppose that groan I heard was my imagination."

Joe pulled down the covers and slowly swung his feet to the floor. The pain wasn't as intense, but he had to hold back a grunt before peering up at her.

"Carly, I'm okay...really."

Her expression told him she wasn't convinced.

"I'll be in the kitchen, tough guy."

Waiting until she'd departed the hallway, he let go a softer groan.

"I've got to do this. Carly can't babysit me all day."

Careful not to make any sudden moves, he leaned to his right and pulled his T-shirt and jeans from the foot of the bed. Still damp, their coolness against his skin provided a small amount of relief to his aching body. Deliberate steps carried him out of his bedroom. With each step taken, the agony lessened. Movement was the cure-all. The more he moved, the less he would hurt—or so he wanted to believe.

Carly was seated at the dining table sipping coffee when he emerged from the hallway. Another cup sat on a placemat in front of the chair on her left.

Joe pulled out the chair and took his time sitting down.

Carly said nothing, watching her friend and sipping her coffee. She set down the cup when he was situated.

"I have some information I'd like to discuss with you if you're up to it."

"I'm all ears." He picked up his coffee.

"At Prospect Lake Park…one of the arms belongs to a white female, approximately mid to late teens. The other is from an Hispanic male about the same age."

"Go on."

"The legs belong to an Asian female and a white male, both mid to late teens."

"I knew it," he mumbled.

"Knew what?"

"I had a feeling we were looking at four victims."

Cold realization formed on Carly's face. "And those we discovered at Cooper's Bayou might mean as many as eight."

A troubled nod was all Joe could offer.

Carly got up and went to the kitchen to get more coffee. When she'd returned and finished with the refills, she sat down and stared into the dark liquid swirling in her cup.

"I don't know about this one, Joe."

"What don't you know?"

"We could be looking at weeks or even months of chasing this guy. I don't know where to begin."

"Easy, Carly. Don't speculate yourself into a hole. I know it looks grim, but you're at the beginning. Do what you always do. You'll find a lead. You'll find something to help you pick up his trail."

"But when? There are no clues, no witnesses, nothing! In the meantime, people are dying!"

Joe reached over and laid his hand on hers. "You'll catch him."

A hint of doubt flickered behind her emerald eyes.

"I know you will."

She didn't speak.

"How is Dani doing on that list of runaways and missing persons?"

"She was still on it when I left the station."

"I was wondering what happened to Little Mary Sunshine."

Carly flashed a disgusted look. "You're being a little harsh, aren't you, Joe?"

"At Cooper's Bayou Park I tried to explain to her how bad I felt about David getting shot, and that I took the blame for it. Everything I said went in one ear and out the other."

"I'll have a talk with her."

"Don't bother. Just let her believe what she wants. I'm through talking"

Carly felt bad for him. In law enforcement, a mistake resulting in the injury or death of a fellow officer was not easily forgiven—a tough place to be for the wrongdoer.

"I've got to be going, Joe. Oh, I stopped by your office on my way here, you know, to see if you had any messages." She stood up and pulled an envelope out of the pocket of her gray slacks. "This was on the floor. There's no name on it, but I figured it was for you."

Joe eyed the envelope as he took it from her. "Thanks."

Carly reached into her other pocket, pulled out his keys, and passed them to him. "Are you going to be okay?"

"Yes, I'm sure this is just a complaint from one of the residents."

"I was talking about your getting around."

Joe didn't answer and dropped the envelope onto the table.

Carly sat down. "Do we need to talk?"

"Shouldn't you be going to work?"

"Joe."

"When you called yesterday, I was in the office." He tapped the envelope. "I was reading the contents of an envelope I found on the floor. That one didn't have a name on it, either. The newspaper article inside was about the trial of a man my partner and I nabbed a long time ago."

"A serial killer?"

"No, an embezzler named Aaron Thewlis. A co-worker caught on to what he was doing, Thewlis tried to bribe him, and when the co-worker refused, Thewlis killed him."

"So, what does that mean to you today...here in Florida?"

"I don't know. The article appeared the day after he was found guilty. Thewlis was a heavy hitter. He had big-money friends and a top-notch lawyer. The trial was drawn out and messy. In the end, he got life instead of the death penalty."

"What became of him?"

"I have no idea."

"Was he paroled?"

Joe shrugged and felt a twinge of pain.

Carly eyed the envelope underneath Joe's fingers. "Well, are you going to open it or just sit there?"

Joe picked up the envelope, flipped it over, and tore it open.

The clipping was smaller than the previous one, had similar hand-torn edges, was not as tinged as the first. Like its predecessor, it was missing a heading identifying the date or the name of the paper.

Joe glanced at it then passed it to Carly.

50

"Thewlis dead," she read, her eyes trained on the ensuing report. "Says here he died in prison...and he was denied every time he was eligible for parole."

"I lost track of him over the years," Joe said.

Carly laid the clipping on the table and slid it over to him. "Did he ever threaten you?"

"I don't think so. Others did, but I don't remember his being one of them."

"How about a family member?"

Joe shook his head.

"Now for the obvious question. Why is someone sending these to you?"

"Maybe the articles *are* the threat."

"You mean that after all these years someone wants revenge?"

"Grudges and long memories are not uncommon. Thewlis was well off and well liked...by those he made wealthy, I mean. It might not be a family member."

"But why you? Why not the judge? Or the prosecutor? Or his lawyer for not getting him off?"

"I don't know. Maybe the others are dead. Maybe my partner, Bill Foster, and I are the only ones left."

"I can request a uniform be posted here if you like. I mean, you do sort of work for the department."

"Technically no threat has been made. I've just been receiving old newspaper clippings."

"I'll come back later. But let me know if you change your mind."

"Carly, you don't have to—"

"I'll come back later!"

"Yes, ma'am. I know better than to argue with you."

She grinned. "Besides, I have to keep you updated on our case."

She rose from the chair and was two steps past him when a soft knocking sounded on the door. She stopped, and looked over her shoulder.

Joe shrugged.

Quiet feet carried her to the door before she peered through the peephole. Again looking over her shoulder, she whispered, "Some short woman."

"It's Leslie. Let her in."

Carly unlocked the door and swung it open.

Confusion wiped away the smile on the diminutive woman's round face.

"Oh! I must have the wrong..." She glanced at the number on the maroon door. "Is Joe Hampton here?"

"Yes, he is. Please come in."

Leslie leaned forward, saw Joe sitting at the table, and stepped through the doorway.

"Good morning, Leslie," he said.

"Good morning, Joe."

"This is Carly."

Confusion again covered Leslie's face.

"She's my private nurse."

"Oh?"

"Now stop that, Joe! I'm Carly Truffant. I'm a detective with the Clearwater Police Department. From time to time, I talk to Joe about my cases."

"Oh!"

"You must be his neighbor."

"Yes...well, I live on the eighth floor. I'm Leslie Symington. I gave Joe a ride home yesterday after his unfortunate accident."

Both of them looked at Joe.

"As you can see, Leslie, he's feeling *much* better today."

Leslie smiled and nodded.

"I'd better be getting back to work. Nice to meet you. I'll see you later, Joe."

Leslie closed the door behind Carly.

"You *are* feeling better, aren't you, Joe?"

"Much better, thank you. Still a little stiff. Would you like some coffee? I'll have to make a fresh pot. Carly only made enough for the two of us."

"Stay where you are. I can do it."

"Everything should be on the counter."

Leslie picked up the carafe from the dining table and went into the kitchen. Joe could hear her preparing the coffeemaker. A minute later she returned and sat down.

"Carly seems like a very nice young lady."

"A very good friend, too." A flashback of the times she'd saved his life entered his mind. "And a good cop."

"How did you meet her?"

Joe was reluctant to tell her the truth. "She was doing an investigation and...asked me for some information."

"Was she the reason you had to break our lunch date?"

"I recently became a consultant for the police department. She needed help with a case she was working."

"You must have been a very good detective."

"I was fortunate to have a lot of smart people working with me."

Leslie folded her hands and leaned back in the chair. "Joe, the reason I stopped by was to see how you were doing. Have you eaten yet?"

"Just coffee so far."

"I'll be happy to fix your breakfast."

"Sounds good."

"What would you like?"

"A Spanish omelet, Belgian waffles, bacon, potatoes, and some wheat toast."

Leslie burst into laughter. "Now I *know* you're feeling better."

"Two over easy with bacon and toast will be fine."

"I believe the coffee is ready." As she stood up, Leslie glanced at the envelope and newspaper clipping by his cup.

Joe picked them up, sliding the clipping into the envelope and laid it next to the placemat. "Do you have a full agenda today, Leslie?"

"No, I'm free all day. What do you have in mind?"
"There's something I'd like to discuss with you."

CHAPTER 9

The question of why a meal always tasted better when prepared by someone else was one Joe didn't care to ponder as he swallowed the last bite of wheat toast. Joyce had spoiled him over the years with her culinary prowess, a fact ever apparent after her passing. His ability to slap together simple, palatable entrees was enough to sustain him, but when the opportunity to dig into the creation of a master presented itself, he was more than happy to oblige. Leslie's breakfast offering was wonderful—better than he'd tasted in quite a while.

He took a final drink of coffee and leaned back in his chair. "That was a fine meal, Leslie."

"Oh, Joe, it was just bacon and eggs."

"I don't know what you did, but it tasted better than when I scrape it out of the skillet."

Pleased by his kind words, Leslie smiled and sipped her coffee. "You said you wanted to talk about something."

Joe sat up, surprised at how little his body ached. "The man you saw in the hall the other day, the one with the red hair, is there anything else you can remember about him?"

"No, other than he was young, thirty or so I believe I said, and he looked lost." Leslie pinched up her face. "Why do you keep asking about him?"

Joe brought out the envelope Carly had given him. He withdrew the newspaper article and handed it to her. "Do you remember reading or hearing about this man when you lived in Philly?"

After studying the clipping, Leslie shook her head. "His name doesn't sound familiar. When did he die?"

"I don't know. He was convicted and sent to prison about thirty-five years ago. As you can see, the name of the newspaper and the date have been removed."

"What does this have to do with the young man I saw?"

"Maybe nothing, maybe everything. Right after you told me you'd seen him, I found an unaddressed envelope on the floor of the office. I'm thinking that he might have slid it under the door."

"This article?"

"A different one. Carly brought me this one. She came by after you left yesterday. She took my keys with her last night and checked the office for phone messages this morning. She found *that* on the floor."

"He was here again?"

"I don't know."

"Was the first one like this?"

"Yes, only it told of Aaron Thewlis being found guilty."

Leslie looked at the article again. "You arrested him, didn't you?"

"My partner, Bill Foster, and I arrested him."

"And he died in prison."

"I never really gave him another thought after he was incarcerated. Over the years I forgot about him, then when Joyce passed away, I...well, this is the first I've heard of him in years."

"Why is someone sending these to you now?"

"That's what I'm trying to figure out."

"It says here that his parents are dead. It only mentions a sister, uh..." Leslie read further. "Anna Denby. Could she be the one?"

"Carly wondered if it was a family member, too. I don't know an Anna Denby and don't know if she's a resident here in town or anywhere in Florida. I can always check around, I suppose."

"I think you should, Joe. This could be serious."

"The thing is I don't remember being threatened by anyone related to Thewlis. Or anyone involved in the case, for that matter."

Leslie stared at him, expressionless.

"What?"

"How many times *were* you threatened?"

"That was a long time ago, and there weren't that many. Most were hollow threats. The rest were never acted upon. No need to worry, Leslie."

"But I *am* worried. You shouldn't take this lightly."

In the past Joe had worried. He'd feared for Joyce's safety more than his own. He knew that some killers blamed everyone but themselves for their bad lot in life. And some were psychopaths. No one or nothing mattered to them.

"I didn't mean to upset you, Leslie. This could be someone playing a cruel game to try to make me feel guilty."

"All the same, I want you to be careful."

"I will."

"Do you need anything from the grocery store?"

"I'm all stocked up, thank you. I do need to call my insurance agent. And I probably should start looking for a new car."

"While you're doing that, I'll clean up and do the dishes."

"Leslie, you've done enough for me already."

"I don't mind." Her brown eyes became serious. "And, Joe, make sure you take a bath today. You're a little ripe."

He watched her pick up the dishes before disappearing into the kitchen. Wondering if an attempt to stand would result in agonizing pain, he paused and stared through the window above the table.

The line of thundershowers Carly had mentioned earlier, a frog-strangling torrent of rain, was passing over the Crimson Conch. Gloomy and gray was the picture. His mood was much the same.

* * *

Alone on his green-and-blue-striped sofa later that afternoon, Joe was still pondering the meaning of the pair of newspaper articles. He figured he'd go to the office and do an internet search of Aaron Thewlis to learn more about the man, but his decision had been foiled by recurring pain in his body. He needed more time to recover—a minor setback resulting in frustration. His only recourse was to wait until the healing was complete, or to sit on his duff and wrack his brain in an attempt to recall the details of the case. He was never one to entertain the patience required for waiting. Meanwhile, he had sent Leslie to his office to retrieve the first clipping about Thewlis's conviction.

Thewlis was a cocky bastard, he remembered. *Goes without saying for some people. He didn't think much of me and Bill. He really believed he was going to beat it. With Daniel Verhooven as his lawyer, he should have walked.*

Joe held a clipping in each hand, glancing from one to the other. Thewlis had too many money friends to remember. He'd need the computer to find out what happened to them. Real friends? Joe didn't recall many coming forward. Didn't recall any at all. And the sister, Anna Denby, why couldn't he put a face to that name? He and Foster must have talked to her.

His phone rang, jarring the thoughts from his head. He'd remembered to bring it with him to the sofa. Too many bouts with pain in the past had made him a smarter man.

"Just checking on you. Feeling any better?"

Hearing Carly's voice warmed him.

"A little. Still hurts to move around. I thought you were calling about something else."

"No, thank god, but waiting isn't doing me any good, I can tell you."

"I know what you mean. What *are* you doing?"

"Taking a crash course in Mutilation One-oh-one. I've been searching the state for cases similar to ours."

"Any luck?"

"None lately...I guess in one sense that's a good thing."

"True, but it doesn't help you. Where's your new partner?"

"Out doing interviews. She came across a couple of missing-person alerts she wanted to explore and left about thirty minutes ago."

"Really? Tell me about them."

"The leg belonging to an Asian female we found at Prospect Lake Park had a tattoo close to the ankle. A Kanji symbol for power I'm told. Dani's checking on a missing Asian teenager from Oldsmar."

"And the other?"

"A seventeen-year-old Hispanic kid from Tampa. He's been missing for about five months. I'm not so sure about that one. The tattoo might give us something to go on."

"Good luck."

"Say, Joe, I was thinking about the article on Aaron Thewlis. If you want, I can run a search and see if I can find out more about him. I can probably pull up the transcript of his trial."

"Nice of you to offer, Carly, but you've got enough going on. Your focus needs to be there."

"I don't mind...really. I can do it after hours."

"After hours? Your schedule isn't set up that way. Thanks, but as soon as I'm able to move without hurting too much I'm going down to the office and use that computer."

"All right, but I'm here if you need me."

"I won't forget. Well, you'd better get to it."

"Joe, I, uh...had a talk with Dani...about you. I did my best to explain the whole situation with David and what happened."

"I really wish you hadn't. What did she say?"

"Nothing. She just sat there and listened. Then she said, 'I understand,' and left."

"The same response, or lack thereof, I got when I talked to her."

"Either she's as unfeeling as they come—"

"Or she's totally *gonzo* for David."

"Gonzo?"

"It's an old expression."

"I take it to mean *attracted*?"

"In this sense, *strongly* attracted."

"Maybe she'll come around after David gets back to work."

"Hope so. I don't like having to deal with another hardhead."

"Thanks a lot. I can tell you're feeling better."

"Keep in touch and stay dry."

"You, too."

Joe laid down his phone, leaned back, and closed his eyes. Many years had passed since he'd been subjected to a multitude of problems. This time of life was supposed to be the golden years. A time to relax and enjoy the benefits he'd worked for once his career was over. Life would always get in the way of the best laid plans, but periodically, not one right after the other. Was he the maker of his own discontent, the source that drew all the unpleasantness in the world to his door? Lately, that seemed to be the case.

Soft rapping on his door pulled him out of his downward spiral and opened his eyes.

Must be Leslie, he thought, taking his time getting up and feeling little pain.

At the door he peered through the peephole. Surprised by the sight, he pulled the door open and both of them hesitated, neither quite certain what to say.

"Mr. Hampton, I...may I come in?"

"Certainly, Dani. Why don't you have a seat on the sofa."

The rookie detective scanned every inch of the living room.

"Mr. Hampton, I went to see Detective Sizemore today, and...I owe you an apology."

"For what?"

"He speaks very highly of you. He said you were one of the...*are* one of the best detectives he's ever met."

"David's a fine young man and a good friend."

"I was wrong to think that..."

"Why don't we sit down."

Joe led her to the sofa and took a seat in the dark blue living-room chair.

"Now, what brings you out on such an ugly day like this?" *What a difference*, he thought after she smiled.

"I was running a search of missing persons," she began. "With so little to go on, we had to start somewhere. By the way, Mr. Hampton, how are you feeling? Sergeant Truffant said you were in an accident."

"Much better now, thank you. And, Dani, please call me Joe."

"Sure, Joe. So, I was running a search of missing persons and discovered that Aiko Misura Toyama, eighteen, of Oldsmar went missing six months ago. According to her profile, she has a tattoo of a Kanji power symbol on her right ankle."

CHAPTER 10

Joe was not a believer in coincidence—never had been. A good many detectives subscribed to this same belief. When something happened, there was always a viable reason. Almost always, anyway.

A test of the principle had been in play for the last two weeks. No more body parts had been discovered by Carly and her team, and no more newspaper clippings had mysteriously appeared in the building manager's office.

Four days after his automobile accident, Joe had recovered enough to hobble down to the office computer and run a search on Anna Denby, sister of the murderer Aaron Thewlis. The answer as to why he was unable to remember anything about her during the investigation and trial became clear. She was married to Cecil Olan Denby, and living in Spanish Fork, Utah. The reason for her absence was not forthcoming, nor was the motivation for her leaving Philadelphia. Anna Corinne Thewlis was a name on a birth certificate, a driver's license, a marriage license, and nothing more. Neither she nor any family members subscribed to the technology of the day. There were no postings on social media sites, no pictures at gatherings for class reunions, company conventions, or weddings, and there was no mention of her belonging to groups such as the Red Hat Society or League of Women Voters. Joe concluded that she must have been a housewife who led a very private life. Her husband, too. Maybe she and Cecil were shy. No law against anonymity. The only picture of her that he was able to uncover was in a high school yearbook. A pretty brunette, young Anna's photo resembled a mug shot—a somber face staring back at him. Joe grinned when first seeing it. She reminded him of a few girls he'd known when he was that age—in a Pennsylvania Dutch sort of way.

After three hours he called off the search. Debating whether to call in some favors owed him by old friends he'd known on the force, he chose not to act, deciding that another time and circumstance might be more worthy of their help.

In the two weeks prior, the only calls he'd received concerning the dismemberment cases were from Carly—to tell him there were no new developments. Dani had delivered one of the calls, and she'd sounded very much at ease. Her demeanor had done wonders for his disposition.

Joe was sitting at his desk in the office going over some old bills when his phone rang. He didn't bother to check the caller I.D.

"Joe, it's David."

"David! How are you?"

"Never better. I've been cleared to return to work on Monday."

"Good for you."

"The time off did the trick, but I need to jump back into the trenches."

He's eager like I was, Joe thought. "I'm sure Carly will be happy to have you back."

"And I'll be happy to be back. Say, Joe, what have you heard on the cases? I've only gotten bits and pieces from Dani."

Joe started at the beginning and told David all he knew, including the unexpected visit from the drone.

"That's all I'm aware of at this point. Seems odd the killer would just stop all of a sudden."

"Maybe we got lucky and he died in a car accident or

something," David mused, "or decided to get out of town. That's a double-edge sword, though."

"You're right. Good for us, but not so much for wherever he lands next."

"I guess it's just wishful thinking."

"That never worked for me."

"It doesn't occur too often in our line of work, does it?"

"Nope, but I believe I know someone who's been doing quite a bit of thinking and wishing at the present time."

Silence dominated the next few seconds.

"What are you talking about, Joe?"

"How many times have you seen or heard from Carly?"

"Since I got out of the hospital? I don't know. Three or four times, I guess."

"Anyone else?"

"Some of the guys at the station called. Dani's been by every couple of days to ask for my take on...are you talking about Dani?"

"Maybe."

"You think Dani is interested in me?"

"Maybe."

"Are you serious?"

"Maybe."

"Joe, would you stop saying *maybe*! Has she mentioned anything to you?"

"No, more in the way she's been behaving."

"What do you mean?"

Joe explained how cold she'd acted toward him the first time they met, and later the absence of expression on her face when he admitted his mistake and feelings of guilt.

"What changed her mind?"

"Not what, who. And that who was you."

"What did I do?"

"She said that in talking to you she realized she'd been wrong to feel animosity toward me. She stopped by sometime back, and we put the matter to rest."

"So Dani likes me. I guess I never saw it because we were always talking about work."

"Women like to test you, David. Always remember that."

"I will." He chuckled. "I have to tell you, Joe, this conversation has been most enlightening."

"And I would prefer it stay between *us*."

"You got it. I'll talk to you soon."

Joe always felt good when he helped his friends. Bringing two young people together was a first for him.

About the time he'd decided to end his work session, there was a rapping on the office door. The door opened before he could get to his feet, and in walked a smiling Leslie, not waiting for him to address her.

"Are you about to wrap it up, Joe?"

"Your timing is perfect."

"Would you like to have supper with me tonight?"

"Well, I'll have to call Meryl and tell her I can't make it."

"Oh." Leslie lost her glow. "I didn't realize you had...is she a new resident?"

"No, Meryl Streep. She calls me whenever she's in town."

Leslie's laughter resounded throughout the office. "Oh, Joe, you are so funny."

The Crimson Conch comedian leaned back in his chair.

"I have a pot roast and was thinking of mashed potatoes and gravy to go with it...and a vegetable. Do you like corn or green beans...or both?"

"Corn is fine. Leslie, it sounds delicious. Should I bring a bottle of wine for the occasion?"

With her brown eyes widened and mouth agape, Leslie brought both hands to her cheeks. "Why, Joe Hampton, were you thinking you might take advantage of me?"

"Hoping."

Together they laughed.

"Does seven-thirty sound okay? It hasn't rained in a few

days and the balcony finally dried off. We could eat outside and watch the sunset."

"No better way to enjoy a meal."

"Then I'll see you at seven-thirty." Leslie turned to leave, then hesitated. "And tell Meryl I said better luck next time."

Although a blanket of stratocumulus clouds had drifted into the area from the south, they hovered well offshore, stretching the length of the pastel western sky.

Leslie and Joe were in the final stages of their pot roast supper, sipping Merlot on the eighth-floor balcony. A periodic southerly breeze swirled about them, making the interval before twilight memorable.

"Oh, Joe, I was hoping for a colorful sunset, but the clouds...we won't be able to see it now."

Joe stared at the massive cloud bank and noticed a glowing strip between the bottom of it and the watery horizon.

"I don't know. We might be surprised before it's all said and done."

"Would you like some more pot roast?"

"No, thank you. Two helpings have me stuffed. By the way, it was very good."

Leslie's round face was aglow. "More wine?"

"I'm okay."

"I whipped up some Apple Brown Betty for dessert."

Joe was focused on the Gulf of Mexico and snapped his head around. "Apple Brown Betty? Really? I can't tell you the last time I had that."

"I'll gather the dishes and go get us some."

"Before you do, take a look." He pointed to the west.

The sun had dropped beneath the intrusive charcoal clouds and sat atop the Gulf. The underbelly of the billows now burned bright red with thousands of sunbursts glistening over the top of placid blue waters. Lasting but a few minutes, the sun's brilliance was swallowed by the now darkened expanse as the scarlet brocade of clouds continued their solemn sojourn north.

"Joe, I..." Leslie stood captivated by yet another of nature's miracles. "I don't believe I've ever seen a prettier sunset."

"I ordered it especially for you."

Leslie ignored him, entranced by the fading illumination, bringing the birth of twilight.

"How about we head into town, find a nightclub, and dance the night away?"

"W-What?"

Joe let loose his laughter.

Leslie was still enthralled by the natural work of art. Then she realized what he'd said. "Oh, Joe! You're teasing me!"

"And enjoying every minute."

"I'll go get dessert."

She picked up the plates from the TV trays and disappeared into her darkened condo.

Joe took notice of the assortment of lights defining the streets and buildings of Clearwater Beach. For the first time since he could remember, he was happy. And, in an odd way, he sensed that Joyce was happy for him, too.

His phone rang, a muffled tone emanating from his pants pocket, erasing further contentment. He let go a muffled groan as he retrieved it.

"Joe, are you busy?"

"And if I say yes?"

"Damn! I'm interrupting something, aren't I?"

"Is it important, Carly?"

"I wouldn't have called if...Joe, I really need to talk to you."

Joe looked over his shoulder. Leslie was still in the kitchen.

"Did our boy strike again?"

"No, it, uh...where are you now?"

"Having supper with Leslie."

"Can you break away? I really need to talk to you."

"About what?"
"About your friend Leslie Symington."

CHAPTER 11

Joe stood up and shoved the phone into his pants pocket. Eying the remaining remnants of sunset, he walked inside, closing the sliding glass door behind him.

Leslie was standing at the kitchen counter about to open a carton of vanilla ice cream to place a scoop on top of their dessert. She stopped and faced him when she heard the slight release of his sigh.

"What's the matter, Joe? Couldn't wait for me to bring it to you?"

Joe offered a tight smile. "I've got to call Carly."

"Oh? Is it something to do with...you don't have to go, do you?"

"I just...need to make this call."

"But our dessert."

"I'm going down the hall. Leave the door unlocked, and I'll be right back."

Her expression told him she wasn't convinced. He didn't want to leave and considered postponing the call. Whatever Carly needed to tell him couldn't be that important. What could be so earth-shattering about this delightful woman to disrupt his evening? An impulse to return to the balcony grew stronger.

"I'll have two scoops, please," he said through a feeble grin.

He was nearing the door to the fire escape at the end of the hall before Carly answered.

"Look, Joe, I'm sorry I messed up your—"

"Carly, what is it that you have to tell me?"

"I ran a search on Aaron Thewlis."

"I did, too, and I asked you not to bother."

"I know, but...Thewlis has, or had, a sister, and—"

"Anna Corinne Thewlis. I know that."

"Right. She married a guy named—"

"Cecil Olin Denby and they were living in Utah at the time of the trial. Spanish River or some place. I already know that."

"Uh, yeah. Spanish Fork, actually. I had a hell of a time finding a picture of her."

"The only picture I found was in her high school yearbook."

"Yeah. Me, too."

"Is that all you wanted to tell me?"

Joe heard nothing but dead air.

"Do you know how Cecil Denby died?"

"I didn't come across any information telling me he *was* dead. I didn't get the opportunity to do an extensive search."

"He was killed in an automobile accident. Anna's injuries were extensive, and she spent some time in the hospital."

"What does this have to do with Aaron Thewlis?"

"It was during his trial."

No wonder I didn't remember her, Joe thought.

"After she recovered, Anna came to see her brother twice while he was in prison. He died a few years later."

"Well, that answers some of my questions. What does this have to do with Leslie?"

"I was able to get a look at Anna's hospital records. Just some general information like height, weight, and so on. Joe, in some ways she's a close match to Leslie Symington."

"What?"

"Black hair, brown eyes, five feet three inches tall, lived in Philadelphia."

"And how many other women living in Philadelphia fit that description?"

"Joe, Anna Corinne Thewlis and Leslie Alice Symington have identical birth dates."

"That proves nothing. You're letting your imagination get the best of you."

"Maybe, but there's something else you should consider. Three years after Aaron Thewlis died in prison, Anna ceased to exist. I couldn't find any records or personal information on her anywhere."

"That still doesn't prove—"

"When I searched Leslie Symington, I couldn't find any records or personal information on her *before* Aaron Thewlis went to prison. It was as if she just dropped out of the sky."

Joe said nothing, stymied by her report.

"I think Anna Corinne Thewlis changed her name to Leslie Alice Symington. I think she's living in the Crimson Conch, and planted those newspaper articles for you to find."

Joe's mind raced back to his relationship with Victoria Combes, and how she had lured him into a trap by drugging him so she and her daughter, Cecily Dearmin, could add him to their list of victims.

"Are you certain of this, Carly? Are you *absolutely* certain?"

"Joe, are you willing to bet your life that I'm wrong?"

Seconds of breathing was all that was exchanged between them.

"Thanks, Carly, I'll…let you know how it turns out."

"To hell with that! I'm in the parking lot. What's her unit number?"

"Carly, there's no need for you to—"

"Her unit number!"

"Eight-eleven."

"Give me two minutes. I'm on my way."

Joe slid the phone into his pants pocket and slowly ambled back to Leslie's condo, leaving the door unlocked after he entered.

The light from the kitchen shone a slanted band along the floor to the open sliding glass door and the balcony. When he

71

stepped onto the balcony, he saw two plates of Apple Brown Betty on the TV trays, the vanilla ice cream oozing down the sides.

Leslie stood by the railing staring up at the obsidian sky.

"Carly knows, doesn't she? And now you know."

"Why, Anna? Why did you do it?"

Anna ran her hand along the top of the railing. "You killed my brother."

"Your brother died in prison. I had nothing to do with it."

Anna spun around, the half-light revealing the anger contorting her face. "He was innocent! You arrested the wrong man!"

"He was found guilty. All the evidence pointed to him."

She took a step toward Joe. "His boss stole the money! His boss was the killer!"

"Who told you that?"

"Aaron! And Aaron *never* lied to me!"

"But why me, Anna? Why me, and why now?"

Anna scowled. Before she spoke, an unexpected calmness appeared to conquer her anger. She sighed. "Because the others are gone. I couldn't find them in time."

"All of them?"

"You're the only one left. You're...the only one."

"And now that you've found me?"

Anna's expression spoke of poignant relief. "Remember me, Joe Hampton. Remember me the rest of your life."

The diminutive woman clutched the railing, hoisted herself atop it, and threw herself off the balcony.

"Anna, no!" Joe yelled, bolting to the barrier too late.

He looked over the railing in time to see her crash into the sidewalk leading to the Rec Room.

A woman on the small dock jutting into channel shrieked, then she and three others hurried to where Anna lay.

Shock and disbelief cemented Joe in place, unable to take his eyes off Anna as an eerie dark halo of blood pooled around her head.

Carly burst through the front door, hesitated, saw Joe standing frozen on the balcony, and sprinted to him.

"Joe! What happened? Where's Leslie?"

Helpless to do anything but stare at the horrifying scene below, Joe felt the pain of loss tear through him.

"Down there."

Carly pulled out her phone to call dispatch for an ambulance and the Criminal Analysis Unit. When the call was completed, she wrapped her arms around Joe and held him a couple of minutes.

"Come on, Joe. Let's go."

Broken in spirit, he permitted her to lead him out of the dimly-lit condo to the elevator. After a short ride, she took him home.

Sitting beside him on the sofa, Carly held his hand and allowed him to settle for a while.

"I have to go downstairs and secure the area, Joe. Are you going to be all right?"

Joe nodded.

"Did she jump?"

Joe nodded again. "She knew that we found her out. She blamed me for the death of her brother."

"Now you try to relax, and I'll come back as soon as I can."

Joe turned and stared into her emerald eyes. "I'll be okay."

Carly got up, asked him for his keys, and quietly left him.

Closing his eyes and leaning back, Joe couldn't rid his mind of the sadness shaping Anna's face right before she leapt. In all his years of police work, and of all the felons and malcontents he'd encountered, none had taken a piece of him like the soft-spoken beauty he once adored. Her curse of this memory would never be forgotten.

Joe?

Not now, Joyce. Please.

You know it wasn't your fault.

Doesn't help.

She was mentally ill, Joe.

I could have helped her if I'd known.

But you didn't. You can't save everyone.

CHAPTER 12

Two hours later, Carly returned. Joe hadn't moved from the sofa. Double-checking to make certain he was able and willing, she carefully recorded his account of the tragedy in her notepad. His responses to her inquiries were concise and without emotion, pouring forth in a mechanical drone. She was reluctant to leave him when the interview was concluded, but he informed her in his usual polite manner that he had witnessed far greater atrocities, some to those he held in close friendship, and her presence was not required.

"I prefer to be alone," he told her. "I need to sort out some things."

Carly knew better than to object. Preferring her own moments of solitude at times, she understood the necessity of dealing with personal issues in private. Taking a friend into confidence to act as a sounding board was beneficial to a point. Sometimes the need to uncover the reason for an act of self-destruction, even to grieve for the person, called for moments alone. In that sense, she and Joe were one and the same.

Once she'd gone, Joe left his sofa and stretched out on one of the blue chaise lounge chairs on the balcony. His mood was as dark as the western sky, the stars unable to cast a glimmer of hope down upon him. One question continued to reverberate in an endless loop. Had he failed Leslie?

The case against Aaron Thewlis had been solid. The evidence

was undeniable. It all pointed to Thewlis. The prosecution had convinced the jury. The defense hadn't been able to steer them in a different direction. But had he and his partner been wrong? Had they arrested the wrong man?

Joe remained on the chaise lounge, unable to sleep or rid himself of doubt, until the sun-lit stretches of dawn spread into the failing night.

No early morning risers clamored about in the rear of the building this day. The black and yellow crime-scene tape barred all from curious wandering, a doleful memorial to the death of a fellow resident.

The sky was brilliant cobalt, and the sun had lighted this portion of Joe's world when he dropped off to sleep. Far from peaceful, his slumber was haunted by the face and curse of Leslie, AKA Anna Thewlis. *Remember me the rest of your life!*

An aroma far removed but vaguely familiar drew Joe out of his troubled sleep. A Southern delicacy, he recalled, golden brown and juicy, with a stream of gravy flowing down a mound of mashed potatoes. No doubt about its being anything else.

He blinked several times, breathing in the goodness, and stared at the sun, which was sitting just above the horizon. The dreamscape was gone, but the aroma remained along with the keeper of his well-being. A lagging moment passed before he realized he wasn't alone and turned his head.

Carly was sipping water from a clear plastic tumbler filled with ice.

"How long have I been out?" he mumbled.

"I'd say all day. I stopped in an hour and a half ago. I nudged you, but you didn't budge, so I let you sleep."

"Who's frying chicken? It smells delicious."

"I just got back from Cluck-U Chicken Shack. I figured you'd be hungry when you woke up."

Joe yawned. "Mashed potatoes and gravy?"

"Biscuits, too. I bought a bucket because you haven't eaten all day...have you?"

"If I did it was in my sleep."

"Well, I'm starved. Shall we have at it?"

Carly helped him to his feet, and they walked inside to the dining table. She pulled out a chair.

"Sit."

"Yes, ma'am."

She easily found the plates and utensils, and once they were laid on the placemats, sat down and removed the assortment of food from the bag before popping the lid off the bucket.

"What'll it be, Joe?"

"A breast to start, please."

"Mashed potatoes?"

"Save some for yourself."

She piled a mound onto his plate.

"Gravy?"

"A river."

Carly obliged.

"Like some green beans?"

"Just make sure I don't eat the tablecloth."

"And a biscuit, of course."

"Two if there's enough."

"Damn! You don't have anything to drink."

"I'll get some water."

"You stay still. I'll get it."

As Carly left the table, Joe picked up the breast, shoved it into his mouth, and bit off a large piece.

Carly returned with the water, eyeing her hungry friend as she sat down.

"A gentleman would have waited," she teased.

"I don't feel like a gentleman today," he said through a mouthful.

Carly bit into a thigh. "Stupid question, but how did you sleep?"

"I guess I did, but it certainly doesn't feel like it."

"Do you want to talk about what happened?"

"Not much to tell." Joe shoveled a forkful of mashed potatoes into his mouth. "I don't believe Leslie—Anna—ever intended to kill me, but I *am* confused about one thing she said."

"What was that?"

"She said that all the others were gone, that I was the last one, and it took her a long time to find me."

"Don't you think she was sick, Joe? Who knows what she meant?"

"Would she have killed herself if she'd found the judge first…or the prosecutor or any of the jury?"

"Joe, don't do this to yourself."

"And my partner, Bill Foster. I didn't even know he'd passed away."

"What Anna did was as unfortunate as her finding you, Joe. Blaming yourself isn't going to change a thing."

Joe laid the bare chicken bones on his plate, reached into the bucket, and pulled out another breast.

"She cursed me. She told me to remember her the rest of my life."

"It wasn't your fault, Joe."

"I know, Joyce, but I can't seem to get it out of my head."

Carly ignored the slip-up. He was exhausted, maybe a bit traumatized. She'd never experienced anything so horrendous, so who was she to correct him? But she would make a mental note of his error and listen more closely to him.

"Has our boy left any more surprises?" Joe asked.

Carly stopped eating, surprised by the question, unsure whether the truth was what he needed to hear at this time. "Yeah, he did. This morning at Allen's Creek Park off the foot trail."

Joe swallowed a bite of chicken then leveled serious eyes. "More of the same?"

"This time it was a pair of torsos, male and female. No arms, no legs, and no heads."

"Torsos? How do you sneak torsos into a park...even in the middle of the night?"

"Three condo buildings sit near the park. He had his pick of any parking lot. Most likely used the one next to the foot trail."

"What were the races of the torsos?"

"Preliminary said the female was Caucasian, the male Hispanic. Not positive, though."

"Wasn't one of Dani's missing-persons alerts an Hispanic male?"

"I believe so."

"Any decay on them?"

Carly nodded.

"No other parts?"

"We didn't find any. We were visited by the drone again."

Joe laid down the green beans he'd stabbed with his fork. "Is Allen's Creek Park close to Cooper's Bayou Park?"

"About five miles away, and about six from Prospect Lake Park."

"Dani talked to you about the range of those things, didn't she?"

"As I recall, she said the range of the most sophisticated non-military models was a little more than four miles."

"So our boy had to be within range of the park. He had to know when you were there."

"Along with the twenty or so other people nosing around. We talked to all of them."

"Notice anything unusual?"

"Not really. No one was acting suspicious."

"Was anything out of place? A bench moved, a sign down, anything like the positioning of the limbs at Cooper's Bayou?"

"Well, facing the torsos from the foot trail, the male was above the female."

"You mean on top of?"

"If the bodies had been intact, the feet of the male would have almost touched the head of the female."

Joe picked up his fork and ate the green beans. "Maybe he's hinting at male domination, saying men are above women."

Carly forked a portion of mashed potatoes into her mouth. "And maybe it's part of his taunting routine, mainly to piss me off."

"Why are you taking it personally?"

"Dani and me. Female detectives. If he *is* spying on us with the drone, he's seen us at least twice."

"True. He could be saying, 'Catch me if you can,' and this time, 'I'm smarter than you,' by implying men's superiority over women."

"If that's the case, then he screwed up royally. Dani took several pictures of the drone while it was hovering over us. She's researching the make, model, and where to buy them as we speak."

"She's a smart young lady."

"Is that so?"

Joe caught himself and stopped eating. "But not as smart as her boss."

"That's better."

They continued to work on the feast with little interruption of conversation, Joe making up for the two meals he'd missed.

Carly sensed that getting his mind off Anna Thewlis would definitely aid in the healing process—how long it took would be up to him. Remaining unfettered, or maintaining the appearance of being unfettered, was starting to drain her. The mutilator was acting at will, leading her team on a chaotic chase, and at present they were helpless to stop him. She longed for David's return.

CHAPTER 13

Carly left two hours later.

Joe had assured her that he felt much better after eating and thanked her profusely for thinking of him. Fact was, he felt better all the way around. Talking with her about Anna Thewlis had released much of the guilt that was plaguing him—enough so that he wouldn't bear responsibility for Anna's actions. Erasing the memory of her face and the curse she had leveled at him before jumping off the balcony might take longer. For now, he was focused on the New Age technology harassing Carly's investigation: the drone. Carly and Joe had agreed that the killer was using the contraption to spy on them. No doubt a method concocted by a millennial mind to rub their faces in it.

Conventional avenues that once had been effective in catching such a perpetrator were now outdated. A handwriting expert employed to analyze notes and letters, even messages created on typewriters, would be powerless in this case. So would be the genius-of-the-internet technician in locating the cryptic paths and back doors disguised in computer-speak. A new breed of nerdishness had evolved—the aerial voyeur—a punk whose intelligence was misguided and lost in the putrid bowels of self-gratification. Only this punk had taken it a step further by committing murder.

Joe was surprised when his body demanded more rest. With no practical reason to resist, he surrendered, hoping his dreams, if there were any, would not include Anna Thewlis.

On this night, his wish was granted.

Telephones had become a source of aggravation during Joe's career. From beat cop to detective to captain, whenever the reprehensible sound found his ears, bad things usually followed. His cell phone was the violator at the moment.

"Joe, it's David."

"David! How are you doing?"

"Fine, but the real question is, how are you?"

"Maintaining. You...know what happened?"

"Yeah, and I'm sorry."

"I never saw it coming. You know, David, I wanted my retirement to be peaceful and spent enjoying life with Joyce. So far it hasn't worked out that way."

"Joe...I don't know that I should be telling you this, but I helped Carly do the background check on Anna Thewlis."

"She didn't mention it to me."

"Anna Thewlis had a rough life. After her husband died in the auto accident, she found out about her brother while she was still in the hospital. After she got out, she saw him only twice before he died."

"I know."

"Did you know that she wound up in a mental institution?"

Anna's curse resounded in Joe's head. "That I didn't know."

"She was released four years ago."

"So that's what she meant."

"I'm sorry, Joe, but after I talked to Carly this morning, and she mentioned what a rough time you were having, I felt like you should know."

"It certainly clears up a lot. Now I understand why she said it took so long to find me."

"Joe, this is off the subject, but I don't guess you've talked to Dani lately."

"Not for a few days. Why?"

"We had a date last night. At least, we were supposed to. She called around seven-thirty and said she was going to be late. She was on her way to The Drone Zone to talk to the manager. She never called me back."

"Did you call her?"

"Three times, but I got her voicemail. I even texted her twice. Carly said she didn't show for work today."

"Where is The Drone Zone?"

"In Palm Harbor. It's one of the few places in the area specializing in drones."

"Feel like taking a ride?"

"I was hoping you'd say that."

"Give me thirty minutes. I need to take a shower."

"I'll stop by Dani's apartment on the way."

"Better call Carly. She may want to meet us there."

Joe remained in bed a moment after finishing the call. He didn't know Dani that well, and his first impression of her had not been the best, but nothing about her signaled a tendency toward irresponsibility. Even as a rookie detective her attention to details and thoroughness in amassing information was admirable. If there were questions concerning potential or attitude, Carly would have already addressed them. In short, if she were a problem child, she'd be on her way out of Homicide by now.

Pulling off the covers, Joe swung his feet to the floor. A hot shower would feel good.

Joe was noticing how much better he was able to get around as he waited for the young detective outside under the concrete roof by the entrance.

A black Mustang GT roared up to the walkway.

"Hop in, Joe," David said.

Joe hurried to the passenger side, opened the door, and slid into the black leather seat.

"Nice car."

"Thanks. I'm not officially back to work yet. This machine's faster, anyway."

David wasted little time in getting them from the parking lot of the Crimson Conch to Memorial Causeway. A pensive expression was etched on his face. He didn't speak again until they made the turn onto North Fort Harrison.

"Dani wasn't home when I stopped by her apartment. I talked to a couple of her neighbors. They haven't seen her since yesterday morning."

"Has Carly heard from her?"

"No. She tried calling Dani, but no luck. She's on her way to The Drone Zone."

"Where, exactly, is this place?"

"On the corner of Palm Harbor Boulevard and Alderman Road." David sighed. "I don't like it, Joe. I've got a bad feeling."

"It does seem odd that she wouldn't contact someone."

"Odd is putting it mildly. Dani's not one to venture off on her own like…"

"Like someone we know?"

"She's a rookie, but she knows better." He pulled the Mustang to a halt for a red light at Sunset Point Road. "Damn it, Joe, she knows better! Something's wrong!"

"Don't get yourself all worked up, David. We don't know for sure."

Joe could tell by his hard look and body language that David wasn't buying a word of it.

He wasn't, either.

Communication was essential no matter the situation—a point pounded into a rookie's head from the beginning. Carly must have seen something exceptional in the woman to let her conduct an interview alone. Or maybe Carly hadn't known about it. Taking the initiative was one thing; acting foolhardy was entirely different.

The light changed, and David sped off.

Traffic was moving at an even pace, and Joe was thankful for small favors. David was on edge—a traffic jam might push him too far.

"So where is Dani from?" Joe asked.

David glanced at him, surprised. "What?"

"Did she come from another department? From another city? Where?"

"She's from Melbourne. She moved here, to Tampa, I mean, and went to South Florida to get her degree. She applied at several departments, Clearwater hired her, and she moved here. She was on patrol for seven years, took the test, and joined us."

"She moved up pretty quickly. She must be intelligent."

"Exactly, and that's why she would *never* do a dumb thing like..."

Joe had no comeback this time. Dancing around the obvious was a fool's game. David was no fool. But until they knew for certain, nothing good would come out of thinking the worst.

They were almost to Michigan Boulevard when David's phone sounded.

"See who it is, will you, Joe? I have a feeling it's Carly."

The caller I.D. agreed.

"Joe! Why are you answering...what's wrong with David?"

"Nothing. I just needed to get out of the house. He stopped by, so I...forced him to go with me."

"I can tell you're feeling better. Do you know what we're doing here?"

"David filled me in."

"I'm at The Drone Zone. It's closed. The fellow at the business next door said the owner hasn't come in yet. Where are you?"

Joe lowered the phone. "Where are we?"

"About ten minutes away," David said.

"Ten minutes away," Joe repeated.

"I'm waiting on Parton to call me with the owner's home address. I'll meet you here or call you before I leave."

"What did she say?" David asked.

84

"She's tracking down the owner."

Joe saw David's knuckles turn white as he gripped the steering wheel.

A certain amount of speculation always managed to work its way into an investigation, though evidence, witness testimony, and research were the mainstays for success. Over-speculation was detrimental. In spite of his many years of experience, Joe felt the owner of The Drone Zone and the mutilator were somehow connected—if not the same person.

The phone rang again.

"Joe, the owner's name is Adrien G. Hockenfuss, and he lives in Ozona. Take Tampa Road from Palm Harbor Boulevard and head west. Look for Tangelo Street. It's near the end of Tampa Road on the left. His house is at the end. I'm leaving now."

Joe laid the phone on his lap. "Carly said to head west on Tampa Road to Ozona."

"Damn! We just passed it!" David growled.

He looked for a place to turn around, and a break in the traffic. An entrance to a small professional building appeared on the left side of the street. Cutting a hard left turn, he wheeled the car into the mouth of a driveway, barely missing a chain link gate, the rear tires squealing and close to breaking loose. He corrected his oversteering in time, the Mustang chewing up the grass on the right of way as it left the asphalt and jerked them back onto the road.

Joe was plastered against the seat as David accelerated into the median, passing car after car, and coming close to clipping the rear end of a silver Audi A3 as they slid into the right turn at Tampa Road.

"I'm not familiar with Ozona!" Joe shouted. "We're looking for Tangelo Street!"

"Pull up a map on my phone!" David ordered.

"I don't know how to do that!"

"Damn it, Joe, when are you going to join the twenty-first century?"

Joe ignored him, keeping a close watch on the cross streets they were racing by.

The Pinellas Trail was free of pedestrians and bicyclists, fortunate because David didn't bother to slow down.

Spying a sign for Marie Street on their right, Joe caught sight of the one for Tangelo Street shortly thereafter. "There it is, David, the dirt road on the left!"

David jammed on the brakes and screeched a tight left in front of a blue Dodge Ram heading in the opposite direction, its blaring horn signaling the driver's anger. A white curtain of dust rose behind them for a block and a half until they stopped beneath the canopy of live oak trees. At the end of the road sat a small white wood-frame house.

David left the motor running. "We'll wait here for Carly. She shouldn't be too long."

Joe nodded.

David set his eyes on the house. "I hope we're not too late."

CHAPTER 14

Carly pulled alongside them five minutes later, lowered the tinted window on the sedan, and nodded. Joe was glad to see her. In another five minutes David would have ripped the steering wheel off the column. They followed her to the end of Tangelo Street and stopped. Once they exited the cars they huddled together on the edge of the lawn.

"Now remember," Carly began, "we're here to inquire about Dani and nothing else." She focused on David. "She only went to see this guy because he sells the same model drone that's been buzzing our crime scenes. We don't know that he's the pilot."

David positioned his badge and automatic on the black belt encircling his jeans. With his black polo shirt and gray running shoes, he lacked the professional appearance of a detective, but his six-foot frame, defined muscular physique, and steel-blue eyes suggested that a person would be foolish to cross him.

The trio followed the concrete walkway, broken in several places, to the screen door of the white house.

Carly announced their presence with several hard knocks.

Seconds passed.

No one answered.

Carly pounded on the screen door again.

Joe ventured away from the pair and peered around the side of the house. In the rear, a structure half the size of the main house but constructed of the same wood siding, stood alone in the overgrown St. Augustine grass. A white van was parked beside it. As he was about to bring it to their attention, the front door opened.

Behind the screen, sunken brown eyes, a pointed nose, close-cropped hair, and protruding ears defined the milky face of Adrien G. Hochenfuss. No more than five-and-a-half-feet tall, his skeletal frame spoke more of a prepubescent teen than a man of twenty-five.

"What is it?" he asked in a raspy, squeaking voice.

Carly held out her badge. "I'm Detective Sergeant Truffant, Clearwater Police Department. This is Detective Sizemore, and Department Consultant Joe Hampton."

Joe nodded.

David stared.

Hochenfuss was unmoved.

"You own The Drone Zone, is that correct?"

"Yes."

"We need some information on the Shuzu Shade Four Pro drone. We understand that you're the most knowledgeable person in the area concerning these types of aircraft."

"My knowledge *is* extensive, but tell me, Detective, do you always go to such great lengths to acquire general information? One could easily have one's questions answered by searching the internet."

"True, but I like to hear it from an expert."

Hochenfuss didn't reply.

"How many of these drones have you sold recently?"

"Next to none. Their cost is far beyond what most of the so-called pilots can afford."

"And what *is* the price?"

"Thirty-six hundred dollars. I would have thought that your charge would have informed you."

"My charge? Oh, you mean Detective McMasters. I haven't seen her today."

"She inconvenienced me with a bundle of questions and wrote down everything I said."

"She's very thorough. There's not much data missing when she files a report. Has she been by to interview you today? I usually see her first thing in the morning."

"I have had no intrusions...until now."

"Strange. It's not like her to go off without... Well, anyway, I was wondering if you might give us a demonstration of the Shuzu Shade Four's capabilities. It would help us a great deal with our investigation."

"Detective, I must conclude that you've been by my shop. Have you given any thought as to why it was closed?"

"Not really."

"I happen to be dreadfully ill."

"Oh, I see. One final question. When Detective McMasters spoke to you, did she request a demonstration of the drone?"

"No. Now if you don't mind—"

"Are you married, Mr. Hackenfast?" Joe asked.

"The name is Hochenfuss, Adrien G. Hochenfuss, and no, I am not married. Why do you ask?"

"I thought maybe your wife might open your shop so we could have a look at the drone."

Hochenfuss let go a sigh. "I really *don't* care to continue further with this inane prattle. Now good day."

After the front door slammed shut, the trio walked back to their cars.

Carly squared up to Joe. "Mr. Hackenfast? Are you married? What was that all about?"

"A little jab to rattle him. And to find out if he's a one-man operation."

"He's lying," David muttered.

"About what?" Carly asked.

"Everything. He knows where Dani is."

"How do you know?"

"I can feel it. That little shit is our guy."

"There's a small building out back with a white van parked beside it," Joe said. "Might be a workshop."

"Let's have a look," David said.

"Hold on," Carly said. "We don't have a search warrant *or* probable cause."

"Dani is our probable cause. How about I just look through the windows?"

"I didn't see any windows," Joe said.

"We can't leave until we know if he's got Dani."

"David, do I need to explain a person's rights to you?" Carly said.

With his brow furrowed, David glowered at her. "I'm going to have another talk with him."

"No, you're not! End of debate!"

The standoff was short-lived.

"Is that an order, Sergeant?"

"Yes, it is, Detective, and if you disobey me, I'll have your badge. Now let's go."

Joe followed David to his Mustang. David's sour expression worsened. They pulled away from the wood-frame house at a conservative speed, maintaining a respectable distance behind Carly. They knew she was watching them.

"You know he's got her, Joe."

"I don't know any such thing, but I agree with you."

"She's going to die if we don't go back."

She may already be dead, Joe thought.

A small puff of dust several yards in front of them signaled that Carly had turned onto Tampa Road.

Joe reached over and laid a hand on David's shoulder. "Give me time to get out of the car."

"Carly gave us an order, Joe."

"She gave *you* an order. I'm going to have a look inside that building."

"All right, I'll drive to Palm Harbor Boulevard, and then turn around. That should give you enough time."

Joe unlatched the door and swung it open.

David got out and went to the rear of the car.

"What're you doing?" Joe asked.

Lifting the trunk lid, David pulled out a jack handle. "Take this in case you have to force your way inside."

Joe took it from him.

"And for protection," David added.

Joe stared at the young detective. "Remember, I forced you to let me out."

"Oh, yeah, *everyone's* going to believe that story."

Joe began his trek back to the white, wood-frame house. Staying on the left side of Tangelo Street, he noticed a home set way off under the oaks. He'd missed it on their way in.

Half a block later, another home, equally distant from the road, appeared on the right. This one he hadn't missed. From there, palmettos, young Sabal palms, ligustrum, and undergrowth formed passable barriers on both sides.

Perfect, he thought. *I'll cut through the woods and come in behind the building and the house.*

If the anemic-looking Hochenfuss was as sick as he claimed, Joe would have no problem poking around—even if breaking and entering *was* necessary.

When the house he'd seen on the right was out of sight, Joe veered left into the woods by following a trail created by nature. Not always concealed by the camouflage, he felt that the safe-guard of foliage was suitable for his covert operation—until he reached the Hochenfuss property. He'd only taken a quick look in the backyard, but what he saw was a wide-open area, thirty yards or more, of uncut grass. He would be out in the open until he got inside the building.

Joe's wandering through the last bit of woodland lasted only a few minutes before the small building and white van came into view. He stopped a good ten yards from the grassy perimeter, unexposed, and debated the next route to take. Knowing the building sat perpendicular to the house with the door facing the rear, he considered using the van as a shield if no other entrance existed. He took a moment to search for any sign of movement.

Or should I go straight to the rear of the building and approach the entrance from the far side, he thought, and paused. *Six of one, half-dozen of the other, I guess.*

He sprang from his woodland cover and hurried to the back wall of the structure. After a few seconds to catch his breath, he glanced down at the jack handle. Gripping it tightly in his right hand, he eased around the corner and slowly slid along the far side. When he reached the front corner, he cautiously stuck his head out, eyes riveted on the house, and strained to detect the presence of the man he hoped to avoid. The house was quiet, so he stepped up to the door, only to find it secured by a padlock. In a single motion, he rammed the jack handle behind the hasp and slammed down hard, grimacing at the groaning and popping noise when it broke loose. He leapt inside, shut the door, and waited. The only sound he heard was his own breathing. In the ensuing seconds, he came to realize something he'd neglected to consider. Without windows, the inside of the building was dark.

Dammit! *I can't open the door*!

Careful not to drop the jack handle, Joe reached out with his right hand. He felt the exposed two-by-fours of the building's frame, but no light switch. Locating the door frame, he inched his hand to the right, then up and down. No luck. On the other side of the door, his left hand found the switch. A bare bulb came to life, probably sixty watts, judging by its intensity, but not enough to eliminate the shadows lining the perimeter.

Unused chairs and a dining table sat against the wall on the left, a dusty lawnmower and gas can beside them. Boxes against the back wall stacked two-high and two-deep jutted out from the shadow line, and a workbench the length of the wall stood on the right. A pair of adjustable desk lamps and various tools were scattered atop the bench, as well as the parts of two partially constructed drones. One fully constructed drone with a controller positioned beside it sat apart from the others.

If he knows how to take them apart, then I'll bet he knows how to fly them. Joe grinned. *Better than most of the so-called pilots.*

Fascinated by the aircraft, the rotors that propelled them, and the cameras used for observation, Joe knew that the real reason for his illegal pursuit was nowhere to be found. Hochenfuss playing with drones didn't prove that he was a killer—or that he was holding Dani captive.

Joe started for the boxes that were stacked against the back wall, taking slow and deliberate steps and thinking there might be a hidden door. Not knowing the degree of intelligence Hochenfuss possessed, he refused to fall victim to a booby trap by underestimating the man. As he neared the row of cartons, he felt the floor beneath his left foot give, followed by a high-pitched squeak. He froze, believing the worst, and expecting the floor to collapse. Seconds of heavy breathing later, he stepped back. Again pressing his foot to the floor, he felt the weakness and heard the squeak. Sliding his foot forward, he located the handle ring.

After quickly scanning of the room, he bent over, grasped the ring, and tugged as hard as he could. A section of the floor opened to reveal a darkened pit, the first few rungs of a ladder barely visible. The foul stench escaping from the hole doubled him over with the dry heaves.

I don't like this.

Joe stepped down onto the ladder, and, taking a deep breath, descended into the darkness. Anticipating a rotten rung and a quick flight to the bottom, he hoped his effort would not be in vain. Once his foot found the floor, he exhaled, again overcome by the malodorous smell and the revolt of his stomach. Adding to his distress once more was the lack of illumination.

"Well, let's see," he whispered. "Light switch on the left up there, light switch on the left down here?"

The room lit up like daylight.

What he saw when he looked to his right took him aback. He froze, staring, struggling to comprehend the grisly scene.

Taking in the middle of the room, he saw a stainless-steel examination table that was filthy with smudges of dirt and the encrusted blood of those unlucky enough to have been placed on it. Grimy saws, knives, and scalpels of various shapes and sizes hung on the right wall. Against the left wall sat a row of four freezers, the contents of which was easy to guess.

Against the back wall was a large metal dog cage. Inside, a woman was constricted into the fetal position, quivering, whimpering, and naked.

"Dani?"

The woman snapped her head around. A path of coagulated blood ran from her blonde hair down the side of her face.

"Oh, god, Joe, please help me! Please help me!"

Joe hustled to the cage, noticing that another padlock secured the door. Hesitating, he eyed the rusty lock then began pounding on it with the jack handle. After six or seven ear-splitting strokes, it broke loose.

Joe threw open the door and Dani crawled out.

"Come on! Let's get out of here!" he shouted.

Dani latched onto him.

"He hit me, Joe! He hit me and knocked me out!"

They rushed past the examination table to the ladder, Joe motioning her to go first. Dani grabbed the ladder and placed her bare foot on the first rung. When she looked up, she screamed.

Hochenfuss stood above the opening, staring down at them.

"You were foolish to come back, old man," Hochenfuss squeaked. "*Very* foolish."

The trap door slammed shut, and the sound of objects being drug across the floor rumbled above them.

CHAPTER 15

Dani yanked her hands from the ladder and threw her arms around Joe, her naked body quivering uncontrollably.

"What're we going to do? What're we going to do?"

Joe fished through his pants pocket and pulled out his phone. "I'll call David. He should have returned by now."

"What if Hochenfuss decides to come back and kill us?"

"He won't. Not with all that hardware hanging on the wall." Dani peered around him at the cutlery.

Joe brought the phone to his ear. "Come on, come on."

"Joe! Where the hell are you?"

"Trapped beneath the floor of the building behind the house! Dani is alive!"

"I'm on my way!"

"Call Carly! Tell her to get some help! I don't know what this maniac is planning to do next!"

Joe pocketed his phone and gently stroked Dani's hair as he held her. "They're coming. We'll be all right." He began a slow scan of the room, looking for a sheet or something to cover the terrified woman.

"I thought I was going to die," Dani sobbed. "I didn't think anyone would..."

"You can thank David when he gets here."

Dani tightened her hold on him and continued to cry.

Joe was still searching the room when the rumbling above

them started again. He raised his eyes to the trap door when it was lifted, noticing immediately that no light shone through the opening. What he *did* see was a small canister as it fell. He jerked Dani away from the ladder just as the metal cylinder hit the floor, rolled a few feet, and started to release a cloud of white smoke.

"Tear gas!" Joe shouted, pulling Dani to the far side of the room while fumbling for his phone.

David answered at once.

"Joe, the son of a bitch used tear gas up here! I can't see a damn thing!"

"Down here, too!" Joe coughed, his eyes tearing.

"I'm coming to get you!"

"Watch out! There's a trap door in the floor near the back wall! And I don't know where Hochenfuss is!"

Dani started to heave and spasm as she coughed.

Joe shoved the phone back into his pocket. "Come on, Dani! We're getting out of here!"

With tears flowing down their burning faces, they struggled blindly through the gaseous fog until they stumbled upon the ladder. Dani took the rungs two at a time with Joe close behind, gasping and choking as they fought to escape.

Wavering when he neared the opening, Joe felt his body weaken, the fire in his lungs intensify, and his will to survive being ripped away.

Keep going! I've got to keep going! his mind screamed, but another step wasn't possible, and he felt himself teeter backward, his grip on the ladder loosening.

Two large hands suddenly penetrated the fog and grabbed his wrists, dragging him out of the pit, through the room, and into the sunlit yard.

With clean air rushing into his mouth and nostrils, Joe returned from the oppression of unconsciousness. The long blades of grass cradled him, and the sky was the bluest he had had ever seen it. He coughed twice.

"Where's...Hochenfuss?" He heard Dani cough.

"I don't know," David said, coughing as well. "The van was gone when I got here."

"Can't let him...get away."

"Carly called the Pinellas County Sheriff's Office. They're looking for him." David snapped his head around at the sound of a vehicle accelerating.

A white van shot out from among the live oak trees, fishtailed onto the white dirt road, and sent a plume of dust high into the air.

"Damn it! I drove right past him!"

Joe heard Dani cough again. As he labored to sit up, she sprinted past him wearing David's dark blue rain jacket, which was long enough to hide her embarrassment.

"Dani, what're you doing?" David shouted.

Joe turned in time to see her disappear into the building. Seconds later she emerged carrying a drone and a remote controller.

"I'll try to spot him from the air!" she shouted, coughing two more times. "Call Carly and tell her to be ready!"

Dani set the drone down on the ground, grabbed the remote controller, and brought the aircraft to life. Buzzing loudly the drone slowly rose to a height well above the nearby oak trees. She continued to work the buttons. The drone dipped, rose again, then cut a sharp right turn downward.

"Dammit!" Dani bellowed.

She righted the drone and steered it up and away from them toward Tampa Road.

"Which way did he turn?"

"I couldn't tell!" David yelled. "Too much dust!"

Dani focused on the controller's viewing screen. "I see an intersection. I'll go higher and see if I can...there he is! He's heading left! I mean...I think he's heading south!"

David was already on the phone to Carly. "We think he's heading south toward Dunedin on whatever road it is! Where are you?" He lowered the phone. "She's a little north of us. Says she just turned off Marie Street onto Mississippi Street. Hochenfuss is on Orange Street."

"Wait!" Dani hollered. "He spun the van around! He's headed back the other way! I think a deputy is after him!" Dani paused. "It *is* a deputy! He's getting closer and—" A beeping sounded from the controller. "Oh no! The battery's going dead!"

David relayed the message to Carly.

Joe tried to get to his feet and tumbled over on his side.

"The deputy is gaining on him!" Dani reported. "Wait! Another car pulled out of a side street! It must be Carly!"

David raised the phone to his ear. "Carly?" He strained a hard look at the ground. "Carly!"

"If that's her then she's right behind the deputy! It looks like they're closing in! Wait! The van just turned right and almost lost it! Now they're getting close to him again!"

The beeping continued.

"What're they doing now?" David yelled.

"Oh, no!"

"What's wrong?"

Dani looked up, her eyes wide. "The screen is blank. We've lost the drone."

Joe made another attempt to get off the ground and failed.

"Carly?" David said. He looked at Dani. "All I hear is a car accelerating."

Dani let the remote controller slip from her hands, went to Joe, and helped him up off the grass.

"Are you okay?"

"I've been better." He wiped the remaining tears from his cheeks with the back of his hand.

"Let's get you in the car." She took him by the arm and led him to the passenger-side of the Mustang, opening the door and easing him into the seat. "You don't look so good, Joe."

"That should tell you how bad I feel. How are you?"

Dani smiled at him. "I've been better."

David was no longer holding his phone when he joined them. "Carly said that when they got to the Pinellas Trail, a woman on a bicycle pedaled out in front of Hochenfuss. He swerved and missed her, but the van flipped over five or six times before crashing into the fence of a marine supply yard. They couldn't get him out after it caught fire."

Dani and Joe lowered their heads.

"I remember seeing a hospital a little north of here on Palm Harbor Boulevard. I'm going to call for an ambulance so both of you can get checked out."

"I'm okay, David. Joe needs looking after, though."

David clasped Dani's shoulders with his huge hands. "Detective, I am the senior officer at this crime scene, and I'm ordering you to the hospital. Understood?"

"Yes, sir."

"By the way, Rookie, you handled yourself very well today, all things considered."

"Thank you...David."

He squeezed her shoulders, retrieved his phone, and left them.

"Get her some clothes, will you, David!" Joe bellowed.

David acknowledged by waving his right hand.

"Can't have you walking around naked all day."

Dani knelt down beside him. "Thank you for getting me out of there, Joe."

"We helped each other get out."

"I...I really screwed up yesterday, and I'm afraid that Carly, uh, Sergeant Truffant, is going to kick me out of Homicide."

Joe studied her through bloodshot eyes. "She's not going to be happy with you, that's for certain. And she'll probably chew your ass and issue a reprimand."

The young detective never looked away.

"Did you learn anything from all that happened?"

"I sure did. I learned that I shouldn't act impulsively just to impress my superiors."

"What else?"

"To always be on guard because you never know what might happen."

"Right, and never forget that communicating with your fellow detectives is very important. They've got your back, and you've got theirs."

"Thanks, Joe."

"If you tell Carly that you won't go off by yourself again, I think you'll be all right. If she gives you any trouble, tell her to talk to me."

"I will." Dani reached over and took his hand. "Thanks again. I really thought I was going to die."

"Don't feel alone. When that trap door slammed shut, I didn't know what to expect."

"But you were so calm and...level-headed."

"Are you kidding? I think I wet my pants."

Dani laughed then quickly brought a hand to her mouth.

Joe grinned. "Let's not tell Carly, okay?"

"It'll be our little secret."

CHAPTER 16

Joe was sitting on a bench behind the condominium building the next morning, gazing at the placid blue-green water in the channel. He was feeling better than he had the previous day, but more time for recuperation would be necessary before he returned to his old self. He raised a mug of coffee to his lips, took in a fair amount, and pondered the doubts that plagued him. The events of the last eight months were calling into question his current station in life, and suggesting a reevaluation of his future course. As much as he wanted to forget the traumatic experiences that overshadowed his illustrious career, forces beyond his control seemed determined that he keep repeating history—an unjust price to pay for doing his job so well. *Whether leading a good life or bad*, he concluded now, *no one escapes their past. They can only endeavor to be an admirable example or strive to become a better person.*

Joe sighed and lowered his mug. He knew he had to move forward. His biggest obstacle was choosing a direction. Lost in these doleful musings, he failed to hear the approaching footsteps.

"Beautiful morning, huh?"

He flinched, then relaxed when he recognized his friend's voice. "You shouldn't sneak up on an old man like that."

Carly sat down beside him. "You're not feeling sorry for yourself, are you?"

"Not sorry. Confused, perhaps. Maybe a little lost."

"Want to talk about it?"

Joe drank more coffee. "How's Dani doing?"

"Oh, she showed up bright and early for work this morning."

"I'm surprised."

"I sent her home. The doctor hasn't cleared her yet. She has a mild concussion from where that bastard Hochenfuss hit her on the head."

"Tough kid. Reminds me of another hardhead."

"You're one to talk."

Joe grinned.

Carly grinned as well.

"I suppose you'll see to it that she understands the error of her ways, once she returns to work?"

"You mean chew her ass for the dumb stunt she pulled? You bet I will. She's a rookie. She shouldn't have gone to interview him alone."

"You were short-handed. She was just trying to be helpful."

"She damn near got herself killed, Joe! If David hadn't called me, we might still be looking for her!"

"Remember when you and I first met? You called me a nosy old goat because I was poking around so much."

"That was different. I was in a bad mood because Tim and I were having problems. And I didn't know you then or how good you were at solving crimes."

"Do you honestly believe that *I* didn't screw up when I was a rookie? And how about you? Tell me that *you* didn't pull a bonehead or two."

"I get your point, Joe, but she has to understand how serious the consequences can be."

"She *does* understand, Carly. She told me as much in Ozona. She's a good person, and she'll make a good detective."

Silence surrounded them.

"I thought you'd be in Ozona, going through everything Hochenfuss owned," Joe said.

"We took care of that last night...and early this morning.

The tear gas created an awful mess."

"When I was in the pit with Dani, I saw four freezers. I guess they were full?"

"Unfortunately. A sheriff's office forensics technician told me they found four complete bodies, and parts of others. There may be as many as ten victims."

"Wonder how long this guy had been operating?"

"Who knows? He could have been dumping body parts all over the state."

The gruesome notion carried them through a few more moments of silence.

"Joe, want to hear something ironic?" Carly asked.

"Why not?"

"When the deputy and I were chasing Hochenfuss, right before he flipped the van at the Pinellas Trail, we were on Pennsylvania Avenue."

Joe turned to her wearing the trace of a grin. "You're joking."

"I wouldn't joke about something like that."

"What a coincidence."

"Maybe, but I don't think so. I think he was doomed the minute you got involved."

"And I think you're stretching it a bit."

"I've been carrying a bad feeling around with me all morning, Joe. I'm thinking that you're going to leave…maybe move back home."

"What brought this on?"

"I saw how you were acting after Anna Thewlis jumped. You were blaming yourself. You still blame yourself."

"Carly, if I'd had any idea—"

"But you didn't. And even if you had, it wouldn't have helped. She was a sick woman."

Joe hung his head.

"You have to face the fact that you can't save everyone."

Joe raised his head and looked into her eyes. "You sound like Joyce."

"Then maybe you should listen."

"Carly, I moved here because…I moved here because this was where Joyce and I wanted to spend the rest of our lives together. She died before we left Pennsylvania. I decided to come anyway, because I couldn't stay there without her and I wanted to get away from everything that reminded me of my job."

Carly shifted around and moved closer to him.

"At first everything was fine," he continued. "I loved the area, people were friendly, and the clean air was unbelievable. Sure, I missed Joyce, but I was adapting. Then what happens? I'm dragged right back into the life I was hoping to escape. Yes, it was exciting at first, but then I realized…"

"Joe, if you hadn't helped us find Beth Randolph's killer, then we would have never known about The Committee. And what about Victoria Combes and her daughter, Cecily Dearmin? Okay, maybe that was a fluke, but we caught two serial killers with your help. And I can't thank you enough for helping David track down Rogan Cavanaugh. Remember, I was about to stand trial for murder."

"David may not agree with you. I got him shot."

"Believe me, Joe, he's behind you one-hundred percent. And this latest case…besides lending your knowledge and expertise, you saved a rookie's life."

"Carly, I appreciate everything you've said, and I couldn't ask for two better friends than you and David."

"Don't forget Dani. I'm sure she holds you in the highest regard."

"The point I'm trying to make is I don't want to track down killers anymore. I'm tired, and I've decided to resign from the consultant's position."

"I really wish you'd take more time to think this over. Give it a few more days before you decide what you're going to do."

"Carly, I'm done. And I *am* thinking about moving. Not back home…I don't know where. All I know is I can't continue to live like this."

Carly ceased her campaign. She knew it was futile to continue the argument. In her time in law enforcement, she'd known a few who'd arrived at a similar conclusion. When there was nothing more a person could give, it was time to walk away.

"Joe, I need a favor.

"Certainly. What is it?"

"Promise me you'll wait two weeks before you make your final decision."

"I'm sorry, my friend. No promises."

She cupped his chin with her hand. "Promise me."

He grinned. "Okay, I promise."

Carly laid her head on his shoulder as Joe returned his gaze to the channel.

Together, they watched the sunbursts glistening atop the blue-green water.

ENGLEWOOD

CHAPTER 1

Joe was well past the toll booths and about to drive onto the ascending stretch of the Sunshine Skyway Bridge when the sun pushed above the eastern horizon to his left. His new white Toyota Camry LE carried him effortlessly up the mountainous incline as he made his way south in the direction of the place he'd chosen to spend a week alone. He needed to experience the elation of discovering new surroundings, of meeting new people, and most of all, to decide whether he would continue living in Clearwater Beach at the Crimson Conch Condominiums.

Too much had happened to him in recent months. Some of it had been good, like his latest friendships with Detective Sergeant Carly Truffant, Detective David Sizemore, and Detective Dani McMasters, but most of it added to a lingering depression that began when his wife Joyce died. Friends and acquaintances had been murdered. Those he had trusted to get near had deceived him. And he had almost been killed twice, compounding his misery, as if the evil from a past he so wanted to escape was shadowing him every step of the way. The hopes and dreams he'd had for this time of his life were never to be. He had wanted to reward Joyce for being so understanding of his demanding career by living their golden years in the sunny retreat they'd always dreamed about. They would finally have the freedom to pack up and travel to parts of the country they'd only read about when they were younger. When Joyce became ill, their plans had quickly gone the way of unrealized expectations. Never again would he witness the pastel skies and fiery brilliance of a setting sun with her—a cruel twist of fate he felt they hadn't deserved.

The brilliant rays of the rising sun were illuminating the horizon when Joe reached the top of the bridge. Usually midnight blue and mysterious, the waters of Tampa Bay rippled a deep cerulean, soon to become a glistening blue-green, as the sun climbed higher.

Wish you were here to see this, Joyce, he thought. Musing a second later, he thought, *Of course you can see it. What I meant was I wish you were here to see it with me.*

Joe had gotten away early to get a jump on the morning rush-hour traffic, knowing full well that he would become a part of the rat race when his route intersected with Interstate 75. Not caring to compete with those in their frenzied dash to wherever, his plan was to get off at State Road 681 and continue until he hooked up with U.S. 41 near the town of Laurel. Continuing south on the Tamiami Trail at a much slower pace would guide him through Nokomis, Venice, South Venice, and, eventually, to State Road 776 and Englewood, his destination. If he got hungry along the way, he'd stop for breakfast. If not, he'd stay the course, taking in all the never-before-seen surroundings until he found Beach Road and crossed over Lemon Bay to Manasota Key. Traveling north from there would lead him to the Sandpiper Shore Cottages, his hideaway on the coast of the Gulf of Mexico.

I'll have all the peace and quiet I need. And plenty of time to do whatever I want while deciding what I'm going to do when I get home.

The thrill of being in the lead car on a roller coaster raced through Joe as he sailed down the far side of the bridge. Once his car leveled out and the excitement was gone, the vision of his new friend materialized in his mind, bringing a grin to his face. She didn't want him to leave.

The bond between him and Carly had strengthened in a relatively short period of time. He found it difficult not to be drawn to someone who'd prevented him from being killed. Her devotion to him was more in line with a pupil seeking answers from a mentor, though her treatment of him was akin to a daughter keeping watch over her father—something he didn't mind.

I'm going to a part of this state where I've never been, Joyce. I've heard that the southern part is quite different from the central and northern parts.

Joyce didn't encourage him this time, and he wondered why. He was heading in a different direction, literally and figuratively. Maybe that was the reason. He knew she would always be with him. Perhaps the time had come to face the future and keep moving forward.

"Thanks, Joyce," he whispered. "It took a while, but I'm going to be all right."

As he glanced to his left at the bold sun spreading its light over the sea and sky, he felt the bonds of indecision release, and his indomitable spirit urge him on.

A familiar feeling stirred inside him. "I'm hungry. Let's see what the next exit has to offer."

Exit 5 at Terra Ceia would lead him to U.S. 41 and Palmetto. Deciding to travel a little farther down the road, he motored toward Interstate 75. Eventually joining the masses heading south, he held his own until he was nearing Exit 220, and a road sign caught his eye.

"Cracker Barrel! That's it!" he said.

The sheer thought of the eatery reminded him of the first time he and Joyce had visited one in Pennsylvania.

Following the long line of cars into the cut-off and then the few in the caravan leading to the restaurant took a minimum of effort, and for that he was grateful.

Settling into a booth, a steaming and wonderful tasting cup of coffee preceded his order of the Sunrise Sampler. Once he'd dug into the bountiful breakfast, a familiar thought crossed his mind.

I still can't get over how much better a meal tastes when someone else has cooked it. He grinned and marveled at how good he felt before shoveling another forkful of biscuits and gravy into his mouth. *I'm really going to enjoy this trip.*

Gearing up for the remainder of his drive, Joe steered his Toyota back to the I-75 shuttle heading in a southerly direction.

The scenery along the interstate was an endless wall of pine trees, oak trees, and scrub brush, interrupted by storefronts, warehouses, and nurseries, as well as the occasional interchange to break the monotony.

Time was of no importance and passed quickly. Joe figured his exploring foreign territory had something to do with it, but he was happy when he came upon the road sign for State Road 681. Leaving the high-speed ribbon to the commuters in exchange for an easy ride with the locals was more to his liking. Eventually picking up U.S. 41, passing through the communities of Laurel, Nokomis, and Venice, heightened his longing to get to the Sandpiper Shore Cottages on Manasota Key, just outside of Englewood. He was surprised at how soon the cut-off for Englewood Road came into view and noticed the same topography of trees, businesses, and side roads remained the norm in each community.

I guess it's the same everywhere, but I can't believe the number of pine trees I've seen on the way down here. And I thought Pinellas County had a lot.

Much to his delight, he reached the city limits sign for Englewood a few minutes later. His first impression was that the town would be a strong candidate for relocation should he decide to leave Clearwater Beach. The sight of several condominiums clumped together reminded him of the Crimson Conch—and Carly.

As he had promised her, he had held off on making a decision about his future, but promised himself now that by the time he was ready to return home, a decision *would have* been made. In the meantime, he was going to benefit from taking in the usual sights along the Florida coastline—different, yet the same—and soak in the serenity of the Gulf of Mexico to help clear his mind.

Joe laughed out loud as he turned onto Beach Road, the avenue leading to the barrier island and his retreat. He could feel the excitement building inside him as he was about to cross the bridge over Lemon Bay, happy that he hadn't been misled by what a couple of natives had told him. The water did look clearer and greener the farther south one traveled. As he was approaching another small bridge over the bay and nearing the intersection on the island, he spotted a small building sitting alone on his right. Flapjack's Bar looked and sounded intriguing. *Might be a good place to unwind later.*

Slowing for the roundabout, and the right turn to follow, Joe sighed and felt his body relax. Nothing or no one was going to upset him during this week. A smile crossed his face as he began his search for the Sandpiper Shore Cottages.

CHAPTER 2

Finding the dirt road leading to the cottages was as easy as checking in. A lean, tan woman with wavy black hair and a welcoming smile assisted him in the order of business, then gladly directed him to the dwelling he'd chosen, the one on the row's end nearest the water.

Once he'd removed his suitcase and other necessary items from his car, Joe stood on the screened-in porch and looked out over the Gulf.

Amazing, he thought. *I'm not that far away from Clearwater Beach, but I feel like I'm in a different part of the country.*

He left the porch and the weather-worn wooden deck nestled against the cottage and strolled a few steps through the sun-baked grass toward the water. The rhythmic breaking of the waves over the rocks lining the edge of the beach filled his ears, lifting his already heightened spirits. He imagined the brilliant sunset to come and the contrasting pictures he'd enjoy every night.

The passing moments were of no consequence as Joe took pleasure in the surroundings. Birds called to one another as they fluttered from tree to tree. The subdued chatter of other visitors drifted out from nearby cottages. An open breeze warmed by the sun brushed across his face. It was as if the moment had been created just for him. A special occasion designed to right his attitude and remind him to embrace each day.

Joe drew a deep, rewarding breath and released it little by little.

"I don't believe it," he whispered. "I'm hungry again."

The dark-haired woman who had checked him in had recommended several places to eat. Lazing in the middle of paradise, he had no intention of preparing a meal. A smile had brightened his face when she mentioned the White Elephant Pub, so he decided to give it a try. He ambled back to the cottage, not bothering to check the time, and locked up before he left.

A thin veil of white dust drifted behind Joe's Camry as he stopped at the intersection of Beach Road. Turning right, he brought the car up to speed and watched for the roundabout that would lead him back to the mainland. He'd been told that the White Elephant Pub was south of the intersection and bordered on Lemon Bay. True to the instructions given him, his destination appeared a short time later.

"There it is," Joe whispered. "It's bigger than I thought it would be."

Leaving Beach Road was no problem as he rolled into the sandy parking lot.

Joe felt right at home when he crossed the threshold and had planned on grabbing a beer at the bar while he waited to be seated. After a few minutes, he was led to a table in the rear and seated near the exit to a wooden deck outside with more tables. The pub looked like others he'd frequented over the years, yet revealed a common Florida ambience.

Soon his red-haired server appeared, and acted as though she'd been waiting for him.

"Well, how are you today?" she said. Her smile reminded him of Carly.

"If I was doing any better, I couldn't stand myself."

The redhead laughed, her blue eyes sparkling, and handed him a menu. "Couldn't ask for much more, could you? While you're checkin' out the food, I'll get your drink. What'll you have?"

"Iced tea."

"I'll be right back."

Running his eyes over the menu, unsure of what he wanted to eat, Joe kept glancing at the outdoor tables and the two small docks provided for those who chose to arrive by boat.

He imagined himself behind the wheel of a Sea Ray SLX 230, navigating the placid waters of Lemon Bay, at times venturing into the Gulf to fish. No big-city headaches and no condo to call home down here, he decided. A small house or cottage was more in keeping with the lifestyle of the locals—simple and easygoing. A community of friendly people going about their business and not sticking their noses into his—or vice versa. Perfect in every way.

"Here's your iced tea," the server said. "You look like you're ready to order."

"Oh! Yes. I believe I'll have the grilled grouper trunk. Is that a type of burrito?"

"It's grouper, rice, and broccoli wrapped in a flour tortilla."

"Perfect."

The server smiled again, took the menu, and left.

Joe decided to head over to Flapjack's Bar for a couple of beers after he finished his meal.

I shouldn't need any supper after all I've had to eat today.

The grouper trunk was delicious, and left Joe wishing that one of the restaurants in Clearwater Beach offered them. Maybe he would mention it to the manager of Frenchy's the next time he went there.

Only a few cars sat in the sandy white parking lot when he arrived at Flapjack's. As other cars sped by on Beach Road, Joe walked to the weathered wooden door of the blanched, free-standing building. The door groaned when opened and closed, and Joe paused to familiarize himself with the surroundings.

Like so many bars, this one had several tables, each with four chairs, scattered throughout the room. The bar and a half-dozen bar chairs sat against the back wall. Three booths with worn padded seats hugged the wall on the right, and a vintage Seeburg 220 jukebox rested against the left wall near the bathrooms.

Joe grinned as he ambled through the maze of tables and claimed a bar chair.

A brown-haired woman on the young side of fifty carried her stocky body to where Joe was seated, wiped the counter with a bar towel, and matched his grin.

"What can I getcha, mister?"

"A draft will do. Whatever's closest to your hand."

She turned and left, flipping the towel over her shoulder.

Joe eased his chair around. He imagined the place brimming with older men and women, a cloud of cigarette smoke hanging in the air, the decor a telling sign. He could see some of them laughing, some who weren't, and some attempting to drown their sorrows. No rowdy behavior would be tolerated in here. Relaxing was all this crowd had in mind. He heard the bartender return and wheeled around.

"Would you like to run a tab?" she asked, setting the glass of beer on the bar.

"Works for me."

"You don't look familiar. This your first time here?"

Joe wrapped his hand around the glass. "I guess it shows, huh?"

"Newbies are easy to spot. I know pretty much everyone who stops in."

Joe took a sip. "I'm Joe. I'm visiting here from Clearwater Beach."

"I'm Sammi. Samantha, actually. Pleased to make your acquaintance."

She offered her right hand. He took it.

"So, Sammi, I'm curious. How did the owner decide on the name Flapjack's?"

"My father, John Calloway, owns it. My stepfather, actually. When he was younger, he picked up the nickname Flapjack because he loved pancakes. Still does."

"And being his name was John..."

"Flapjack only seemed natural. When he retired and bought this place, he renamed it Flapjack's so all his friends would know he owned it. Pretty much everyone who grew up around here knows Dad."

"It's a nice place. Has a good feel about it."

"I think so. It's the only place I ever worked. Dad's a good man. He took good care of me and my mom."

"Will your dad be coming in sometime today?"

The friendliness brightening Sammi's face disappeared.

"No, I, uh, don't think so, Joe."

"That's too bad. I'd like to meet him."

Sammi leaned forward and wiped an imaginary spot off the counter beside his glass.

"We had a death in the family. My sister, stepsister, actually, was killed."

"Oh, I'm sorry."

"Dad hasn't gotten over it yet."

Joe took a long drink of beer and looked down at the counter.

Sammi gazed over Joe's shoulder. "I'd better go check on the other guys."

She left him and moved from behind the bar to a trio of men sitting at one of the tables. Joe heard two of the men laugh. He looked in Sammi's direction and saw her heading toward a couple in one of the booths. When she turned back, there was no mistaking the grin on her face.

Returning to the bar, she leaned against it.

"So what do you do for a living, Joe?"

"I'm retired. I used to be on the Philadelphia police force."

Sammi straightened up, her mouth a circle of surprise.

"No foolin'? Dad was a deputy here in Englewood for almost forty years."

"Is that a fact? Please pass along my condolences and tell your dad I'd like to meet him. I'll be at the Sandpiper Shore

Cottages until Sunday."

"You'll come back before you leave, won't you, Joe?"

Joe nodded. "Count on it."

CHAPTER 3

Although he felt sorry for the man he'd never met, Joe saw no reason to dwell upon the death of John Calloway's daughter. He had his own problems to consider but pushed them aside when he returned to the cottage. He'd remembered to bring a bottle of Evan Williams whiskey, and with a half-full glass on the rocks in hand, he sat down in a yellow folding chair on the porch to enjoy the steady breeze blowing off the Gulf. The more whiskey he drank, the stronger the urge to leave Clearwater Beach and move to Englewood grew. Was it the lure of the friendly people in a smaller town that seemed so inviting? He'd come to Florida because it was Joyce's lifelong dream. He had no regrets, and took to life on the beach right away. Joyce not being with him had been difficult in the beginning. And the compacted housing of a condominium challenged the privacy and freedom of owning a house. But he was happy—to a degree. A squawking seagull gathered his attention.

I could easily fit in here, he thought. *And live in relative obscurity.*

By the third glass, he'd set aside the thought of relocating and focused on the panoramic picture unfolding as the day ended. The light began to fade as the searing red-orange sun sank into the vast, dark expanse, dimming the pastel blues, yellows, and greens splashed across the western sky. Although the undying brilliance of the sun remained unchanged, the picture presented at sunset was exactly as he had imagined it would be.

Joe sighed. One more drink would do the trick. He was starting to feel the weariness of travelling and knew that sleep would overtake him soon. One final toast to the remnants of the day, followed by a pleasing chorus of night sounds, would make for an ideal memory. As he poured another drink, he thought of Carly and David, and let go with subtle laughter when he recalled the youthful exuberance of Dani McMasters. He missed them already, and yet, he didn't seem to mind.

"They have their whole lives in front of them," he whispered. "I'm going to enjoy what's left of mine."

Joe was surprised when he opened his eyes and discovered daylight glowing around the edges of the bedroom drapes. Contented that he'd slept undisturbed, he yawned and stretched. In no hurry to begin the day, he wondered why he couldn't get a good night's sleep at home.

Giving no more thought to the question, he kicked off the covers, got up, and selected a comfortable dark blue T-shirt and broken-in pair of khaki trousers, then ambled barefoot to the undersized kitchen. As he leaned against the kitchen counter, he realized he'd forgotten to bring coffee. He waited long enough to yawn again, then decided to take a shower before heading to the office to inquire about a restaurant for breakfast.

Three solid raps sounded on the front door before he could take a step. As usual, innate curiosity urged him to answer.

A man with a tanned, weathered face and lacking all but a ring of thin, white hair stared Joe straight in the eyes. A few years older, but about the same height, he grinned slightly before speaking.

"You Joe Hampton?"

"I am."

"I'm John Calloway."

Joe eyed him a second, remembering Sammi's kind words

regarding her stepfather. "Would you like to come in?"

"Don't mind if I do."

Joe immediately picked up on his gray, sweat-stained polo shirt, faded jeans, and dirty white sneakers as he entered the cottage.

Calloway turned and faced Joe, wasting no time.

"Sorry ta barge in on ya like this, especially since we don't know each other, but my daughter told me ya stopped by the bar yesterday."

"Flapjack's is a nice place, John. I like it."

"It's not much, but it suits me."

"I'd offer you some coffee, but I forgot to buy any."

"Ya look like ya just woke up. Ya eat yet?"

"No. Any place special you like to go?"

Calloway lowered his head. "Look, Joe, I don't mean ta bulldoze ya, but there's somethin' I'd like ta run by ya. Would ya be willin' ta let me take ya out ta breakfast?"

Joe hesitated, sensing that he was about to be dragged into a compromising situation.

"Does it have to do with your daughter? I don't mean Sammi."

"Livie was the best thing ta ever happen ta me. Don't get me wrong. I love Sammi, but Livie...she was special."

"I take it that Livie is short for Olivia?"

Calloway grinned. "Sammi said ya were sharp. She's real good at readin' people."

"Why come to me, John? In fact, how did you even find me?"

"Well, when she got home last night, she told me that ya were a cop in Philadelphia. Her son, Randy, my grandson, lives on his computer. He looked ya up and, well, I never knew anybody that was as good a cop as you. As far as findin' ya...I still know a few people around these parts. And ya did mention ya were staying at the Sandpiper Shore." Calloway paused.

"I thought maybe ya might, you know, wanna listen to my story."

I don't believe it, Joe thought. *It just never ends.* "Englewood P-D not having any luck?"

"Englewood never hadda police department. It's the Charlotte County Sheriff's Office. They're doin' their best. The lead detective is a good man, but...well, there's some complications."

"What kind of complications?"

"My son-in-law was the last ta see Livie alive. His alibi is lame, Joe. I've heard better excuses from a fifth-grader."

"Is he the only suspect?"

Calloway shook his head. "One of the problems, though, is that he and the detective went ta school together."

Joe winced. "I'd really like to help you, John, but I've been out of the loop for a while. And I don't know the first thing about Englewood."

Calloway shook his head again. "I understand, Joe, but would ya do me the courtesy of hearin' me out over breakfast?"

"I can't make any promises."

"I understand, but I'd appreciate it."

Joe went to the bedroom to put on his favorite black running shoes.

Here we go again, he thought.

John Calloway said very little after they left the cottage and even less as he steered his brown Dodge Ram onto McCall Road when they reached the mainland. Minutes later, they pulled into the parking lot of the Country Hound Café.

Joe couldn't help but grin. "Do you eat here a lot, John?"

"They know me. If I'da had any brains, I'da bought this place 'steada Flapjack's."

The walk to the front door was short. Calloway never broke stride after they entered, leading Joe to a two-seater table in the rear of the quaint establishment. Joe figured it must be his table and pulled out a chair.

The aromas embracing him caused Joe's stomach to growl. People around them chattered away as they enjoyed their meals, believing all to be well in the world. In their world, it was.

Joe leaned forward to ask John about his daughter when a

stocky young, gum-chewing redhead walked up and laid a menu next to him. He smiled when he saw the sad-face bloodhound on the front.

"Flapjack! I ain't seen you in a while. How ya doin'?"

"Doin' okay, Trish. How 'bout you?"

"'Bout the same. This place liked to killed me yesterday, though." Trish froze, her eyes wide, and bit her bottom lip. "I'm sorry, Flapjack. I forgot about...you know."

"No need ta worry, darlin'. This here is Joe."

The server relaxed. "Hi ya, Joe."

"Nice to meet you, Trish."

"What can I get you to drink?"

"Coffee is fine."

"This together or separate?"

"All on one," Calloway said.

Trish smiled at Joe, cracked her gum, and left.

"So, Joe, as I was tellin' ya, one of the problems with the case is that my son-in-law, Phil Bridgewater is his name, and the sheriff's detective are buddies."

"I would think there would be a conflict of interest," Joe said. "Did you speak to the detective about it?"

"I gave it some thought. But that might cause another problem. Ya see, Phil's daddy used ta be a defense attorney. We locked horns a few times back in the day. It weren't pretty."

"And you think he might interfere with the case somehow if you suggest the detective might show favoritism?"

"I can almost guarantee it. He's still gotta lotta clout around here."

Trish returned and set two cups of coffee in front of them before pulling out her pad and pen. "Whatcha gonna have, Joe?"

"Two over easy, bacon, and wheat toast."

"Grits, potatoes, or hash browns?"

"Potatoes."

Trish cracked her gum, picked up the menu, and turned to leave.

"Wait a minute." Joe looked at Calloway. "Aren't you having anything?"

"Oh, I already know what he wants," Trish said over her shoulder.

Calloway stared at his steaming black coffee a second before taking a healthy pull.

"Joe, my Livie was stabbed fifteen times and left ta die. I don't know who did it. I want ta believe I know, but truth is, I don't know fer sure."

"Your son-in-law?"

"Never did like him. Rich kid in his fancy boat. Thinks he's a fishin' guide. Barely made it outta high school. His old man set him up in business. I don't know what Livie ever saw in him."

Sounds like the classic love story, Joe thought. "How long had they been married?"

"More'n twenty years."

"Any children?"

"Nah. Never did know why. Livie wouldn't tell me."

"John, are there any more problems that you haven't mentioned?"

"There was talk…" Calloway cleared his throat. "There was talk that Livie was screwin' around, and that one of her lovers killed her."

Joe hesitated, attempting to find the right words for his next question. "Look, John, there's no easy way for me to say this, but if you want my help, I have to ask."

"I know. And the answer is no, she wasn't screwin' around. Not to my knowledge."

Joe knew a smart woman wouldn't tell anyone anyway. But in a small town she wouldn't have to. "How long had Olivia and Phil been having problems?"

"Two or three years, I guess. Livie had mentioned gettin' a divorce more'n once."

"I'll bet that didn't make Phil happy. Or did it?"

"Accordin' ta what I was told, Phil didn't like to lose...ta anybody."

Joe had another question ready when Trish walked up holding two plates.

"Two over easy, bacon, potatoes, and wheat toast for you, Joe." She offered a smile as she set the plate in front of him. "And the usual for you, Flapjack."

As he removed the silverware from inside his napkin, Joe noticed that four pancakes dripping with butter surrounded by four sausage links filled the plate in front of Calloway.

CHAPTER 4

On the way back to the cottage, Joe learned from John Calloway that the body of Olivia Bridgewater had been discovered three weeks earlier in Stump Pass Park by a couple out for an early morning stroll. Appearing to have washed ashore on a narrow strip of beach, she hadn't been in the water very long, according to the coroner's report, leading to the conclusion that she was dumped into Lemon Bay. Joe didn't question how Calloway came by this information. Since Olivia and her husband, Phil, were having marital problems, and he operated a charter fishing boat, it was easy to assume that he was the killer. But a good detective never assumed anything—especially when it came to murder. The truth lay in the proof.

A half-hour after the ex-deputy nicknamed Flapjack dropped him off, Joe climbed into his Toyota with the idea of visiting the park to take a look around. He hadn't agreed to assist the man in any way and was still questioning why he had accepted the offer for breakfast. Though he hated to turn down a fellow officer, he was on vacation and had come to Englewood to relax.

As Joe headed south, he passed the roundabout leading to the mainland, glanced at the White Elephant Pub a minute later, and continued on to the cul-de-sac near the beginning of the park. A small parking lot bordered each side of what was now Gulf Boulevard. He swung around the cul-de-sac and backtracked until he located a parking space. After paying the parking fee, he strolled to an opening carved into the sea grapes and mangroves, and the head of a sandy white trail. Catching sight of the Florida state flag waving in the breeze atop a flagpole, he grinned when he realized the small building behind it housed the restrooms and areas to shower off. Someone had used their head in the initial planning stages.

Joe caught glimpses of several openings in the scrub brush as he ambled at an easy pace, wondering which opening, exactly, was the crime scene. His question was answered when he saw four waist-high stakes protruding from the sand in one of the breaches, along with lengths of black and yellow crime-scene tape, fluttering in the breeze.

Wonder if the S.O. knows the scene has been compromised? he thought. *Easy to see how the couple found Olivia, though. Even from here.*

Joe did a slow scanning of the opening and the plots of scrub brush on either side. If Phil Bridgewater had killed his wife, why did he leave her here? He looked across the narrow body of water, an arm of Lemon Bay, he guessed, to what appeared to be an island of mangroves and undergrowth. His view of the mainland was blocked. *And if her husband's charter service was located nearby then leaving Olivia 's body on this stretch of beach made no sense. Maybe she was dumped in the water and wound up here at low tide. If so, then why wasn't she carried away at high tide?* Joe shook his head. The most efficient solution would have been to weigh her down and drop her somewhere out in the Gulf. He lifted his gaze as a seagull squawked and swooped low over the island.

Maybe it wasn't Phil Bridgewater who killed her.

Joe felt his frustration beginning to build and headed back up the trail, all but convinced that he was not going to involve himself in investigating Olivia's murder. Though he'd taken a liking to John Calloway, his gut told him this was one case that might never be solved. Too much open ground and water surrounded the crime scene, and there was too much information to be digested in a week.

I'll bet they didn't find a single clue.

And was Olivia really screwing around like the rumors held? No father wanted to believe that of his daughter. But if the rumors were true, and one of her lovers did kill her, then tracking him down could take weeks. Joe shook his head again. The Charlotte County sheriff's office would have to tackle this one without him.

Joe was almost to his car when he spotted a half-dozen young people standing in an opening by the water's edge. Sliding a canoe into the water, two in the group hopped inside and paddled away. A second pair followed soon thereafter. He approached the remaining couple before they had a chance to join the others.

"Excuse me. I wonder if you could help me."

The young man turned around, eying him a second. "I'll certainly try."

"I'm vacationing here, and I want to do some fishing. I heard that Bridgewater Charters is a good outfit, but I can't remember where they're located."

"Almost directly across from us," the young man said, and pointed toward the water behind him. "The charters are all about the same, though."

"Really?"

"It *is* the Gulf, right, mister? One place to drop a line is as good as another."

"I suppose that's true. And I guess there's only one way to get to Bridgewater's from here."

"You got it. Beach Road to McCall Road then take a right onto Placida Road. Stay on Placida until you get to Maryland Avenue and turn right. Stump Pass Marina is at the end. Bridgewater's is close by."

"Thank you."

"Say, mister, canoe canoe?"

"I beg your pardon?"

The young man laughed. "It's a joke. Canoe canoe? *Can you*

canoe?"

"Oh, right." Joe joined him in laughter, but noticed a serious glint enter his eyes.

"Look, mister, since you're not from around here, I think I ought to tell you something. I don't know Phil Bridgewater personally, but I know people who know him. He's not that good a fishing guide. You'd have better luck with one of the guides from the marina."

Joe nodded.

"But if your mind's made up then you should know that he's not very friendly and has a super bad temper."

Though he'd decided against doing an investigation, Joe could feel curiosity building inside him. "Thank you, son, I'll keep that in mind."

As he got into his car and pulled out of the parking area, he heard a familiar voice.

Why are you putting yourself through this, Joe? You already know what's going to happen.

I'm tired, Joyce. I've been chasing criminals for as long as I can remember. I don't want to do it anymore.

But you're the best. It's what you do.

I'm not the best. And weren't you the one who told me not to let the past disrupt my future?

Trapped by my own words. But, Joe, you always stepped up when someone needed help. It's one of the many reasons I fell in love with you.

"Talk about feeling trapped," Joe muttered. "Now I'm trapped by who I am."

"The Boy Scout's Boy Scout" his friends had branded him in his youth. He never cared for the moniker, but there was no denying the truth. To stand at the side of someone in need was the right thing to do, and how he was raised.

Joe sighed. "Guess I'd better contact John Calloway and see what I can do."

He was in sight of the White Elephant Pub when he heard his

phone. Guiding his Camry into the parking lot, he answered, not bothering to check the caller I.D.

"Joe, it's Carly."

"Carly! What a pleasant surprise. How are you?"

"I'm fine. I'm just calling because I..."

Joe's elation faded fast. "Is something wrong?"

"No, I just miss you. That's silly, isn't it? I mean, you've only been gone what, a day or two?"

"How are David and Dani?"

"Couldn't be better, but I'm concerned that their relationship might become a problem in the future. I'll have to keep an eye on them. Otherwise, we're in kind of a lull around here. We've only got one case pending. Dani and her partner are on it. All in all, it's been pretty quiet."

"Let's hope it stays that way for a while. It's always good to catch a breather now and then."

"So what are you up to, besides sleeping until noon?"

"Relaxing. Sightseeing. I'm thinking of doing some fishing."

"You? Somehow I can't picture that."

Joe laughed.

"Well, I guess I'd better be going."

"Say hello to David and Dani for me."

"Sure will." Carly paused. "Joe, you sound good. *Really* good. You like Englewood, don't you?"

"It's a different world down here. People are friendly. Life is easygoing. Yeah, I like it. It's nice."

"Well enjoy yourself, and stay safe, okay?"

"I will."

A smile was set firmly on Joe's face as he motored back onto Beach Road.

CHAPTER 5

The struggle as to whether he would help John Calloway was long over by the time Joe reached the cottage. He lingered a moment after he'd stepped inside, then went to the refrigerator and grabbed one of the dozen bottles of water he'd brought with him. He moved onto the porch, where the neon yellow folding chair sat facing the Gulf. He slid into it, cracked the seal on the bottle, and took a long drink.

Remembering his early encounters with Carly, Joe knew that the lead detective in the Olivia Bridgewater case would not be happy with his involvement. And how much could he actually hope to accomplish during his brief stay?

Sunbursts topping the miles of water before him were a pleasant distraction, leading his eyes to a pair of sailboats far off on the horizon. A steady, salt-tinged breeze, sifting through the screen, enveloped him in a cool embrace, and unleashed a gentle, relaxing calmness. Before long, he drifted off, the water bottle slipping from his hand to the floor.

"Grandma! Grandpa! We're here! We're here!"

The child's voice sounded distant at first, the car doors slamming soon after.

The better part of a minute passed before Joe opened his eyes.

A late afternoon sun burned in the cloudless cobalt sky, its fading brilliance receding across the water. He came to realize that the couple in the next cottage had company, at least three people, judging from the variety of murmurs. He yawned and stretched and didn't care that the day had passed him by as he searched around the chair for the bottle of water he'd dropped.

I need a shower, he thought, and took a drink to chase the dryness from his mouth. *Then I think I'll head to the Lock 'N Key Restaurant for supper.*

In no hurry to leave the porch, Joe looked out over the water, but didn't see the Gulf. His mind's eye was searching the strip of beach where Olivia Bridgewater's body had been abandoned. He decided that when he was through eating, he'd stop by Flapjack's and get John's phone number from Sammi.

He intentionally hadn't asked John for the number because he didn't want to give the man the wrong impression. No sense building up his hopes. After Carly's call, though, he'd felt a revitalization of sorts, like his being in Englewood at this particular time was meant to serve a purpose. And then there was Joyce, always steering him in the right direction and making certain he didn't get lost.

The water pressure for the shower wasn't as strong as it was at home, but Joe was able to enjoy the soaking anyway. He chose a blue-striped dress shirt and navy Dockers as his uniform for the evening, remembering too late that he'd forgotten to pack a pair of dress shoes.

Finding humor in his forgetfulness for a change, he laughed and hoped that no one noticed his running shoes.

He climbed into his car, decked out and hungry, as the dimming of twilight began.

Joe had no idea of the time and felt somewhat disappointed when he saw the line of people waiting in front of the restaurant. He considered searching for another eatery, then thought better of it. The kindly woman he'd spoken to in the office at the cottages had recommended the Lock 'N Key. He decided to take a chance.

Told that he would have to wait at least fifteen minutes to be seated, he ambled into the pub and took a chair at the bar. Fortune smiled on him when he was told that the establishment kept Evan Williams in stock. He sipped a glass of his favorite whiskey on the rocks, of course, while he waited. He spent the time figuring out exactly what he was going to say to John Calloway. Depending upon what information he would be given, and what help, if any, he would receive, Joe decided the best way to approach the man was to be open and honest.

"Who am I kidding?" he muttered. "I'm going to be spinning my wheels and getting nowhere."

As he took a sip of whiskey, he suddenly realized he wasn't alone.

"Hey, Joe."

"Sammi!" Joe straightened up and swiveled his chair around. "What a surprise."

"I thought that was you." She gestured to the thin man beside her. "This is my husband, Herb."

Joe extended his right hand. "Pleasure to meet you, Herb."

Herb nodded and shook his hand. "I'll wait for you in the car, honey."

Sammi stood silent until he disappeared into the crowd. "Herb's not comfortable around a lot of people."

"I thought you'd be working," Joe said.

"Dad is working tonight." A pleasant glimmer appeared in her eyes. "He told me you two had breakfast together. Talking to you had an effect on him I think."

"Sometimes talking about an unfortunate occurrence is what a person needs."

Sammi paused, at a loss as to what she should say next. "Joe, are you gonna...are you gonna help my dad?"

"I'm not sure how much help I can be, Sammi. I did want to talk to your dad again."

"I'm sure he'd appreciate *anything* you can do. Well, I'd best be going. Herb's probably getting antsy."

Joe turned back to his drink and took a longer sip. Glancing to his left, he noticed a server heading his way. The green-eyed brunette was made prettier by her engaging smile.

"If you will follow me, Mr. Hampton."

Joe grabbed his glass and stood up. "Has it been fifteen minutes already?"

The brunette winked at him. "Any friend of Sammi's is a friend of mine."

The atmosphere in Flapjack's was smoky and noisy with chattering people. Unlike his first visit, Joe found it next to impossible to locate a place to sit down until he saw Calloway waving to him from behind the bar. Easing his way through the groups of people planted around the tables, he finally reached the far-right corner of the room. Against the wall and a few feet away from a door marked "Private," Joe met Calloway by a vacant table and shook his hand.

"Good ta see ya, Joe."

"You, too, John."

"Sammi called and said ya might stop by. Pull up a chair."

Calloway said nothing after they were seated.

"Busy tonight. Special occasion?"

"Not really. You should see it on the weekend."

Calloway went silent again.

"John, I went to Stump Pass Park today and had a look around."

"Wasn't much ta see, was there?"

"I don't know how much help I can be."

"Does that mean ya won't help?"

"It means that I can't make any guarantees."

"Ya said that already. But you'll try?"

Joe tilted his head and sighed. "I'll try."

Calloway wasted no time in standing up. "What'cha drinkin'?"

"Evan Williams on the rocks?"

"Jack Black okay?"

"Sure."

Calloway disappeared through the "Private" door, returning seconds later. He dropped a worn brown briefcase on the table.

"That's all I was able ta round up."

He went behind the bar and pulled a tumbler from the shelf. Setting it on the counter, he was about to pour the whiskey when he was interrupted by a customer.

Joe stared at the briefcase, tempted to look inside. He guessed it contained reports and photos, some confidential, and figured he had nothing to lose except his freedom if the lead detective found out. As he further contemplated the consequences of his breaking the law, his attention was yanked to the bar and Calloway's bellowing.

"What in the hell are you doin' here?"

"We need to talk, John."

Leaning against the bar was a brown-haired man standing a good six inches taller than Calloway, his yellow T-shirt stretched tight over his broad shoulders and protruding belly. His brawny arms were acorn-brown, and his huge hands, his fingers splayed, lay flat on the counter.

"I'm through talkin'! Now get outta here!"

"Through talkin'? You haven't stopped runnin' your mouth for three weeks!"

"And I'll keep right on talkin' until they put yer worthless ass away!"

Every man and woman in Flapjack's was staring at the two men. No one dared move.

"Then I'm gonna slap you with a lawsuit! I'll take you for everything you got! Includin' this dump!"

Calloway shoved his hand into his pants pocket and yanked out his phone. "You got one minute ta get outta here, Phil, then I'm callin' the cops!"

"I didn't kill her, John! Can't you get that through that thick head o' yours?"

The staring match between the men lasted mere seconds. The big man pushed himself away from the bar then stopped, slowly turning his head and giving Joe the eye.

"Who the hell are you? Is this your bodyguard, John?"

Joe stared hard at him and didn't blink.

"Get out, Phil!" Calloway yelled.

Bridgewater took a step toward Joe. "What're *you* lookin' at?"

"Not very much," Joe said.

The big man's eyes went wide.

"That's it, Phil, I'm callin' the cops!" Calloway roared.

With his wild eyes still riveted on Joe, Bridgewater turned around and headed for the door.

A collective sigh was released by everyone in the room when the door finally closed.

Calloway returned to the table and set a glass of whiskey over ice in front of Joe.

"I take it that was your son-in-law, Phillip Bridgewater?" Joe asked.

"The one and only. A bigger asshole you'd never want to meet."

Joe picked up his glass and took a healthy pull. "Give me your phone number, John. I'll go over everything in the briefcase and get back to you as soon as I can."

CHAPTER 6

The excitement of witnessing the encounter between John Calloway and Phil Bridgewater was still flowing strong in Joe when he got back to the cottage. He'd intended to go over the contents of the briefcase as soon as he could pull up a chair at the dining table, but after three generous glasses of Jack Black, courtesy of John, and the ongoing adrenaline rush, he decided his concentration would be keener the next day.

Sitting in the yellow folding chair on the porch, Joe marveled at the myriad of stars scattered across the ebony sky, the only discernible difference between it and the midnight waters stretching toward the horizon. The smell of newly mown grass, a pleasantry he'd failed to notice before leaving earlier, intermingled with the salt-tinged breeze pouring in through the screen. Maybe it was the effects of the entire evening, but the only desire that would bring him satisfaction was to laze in the darkness—and reflect. Was this the way it was always going to be? No matter where he went, or who he met, something terrible was bound to follow? Hadn't he done enough? Given enough?

It's what you do, he heard Joyce say. *You're the best.*

"But even the best has the right to call it a day," he muttered.

The steady hum of the vehicle's engine and tires popping pieces of shell embedded in the sandy road pulled Joe out of his mood. He looked over his right shoulder and saw the flood of headlights sweeping across the open yard to the property's end.

Unwilling at first, he finally stood up and turned around.

A dark sedan prowling unhurriedly rolled into the looping right turn and disappeared behind the second row of cottages.

Joe remained still for a moment, hesitant, slowed by the numbing of alcohol, but curious as to the reason for the vehicle's presence and the identity of the driver. The car's unadorned exterior and deeply tinted windows suggested it belonged to a law enforcement agency—more in line with what a detective would be assigned. A clearly marked cruiser would be the usual ride for an officer or deputy on a routine patrol. If searching for someone then a spotlight or high-intensity flashlight would be employed.

I wasn't driving erratically, he thought. *And I didn't notice any police activity in the area when I left Flapjack's.*

Returning to the folding chair and the countless twinkling stars, he allowed the brief encounter to fade away along with his adrenaline and curiosity. The night was too beautiful. Nothing or no one would be permitted to ruin this moment of tranquility.

Joe found it hard to believe the time displayed on his watch. He remembered the wondrous, starry sky and leaving the porch and falling into bed, not bothering to take off his clothes. He smacked his lips in an attempt to water down the desert in his mouth and figured a cold shower and a bite to eat would ready him for an afternoon of reviewing the reports stowed in the briefcase. First on the list of things to do was to get up.

"If I don't get out of bed soon, I'm going to stay here the entire day," he murmured.

Chuckling as the midmorning sun crept from behind the floral drapes and over the tan bedroom wall, he thought of Carly and David.

"They wouldn't believe it if they saw me like this."

Ten minutes later, he got out of bed.

Forty-five minutes later, he was showered and ready to eat

lunch. He ran a hand over the stubble on his face as he stood in front of the dresser mirror.

"I don't think the folks at the Country Hound will mind a little fuzz. Besides, I'm on vacation." He stared a second longer at his reflection. "Maybe I'll grow a beard."

He was two steps from the front door when he stopped and peered over his shoulder. The briefcase was lying on top of the small walnut dining table where he'd left it. As was his habit with the property belonging to other people, he took the briefcase to the bedroom for safekeeping and placed it on the shelf above the clothes rack in the closet. Satisfied that John Calloway's research was safe, he headed back to the living room.

Seeing the obscure silhouette through the frosty jalousie panes stopped him cold. Three heartbeats later came the knocking.

An icy jolt of apprehension shot through Joe for a reason he couldn't fathom. Unless the unknown visitor was Phillip Bridgewater, the last person he wanted to see. He grasped the door knob, exhaled sharply, and swung the door open.

A trim man with clear green eye, and a face that Hollywood publicists would stand in line to promote stared back at him. His white dress shirt opened at the collar and black slacks spoke of someone with something to sell. The automatic strapped to his right hip suggested otherwise.

"Joseph Hampton?"

"Yes."

The man held up his identification. "Detective Seth Probst, Charlotte County Sheriff's Office. May I come in?"

"Certainly."

Joe stepped back to make way for the detective to enter.

"So, Mr. Hampton, what brings you to Manasota Key?"

"I'm on vacation."

"How long do you plan on being here?"

"A week."

"Any friends or relatives in the area?"

"No."

"Just here on vacation."

"Right."

"How long have you known John Calloway?"

"I don't know him."

"You've never met him?"

"I met him for the first time yesterday."

"I thought you said you didn't know him?"

"I don't. Couldn't tell you the first thing about him."

Probst grinned and ran a hand through his dark red hair. "Then you didn't come here to consort with him in any capacity?"

"As I said, Detective, I'm on vacation."

"Did he mention anything about his daughter?"

"I met his daughter, Sammi, at Flapjack's the first night I was here."

"The first night?"

"I saw the bar on my way to the cottages. It looked interesting so I thought I'd stop by."

"Did Sammi tell you about her sister?

"She mentioned her sister had died recently."

"Nothing else?"

"She said that her father was taking it hard."

"How were you introduced to Mr. Calloway?"

"He stopped by yesterday and invited me to breakfast."

"For no reason at all he came to see you?" Probst offered a suspicious grin.

"I told his daughter that I liked the atmosphere at Flapjack's, and I'd like to meet her father sometime. I figured I'd meet him the next time I went there."

"How did he find out where you were staying?"

"Detective, maybe if you told me what this is all about I could better answer your questions."

Probst glanced at his brown oxfords. "Are you a cop, Mr. Hampton?"

"Used to be."

"Detective?"

"For eighteen years."

"Uh-huh. Well, you see, Mr. Hampton, John Calloway's daughter, Olivia, was murdered. Right now, I have no witnesses, no clues, and the only viable suspect is her husband. It's a difficult case, and quite frankly, sir, I don't need any outside interference adding to the problem. Do we understand each other?"

"We do."

Probst was well out the door and into the yard when he turned back to Joe.

"To tell you the truth, Mr. Hampton, I think you know more about this case than you're letting on."

Joe watched him climb into the dark blue sedan and pull away, following the same route as the vehicle from the previous night.

"To tell you the truth, Detective, I used that same line more times that I can remember. And I'd like to know how you found out about me."

Taking a moment, he thought about the briefcase stashed in the closet and floated the notion of giving it back to John. As much as he wanted to help the man, his gut feeling was telling him to rescind his offer.

Joe locked the cottage and headed out in search of a place to go for lunch. He decided to try the mainland and somewhere different with different selections. Bothered by the appearance of Detective Probst, the idea of stepping away from John Calloway's request for help grew stronger.

After leaving Beach Road and heading south, he continued to struggle with his conscience until he came to Placida Road.

"Rob's Pizzeria," he said aloud. "I could go for a couple of slices."

Turning into the parking lot, the question of whether he should get involved with Olivia Bridgewater's murder reemerged. In comparison to Clearwater Beach, Englewood was a small town—but not that small. Sure, people talked. Sure, people helped their friends. But people who helped their friends get away with murder? Though he despised corrupt cops, Joe wanted no part of tangling with them. Even if he *was* helping a brother in arms avenge his daughter.

CHAPTER 7

Joe was up and out the door early the next morning, arriving at the Country Hound Café shortly after it opened at six-thirty. All through his breakfast of waffles and bacon, he kept staring at the table where he'd sat with John Calloway, expecting him to arrive at any moment. Missing also was Trish, the amiable, gum-cracking redhead who'd waited on them. Not unusual for the pair to be absent, he supposed. Life had a habit of getting in the way and disrupting a person's everyday routine. Then again.

The return trip was a blur with Joe's sole focus being on the briefcase. He was going to go over each report thoroughly and pay close attention to every detail before deciding to move forward. Detective Probst had already told him there were no witnesses and no clues, the only suspect being the victim's husband, who happened to be Probst's high school buddy. If nothing in the other reports raised doubts or contained inconsistencies, he would tell John that he couldn't help him. He didn't want to disappoint the man, but he didn't want to beat his head against a wall, either.

A thin curtain of dust followed Joe into the driveway. Laughing and conversation from those staying in the other cottages reached his ears as he got out of his car. He waved at the young woman and a couple his age as they loaded a cooler, blankets, towels, and an umbrella into a silver SUV, then smiled and wiggled his fingers at the boy and girl wearing bathing suits and rubber shower shoes, who were waiting nearby. No doubt the woman and children were the ones he'd heard the day before. He silently wished that he could enjoy a day at the beach.

Maybe I can. There's still plenty of time.

He'd no sooner gone to the bedroom, pulled the briefcase out of the closet, and sat down at the dining table when his phone rang. The caller I.D. bore the number belonging to the Sandpiper Shore Cottages.

"Mr. Hampton, this is Juanita in the office. I have a message for you."

"Really? I can't imagine who it might be from."

"Detective Seth Probst of the sheriff's office would like you to call him."

Joe searched the briefcase for something to write on, eventually grabbing one of the reports and a pen he uncovered. Sounding tentative, Juanita passed along the phone number and bid him good day.

Joe sat back and studied the number he'd jotted down on the corner of the report.

Now what does he want? Could he know about this briefcase? I wouldn't think that John told anyone about it, except for those who got the info for him. I haven't been poking around...yet. So what could it be?

"Only one way to find out," Joe whispered, and picked up his phone from the table.

"Mr. Hampton, I appreciate your getting back to me so quickly." Probst's tone was all business. "I'm afraid I have some bad news."

Oh my god! Joe thought. *Carly? David?* "What is it?"

"Your friend John Calloway was murdered last night."

Stunned, Joe didn't speak.

"Mr. Hampton?"

"Yes, I heard you. How did it happen?"

"I have some questions. I'd like to stop by if you're not planning to run off."

"What questions could you possibly have for me, Detective?"

"I can be there in, say, twenty minutes?"

"Fine. I'll make it a point not to *run off*. And I'll tell you again, I just met John Calloway a few days ago."

Probst grunted. "So you say."

When Joe heard the humming of a car's engine and shells popping under the tires, he didn't move. Curiosity, more than anxiety, whirled inside him as he remained seated on the floral sofa. Seconds later, an obscure figure stood in front of the jalousie door. Joe was on his feet before the first knock sounded.

"Good morning, Mr. Hampton."

A mint-green shirt and navy slacks defined Probst's uniform, standard wear for a detective in these parts, Joe figured.

"Please come in." Joe directed him to the sofa and pulled out a dining-room chair for himself. "Now, how can I help you?"

Probst removed a notepad and pen from his shirt pocket. "Where did you say you were from, Mr. Hampton?"

"Clearwater Beach."

"And where exactly do you live?"

"Detective Probst, is this really necessary? If you're a good detective, and I'm assuming you are, then you've already run a search on me."

Probst's green eyes narrowed. "Are you trying to be difficult, sir?"

"No, I'm trying to figure out why you're so interested in me."

Probst continued to stare.

Joe sighed. "The Crimson Conch condominiums," he said and passed along the address.

"Did John Calloway ask you to come down here and investigate his daughter's murder?"

"No."

"And you never met the man before? Never knew he existed until you came to Englewood?"

"Right.

"Do you know Phillip Bridgewater?"

"I'm going to save you some time, Detective. Night before last I went to Flapjack's. I was having a drink and talking to John when Phillip Bridgewater came in. He and John got into it. John told him to leave."

"Did you confront Mr. Bridgewater?"

"On the contrary, he confronted me."

"What did you do?"

"Nothing."

"Nothing?"

"I'd be a fool to take on someone that big at my age."

"And Mr. Bridgewater just left?"

"After John threatened to call the police."

Probst grinned as he wrote down the information in his notepad. "How about yesterday?"

"What would you like to know?"

"What did you do?"

"Shortly after you left, I went to Rob's Pizzeria for lunch. Then I drove around."

"Sightseeing?"

"It's a beautiful area."

"And after that?"

"I picked up a sub for supper and came back here."

"Go anywhere else?"

"I sat on the porch, had a couple of drinks while I watched the sunset, and later I went to bed."

"So you didn't go looking for Phillip Bridgewater?"

Joe couldn't help but shake his head. "Detective Probst, I am *not* a hired thug nor am I a private investigator. I came to Englewood for a vacation. That's all."

"One final question, sir. Do you think Phillip Bridgewater killed his wife, Olivia?"

The detective's question sparked a necessary hesitation in Joe. He knew it was a trap. There *was* no correct answer. The only good answer was no answer.

"I have no opinion on the matter."

"Why is that?"

"Because I'm not one to pre-judge people, especially those I don't know."

Probst wore a noticeable grin as he stood up. "You're good, Mr. Hampton. Very good."

"Good luck with your investigation, Detective."

Joe saw Probst to the door, then waited in the middle of the room until he heard him drive off, assured that the detective didn't know which way to turn. Even if Probst *was* covering for his buddy, Phillip Bridgewater, now he had a bigger problem. By Probst's own admission, Bridgewater was the lone suspect in Olivia's murder. With the confrontation between Bridgewater and John Calloway in Flapjack's being witnessed by a roomful of people, the popular conclusion would be that Bridgewater killed Calloway.

"So how are you going to cover for your buddy now, Detective?" Joe whispered.

Without another thought, he went to the refrigerator and pulled out a bottle of water, setting it on the dining table as he passed by. Removing the briefcase from the closet, he returned to the table and sat down.

CHAPTER 8

By late afternoon, Joe had gone through every report in the briefcase. Information surrounding the discovery of Olivia Bridgewater's body and the ensuing investigation was unremarkable. Nothing questionable appeared in the autopsy report, but he did note one interesting fact. Of the many knife wounds, those discernible were seven-sixteenths of an inch in length. Why would a man the size of Phillip Bridgewater choose such a small knife? Not possessing so much as a general knowledge of knives, Joe guessed that some type of fillet knife might have been the only weapon within reach during a heated argument. But even that possibility wasn't enough to convince him. Added to Seth Probst's confirmation of Bridgewater being the only suspect was John Calloway's finding fault with his son-in-law's alibi.

You told your buddy, Probst, that you were sleeping on your boat, Phil...alone? Joe shook his head. "That is lame. And why didn't Probst ask you where Olivia was...even if you didn't know?"

Another age-old problem existed: There was no proof that Bridgewater was lying. No matter what the popular consensus in the court of public opinion, without proof there would be no conviction.

Joe leaned back in his chair and folded his arms, carefully eyeing the papers spread out on the dining table.

"I don't see it, John," he whispered. "Nothing points directly to Bridgewater, lame alibi or not. There's no evidence of a fight taking place at their home or on the boat, and the murder weapon has yet to be found. Unless..."

One explanation after another of how the knife might have vanished was considered, including the possibility that Probst had literally destroyed it, piece by piece.

"I've exhausted all the theories I can think of, John. And I don't know where to turn from here."

Joe picked up the reports and put them back into the briefcase before returning it to the closet shelf. On his way to the refrigerator for another bottle of water, he stopped at the kitchen sink and gazed out of the window.

A gathering of clouds slowly drifting north were lining up to make for a beautiful sunset. Tonight, he wasn't interested. Nor would his favorite whiskey bring him comfort. The fact that he'd only recently met John Calloway was irrelevant. Someone had committed murder—twice—and he was helpless to do anything about it.

Joe stood at the window, staring out at the Gulf for forty-five minutes, then headed to the bathroom for a shower. He wasn't as hungry as he'd been during the past few days, and the reason was clear. But he was going to the Lock N' Key to try to eat supper. What he didn't finish he would bring back with him.

Darkness had overcome the twilight sky when Joe pulled into the parking lot. A line of people stood in wait before him. No matter. A beer in the pub would do while he passed the time.

The cold beer tasted good when the frosty mug reached his lips, and he envisioned the pink and juicy slice of prime rib beside the baked potato oozing with butter he would soon carve up and try to eat. Once again, he sensed that someone was standing nearby, watching him. The stocky young redhead wasn't cracking her gum this time.

"Trish?"

"Joe, I need to…" She looked over one shoulder and then the other. "I need to talk to you. Somewhere private."

"Okay, let's go to my car."

"That's not a good idea. Outside…in the parking lot behind the building, maybe."

Joe left his half-full mug and a five-dollar tip on the counter and followed Trish through the crowd. Outside, they worked their way around the building to a host of cars parked in front of a waist-high, yellow, concrete-block wall.

As she had done in the pub, Trish looked over both shoulders. "I don't know if you've heard, but Flapjack is dead."

"Yes, I…found out this morning."

In the faint pouring of light coming from the pub, Joe could see her eyes begin to well up.

"He liked you, Joe. He told me he had a good feeling about you, and felt like you could steer him in the right direction to finding out who killed Livie."

"I liked him, too, Trish. I'm sorry I didn't get to know him better."

"I guess he told you that he always thought Phil killed her."

"He did, but he admitted that he didn't know for certain."

"Yeah. He told me more'n once that he wasn't sure."

An unexpected notion made Joe pause. "Trish, you seem to have known John pretty well. More than someone who only sees him when he's hungry, I mean."

Silence slid between them a moment.

"Joe, can I trust you?"

"I want to help, Trish."

"Flapjack was a good ole boy, and as tough as they come, in a good way. But every now and again… He was married twice. Both his wives died, in case you didn't know. He raised both them girls by himself, and did a good job, too. But later on, after they were grown and out the door, he kinda got to feelin' lonely at times. I got to noticin' when he was feelin' down and, well…" She sighed. "I started helpin' him feel better."

"What are you saying?"

"I went to bed with him every now and again...and I know who killed him."

Joe didn't let his surprise show. "Have you told the police?"

"I can't."

"Why?"

"'Cause Phil killed him, and I'm afraid to tell 'em 'cause Phil is buddies with one of 'em."

"You know for certain that Bridgewater killed John?"

"I was there, Joe. I was in the bedroom when it happened."

"And he didn't see you?"

"He and Flapjack were in the living room. They got to arguin', and then I heard a crash and what sounded like scufflin'. Then it got quiet."

"Bridgewater ran?"

"He must've been drunk 'cause he didn't search the house. I waited, then got dressed and snuck into the living room. That's when I saw Flapjack. I think he was strangled."

"Are you sure he didn't see you? What about your car?"

"Flapjack always came and got me on our special nights. He didn't want his neighbors gettin' any ideas."

Joe stared hard at the block wall, thinking. "Is there *anyone* at the sheriff's office you trust enough to tell them what happened?"

"Nope. I try to avoid all cops 'cept Flapjack. No offense."

"Bridgewater has killed two people. We can't let him get away with it."

Trish arched her eyebrows and glanced to the right.

"What is it?"

"I heard somethin' when Phil and Flapjack were fightin'. Flapjack kept sayin' that he knew Phil killed Livie, and Phil kept sayin' he didn't. Then Phil yelled 'so-and-so killed Livie, you dumb ass!' That was right before I heard the crash and the scufflin'."

"Bridgewater told John who killed Olivia?"

"Yes, but I didn't hear the name. I was slidin' outta bed, and the mattress springs started squeakin'. I thought for sure he heard me."

"I can't let this go, Trish. You've got to go to the sheriff's office and tell them what you know."

"That ain't gonna happen, Joe. If Phil finds out, he'll kill me. And if *he* doesn't, his buddy will."

"Two people are dead!"

"I know!" Trish looked around then lowered her head. "I know."

Joe's anger slowly subsided when she started sobbing. "Don't worry. I'll figure something out. Are you going to be all right?"

Trish sniffed. "Yeah."

"Do you have someplace safe to stay?"

"My apartment. I'll be okay as long as Phil doesn't find out that I know what he did."

"Shall I walk you to your car?"

Trish grinned through her tears. "You're a real gent...just like Flapjack. But you better not. Somebody might see us."

As he watched her disappear around the corner of the building, Joe felt a dull ache begin in his stomach. He couldn't sit by and ignore the two murders, and he couldn't risk putting Trish's life in danger by going to the sheriff's office and telling them what he knew—not yet, anyway. The sound of laughter from a couple preparing to leave the parking lot accompanied Joe back to the entrance.

Once inside, he told the hostess he'd been called away, and went back to a chair at the bar for another cold beer. Minutes passed as his stomachache continued, the beer not helping to change his mood. Seated for dinner a while later, he ordered a Caesar salad with grilled shrimp instead of the prime rib, ate half of it, and took the rest back to the cottage.

His mood unaltered as he took a seat on the porch, a glass of Evan Williams helped him to relax. But the problem weighing him down was as dark as the warm Gulf waters.

CHAPTER 9

Joe found himself in bed when he woke the next morning but lacked the desire to figure out how he'd gotten there. The familiar signs of morning glowing behind the bedroom drapes left him to question how much of the day he'd lost. Not that it mattered.

During his final coherent moment the previous night, he'd decided to give up trying to prove that Phillip Bridgewater was a murderer. He hated admitting defeat, but sometimes nothing or no one could uncover the truth.

Joe rolled over on his left side.

I could get with Carly and David after I get home, he thought. *I'll bet the three of us could figure out something, once they've looked over the reports.*

The idea vanished as quickly as it had arrived. His friends had enough to do without catering to his personal projects—even the murder of an ex-cop.

He threw off the covers and eased his feet to the floor. Still in his clothes, he sat hunched over, catching the scent of salt air heavy on the breeze through the cottage. Unlike when he'd first arrived, the breeze and tropical surroundings no longer held the magic that had soothed his soul. A growing urge to pack up and leave right then began to build inside him, growing stronger with each passing minute. Slowly rising, he plodded to the bathroom to splash water on his face, and felt the cool linoleum floor beneath his feet. At least he'd removed his shoes and socks. A handful of refreshing water opened his eyes to the aged reflection in the mirror. The early stages of a beard were evident now, and it was as gray as the hair on his head. He stared at the stubble, picturing it full and wavy. Imagining the reactions of Crimson Conch residents when they saw him, a smile turned up the corners of his mouth.

He was thinking about how good a shower would feel when a loud knocking on the front door rattled the slatted panes and his serenity. Joe grabbed a towel, dried his face, and took his time in answering, attempting to determine who the blurry figure outside might be. Opening the door provided a surprising answer.

"Detective Probst."

"Mr. Hampton." Probst's hardened face remained unchanged as he looked Joe over. "Did I wake you?"

"No. I've been up for several minutes."

Joe grinned. Probst didn't.

"What brings you to see me today, Detective?"

"There's been a development. I'd like to talk to you about it."

"Okay. Come on in."

"How about I buy you breakfast...or lunch, maybe?"

This is getting stranger by the minute, Joe thought. "All right, let me find my shoes."

For the first time in his life, Joe felt uncomfortable when he slid into the front seat of a police vehicle. Now he had a good idea of what others experienced when being taken for a ride by the law. Only difference was, Joe wasn't sure what was in store for him.

Probst said very little during the trip, occasionally asking Joe if he'd visited various tourist attractions on Manasota Key and around Englewood. Joe didn't mind the small talk, initially believing it to be a relaxed form of interrogation. He wasn't divulging any secrets or betraying any confidences, but he knew the shallow banter was leading up to a subject about which he had very little knowledge—the murder of John Calloway. But he'd been wrong before.

Joe succeeded in disguising his uneasiness until Probst steered the sedan into the parking lot of the Country Hound Café. He hoped that Trish would be equally adept at remaining calm when she spotted the two of them—*if* she had returned to work.

"Ever eaten here before, Mr. Hampton?" Probst asked as they moved toward the door.

"As a matter of fact, I have."

"I like it. And the food is good. Wouldn't you agree?"

"You'll get no complaints from me."

Joe's stomach began to tighten as they approached the entrance. Once they were inside, they paused to search for a table. Joe tried not to appear obvious as he scanned the room for Trish. When he didn't see her, he released a shallow sigh. What he *did* see was a couple seated at the table where he and John Calloway had talked. Another server was chatting with them.

Probst wasted little time in leading him to a table, and they sat down. Folding his hands and resting them on top of the table, the detective appeared to be struggling with how he would begin the conversation. Having experienced the same awkwardness himself at times when he had been on the job, Joe waited.

"Mr. Hampton, I'll get right to the point. Do you know Patricia Nelson?"

"I don't believe I do."

"You did say that you had been here before, is that right?"

"Yes."

"She works here. I thought she may have waited on you."

"I don't recall a Patricia when I was here."

Probst nodded, and ran a hand through his hair. "She's better known as Trish."

"Okay. Trish I remember. I didn't know her last name."

"When you came here with John Calloway?"

Joe's uneasiness increased. Before he could answer, a server with straight black hair and a wide smile walked up.

"Hey, fellas. What can I get you to drink?"

Probst stared at Joe.

"Too late for breakfast?" Joe asked.

"'Fraid so."

"In that case, I'll have iced tea."

"I'll have the same," Probst said.

The server laid two menus on the table. "Be back in a minute."

Probst's eyes never left Joe. "Did you come here with John Calloway, Mr. Hampton?"

"Yes."

"And did he ask you to look into his daughter's murder?"

"In so many words."

"I thought you told me he didn't?"

"You questioned whether I knew John. At the time I had just met him. Then you wanted to know if he'd asked me to come down here and investigate his daughter's murder, which he didn't. He asked for my help when we came here for breakfast."

"And what did you tell him?"

"I told him I didn't know the area and wouldn't know where to begin."

Probst nodded, and looked down at his hands. A moment later he looked up. "Mr.

Hampton, are you aware that John Calloway and Trish Nelson are close friends?"

"I got that impression from the brief time I was around them."

Joe was waiting for him to dig deeper when the server returned with their drinks.

"Now, whatcha gonna have, fellas?"

"I'll have the French dip," Probst said.

"Turkey bacon club," Joe said.

Rapid scribbling, followed by another wide smile, and she was gone.

"Detective, let me assure you that I am *not* here to interfere. Now you said you wanted to talk to me about a development."

Joe noticed Probst's hardened face relax, taking on a look of mild surrender.

"Mr. Hampton, when Livie Bridgewater was murdered, I

lobbied to get the case—big time. None of the higher-ups wanted me near it. Conflict of interest, they said, because of my relationship with Phil."

Joe nodded and took a drink of tea.

"I finally convinced them to give me the case, but I was put on a tight leash. I had to play it straight and by the book. No favoritism. Otherwise, I would lose my badge. And for the record, I'm playing it straight." Probst paused, his eyes locked onto Joe. "I figured I owed it to Phil to clear him if I could. Yeah, he can be an asshole at times. Especially when he's drunk. And his temper has gotten him into trouble before. But I don't think he killed Livie."

"Didn't you tell me that he's your only suspect?"

"Because his alibi is weak. Then John Calloway winds up dead, and I'm back at Phil's house asking more questions."

Joe tensed, hoping more questions weren't coming his way. "What did he say?"

Probst snorted. "He said he got drunk and passed out."

"Are you working that case?"

"No, but I talked to him anyway. I figured he wouldn't lie to me."

"Is that what you wanted to see me about?"

A sigh led Probst to lean forward. "I *did* run a search on you, Mr. Hampton. You were an exemplary detective. That said, I'm going to do something I've never done before, and quite frankly, I hate doing it. I'm going to ask you for your help."

Joe didn't answer, though his anxiety level was spiking.

"Detective Probst, I don't know how much help I can be. As I said, I don't know anything about Englewood."

"No matter. That part I can cover. So, Mr. Hampton, are you in or out?"

The weight of indecision was crushing Joe from all sides. Once again, a person he'd never met was asking for his help. Help in a murder case. The one thing he was trying so hard to escape. Could he trust this man? Or was he being set up to find out how much he knew, then go the way of Olivia Bridgewater and John Calloway?

"Detective, I have no idea who you are, but I'd like to believe that you're a good cop who wants to do the right thing. Before I give you my answer, I have a question for you. I want to know about the development you mentioned earlier."

"Mr. Hampton. Trish Nelson was killed by a hit-and-run driver in front of her apartment early this morning. I know for a fact that Phil Bridgewater had nothing to do with it because we have him staked out. He was on his boat all night."

Joe couldn't believe what he'd just heard, and needed a moment to deal with the news.

"Detective, I spoke briefly with Trish last night in the parking lot of the Lock N' Key. I guess I'm in because you're going to want to hear what I have to say."

CHAPTER 10

After hearing that Trish Nelson had overheard his friend, Phillip Bridgewater arguing with John Calloway, and eventually killing him, Seth Probst's expression changed to one of painful skepticism.

Between bites of his sandwich, Joe questioned whether the hit-and-run death of the friendly server had been the result of her being found out. Once again, Joe pointed out that he didn't know anyone in Englewood—not even the man sitting across the table from him—so he couldn't begin to put a name to the driver.

Probst had barely touched his French dip.

"Mr. Hampton, I didn't know Trish that well. Hardly at all. I don't know if I believe the story she told you."

"I understand your reluctance. I can see where, being friends with John Calloway, she would have it in for Phillip Bridgewater. But she was scared when I talked to her. I've seen that kind of fear before in witnesses."

"Scared of Phil?"

"And you. She was afraid you'd kill her if Bridgewater told you that she had been in Calloway's house when he was murdered."

"She thought I was part of a coverup?"

"So did Calloway."

"I'm not surprised...about Calloway, I mean. Martin Bridgewater, Phil's dad, was a defense attorney. He and Calloway battled each other quite a bit when we were kids. I guess Calloway figured that since I was close to the family, I'd protect Phil." Probst's expression softened, and he shook his head as he chuckled. "Martin almost had a heart attack when he found out I wanted to become a cop. I don't think he's said ten words to me since."

"There are a couple of things we need to consider, Detective. If Trish *was* lying to me, then who *did* kill Calloway? And why? Did he have any known enemies, other than Bridgewater's father?"

"I don't really know. Of course, I always steered clear of the Calloway's."

"How come?"

"Talk. You know how it goes. My friend heard such-and-such, and he doesn't like you so I don't like you. You know how kids are."

"Was it always like that?"

"No. Livie was a sweet kid and grew up to become a fine woman. I often thought about asking her..." Probst paused, and acted as if a memory had broken his concentration. "She was drawn to Phil, though. It was pretty obvious."

"Even with the mutual dislike between their families?"

"Livie took a lot of shit at first. Phil said really mean things to her. Called her names like Livie Lardass and Cow Butt Calloway. It didn't stop her from coming around."

"Bridgewater finally wise up?"

Probst snorted. "Wise isn't a word to use when talking about Phil. As dumb as he was, and still is, he finally figured it out."

"I'll bet the wedding was a lot of fun."

"There never was one. Phil and Livie eloped."

"That must have made the fathers of the bride and groom *very* happy."

"Like spraying a burning house with gasoline."

"Do you think Martin Bridgewater might have killed John Calloway?"

"Interesting thought, but there are two viable reasons why he didn't. First, Martin isn't as dumb as his son, nor as quick-tempered. And two, he's bound to a wheelchair, the result of an auto accident years ago."

"What about those who Calloway put in jail? Surely there had to be some looking for payback."

"There were a few. Big talkers, mostly. I never heard of anyone actually going after him. He was as tough as they come, but fair. Always played it straight. Not someone to call out, though. He had to be tough to handle Sammi."

Joe remembered how much praise Sammi had heaped upon her stepfather.

"She was a handful, was she?"

"Party girl. A real hell-raiser. It was all he could do to keep her out of trouble."

"I talked to her at Flapjack's when I first got here. She didn't strike me as being the rambunctious type."

"She's not as wild as she used to be. She calmed down a little after her mom died."

"So Calloway raised the two girls on his own?"

"They were young women by then. I think they realized what he was going through."

"But Olivia still wound up with Phillip."

"Yep. I always thought that Sammi was better suited for him."

"Because both of them liked to have a good time?"

"Mr. Hampton, for all his faults, Phil is still my friend. But he's a drunk, plain and simple. Sammi's become more responsible as she's gotten older, but even she likes to free the weasel every so often."

Joe smiled at Probst's country colloquialism.

"Detective, no matter how many different ways we look at the situation, there has to be someone else involved. From where I sit, your friend couldn't have committed all three murders."

"I'm with you, Mr. Hampton, and the possibility still exists that he didn't kill anyone."

"Very true. Where Olivia's murder is concerned, he does

have an alibi, as weak as it might be. And remember, Trish overheard him tell John Calloway who *had* killed Olivia, only she hadn't been able to catch the name. Now the only witness to his allegedly killing John Calloway is dead. You had eyes on him at the time, so we know he didn't kill Trish Nelson."

"No clues, no witnesses, no luck. This sucks, Mr. Hampton."

Joe finished the last of his turkey club as their server walked up. She eyed the unfinished sandwich sitting in front of Probst.

"Dip no good?"

"Could I get a box to go?"

"Sure. You want the juice, too?"

"Yes."

"More tea?"

"No thanks."

Joe shook his head.

The server picked up Joe's plate, smiled at him, and left.

By the pensive expression Probst was wearing, Joe could tell that the wheels were turning. He wanted to believe the detective was playing it straight, as he'd put it, but he was reluctant to divulge all he knew. Not until he was certain they were both on the same team.

"Have any plans for the rest of the day, Mr. Hampton?"

"Not really."

"Let's go talk to Phil. I have some more questions, and I want to see how he responds after he finds out who you are. I can read him like a book."

"An interesting ploy, Detective."

Joe was surprised twice during the ride with Probst after they left the Country Hound Café. The first surprise came when he realized they were heading in the direction of Beach Road. Not knowing the exact location of the Stump Pass Marina, he'd guessed it to be farther south of the café. The second surprise was their turning onto Massachusetts Avenue. The young man he had spoken with at Stump Pass Park days earlier had indicated the marina was located at the end of Maryland Avenue,

Bridgewater Charters being located nearby. Maybe he had gotten his streets mixed up. But he had been right about Bridgewater.

A cluster of homes sat on the north side of the two-lane asphalt street. Pine trees, palm trees, and scrub brush abounded in the fenced-in property owned by Charlotte County on the other side until the road ran out. There, the fence jutted inward, and a section of land had been cleared away. An undersized parking lot of white sand and shell partnered with a building that was not much larger than an office and that teemed with mold at its base. Its paint chipped and peeling, a washed-out blue sign by the door read: Bridgewater Charters. A foot path of the same white sand and crushed shell that covered the parking lot ran from the building to a weather-beaten dock. No boat was moored to the dock.

Daddy must have wrangled a deal for the land to help his boy, Joe thought.

Probst pulled into the parking lot and turned off the engine. Neither of them bothered to get out of the car.

"I wonder if he's on a half-day or an all-day charter," Joe said.

"If he has any customers at all," Probst said.

Joe turned and looked at him.

"He's not much of a fishing guide. He could never hold a job, so Martin bought him a boat and got the business started."

At least the kid in the canoe kid got that part right.

Joe stared across the water and saw an island filled with mangroves and undergrowth, similar to the island he'd seen from Stump Pass Park. Curiosity begged for an answer.

"I took a look at your crime scene...where Olivia was found."

"What?" Probst said.

"The barricade tape has been torn down."

"I'm not surprised. It's hard to keep people away. Especially in a place like that."

"Where is it from here?"

"Almost directly across from us."

"On the other side of that island?"

"Actually, there are two strips of land between here and there."

"Hmm."

"Something on your mind?"

"Were you able to determine if Olivia was killed where she was found?"

"No, but I don't think so. And I don't think someone carried her from the parking lot and dumped her."

"How come?"

"We couldn't find any evidence to support that belief."

Joe nodded and waited for the obvious conclusion.

"I think she was brought there by boat."

"Couldn't the tide have left her?"

"She was too far from the water's edge." Probst stared at Joe a second. "You already know that. You were there. Besides, if the tide *had* left her, it would have taken her away as well."

"So anyone with a boat could have provided the taxi service."

"But not just anyone was married to Livie and having marital problems."

"Are you saying that now you believe your friend killed her?"

"I'm saying that I don't *think* he did, but…I wouldn't be doing my job if I didn't consider all the possibilities."

Joe was starting to feel better about Probst. The detective talked a good game, anyway. Now he wondered if Probst would follow through when they finally located Bridgewater.

"Well, look who's here," Probst said.

Joe turned to see a stained and scarred thirty-seven-foot Grady-White Canyon 376 idle up to the dock.

CHAPTER 11

Joe remained shoulder to shoulder with the detective as they strolled to the dock, stopping two steps before Probst mounted it. Bridgewater had caught sight of them before hopping from his boat and was busy tying off the bow line.

"How's it going, Phil?" Probst asked.

"Slow," Bridgewater said. He didn't look up and headed for the rear of the boat.

"I need to talk to you."

Bridgewater didn't answer as he finished securing the stern line and started back toward them. Probst stepped off the dock as Bridgewater joined them.

"I thought I answered all your questions."

"I have some more."

Bridgewater glanced at Joe. "Who's this?"

"Mr. Hampton."

Joe nodded.

Bridgewater replied with a stern glare.

"Let's talk in your office."

"Nah, it's a mess. Out here's fine."

"How's your dad?"

"As ornery as ever. What do you want?"

"And your father-in-law?"

"Cut the crap, Seth. You know he's dead."

"When was the last time you saw him?"

"I don't know. A coupla weeks ago maybe."

"That long?"

"I don't know."

"You didn't go to Flapjack's recently and get into an argument with him?"

"I might have. I don't know." Bridgewater glanced at Joe again. "I been drinkin' a lot lately."

"How come?"

"Business is slow."

"Where were you just now?"

"Out for a spin. Went to the pass and come back. Need ta turn the motors over now and then when they ain't been used for a while."

"No charters, huh?"

"You see anybody?"

"Don't be a smart ass, Phil."

"Then stop jerkin' me around. Whaddaya want?"

"Do you know Trish Nelson?"

"Nope."

"But you do go to the Country Hound Café sometimes."

"Sometimes."

"She works there."

"Good for her."

"She's dead, Phil."

"What's that got ta do with me?"

"She was a good friend of your father-in-law."

"So? You think I killed her?"

"Did you?"

"No."

"Where were you last night?"

"Right here. Slept on the boat."

"Someone fitting your description was seen outside of her place."

Bridgewater glared at Joe. "Who told you that? Him?"

"I'm asking the questions, Phil. *Did* you go to her place?"

"I don't know where she lives."

"Are you sure?"

Bridgewater huffed. "How would I know where to find the chubby bitch?"

"I thought you said you didn't know her?"

Bridgewater's hardened expression didn't change.

"Answer the question."

"I remember seein' her at the Hound, okay? I never knew her name."

"Where's your car?"

"At the house."

"What's it doing there?"

"Livie said I was drinkin' too much, and hid the keys before she..."

"You've been staying on your boat all this time?"

"Pretty much."

"Phil, that's the biggest load of bullshit you've ever fed me. What about food? How'd you get your groceries?"

"When I have to...I have it delivered by one of them delivery companies."

"That could get expensive."

Again, Bridgewater glared.

Joe noticed his jaw tighten.

"You're not planning to leave town any time soon, are you?" Probst continued.

"Just ta go fishin'."

"Well make sure you come back."

"Are you finished?"

"Why, Phil, are you in a hurry to go somewhere?"

"I gotta job later this afternoon."

"I thought you said business was slow."

"First one I've had in over a week."

"Good luck."

Probst turned to Joe and motioned with his head.

Neither of them said a word as they walked the sandy path

until they were about to get inside the car. Probst stood by the door and stared at the boat. Joe looked over his shoulder in time to see Bridgewater unroll a sleeping bag and stretch out on the bow.

"He's lying about something," Probst said.

"What tipped you off?"

"Did you see his jaw tighten? Phil would walk ten miles before he'd call for a delivery. And he's too dumb to call Uber or some other people transporter."

"There's no car in the immediate area. None that I can see."

"Oh, I believe that Livie hid his car keys. But I think someone else is hauling him around. The question is, who?"

Joe slid into the front seat without answering. He had no answer for any of the unfortunate events that had occurred before or since his arrival in Englewood. Maybe it was best that he didn't. He'd come here to relax and consider whether he wanted to continue living in Clearwater Beach—not to become embroiled in solving another murder.

"I've got a few more things to check out, Mr. Hampton, so I'll drop you back at your cottage."

As he came to realize that engaging in small talk wasn't part of Seth Probst's personality, Joe used the quiet time during the ride back to the Sandpiper Shores Cottages to consider his situation. Probst appeared to be playing it straight, as he'd put it, and Joe felt assured that the detective was a competent investigator. He didn't want to delve further into the trio of murders anyway. What he found troubling was the possible existence of a second party—a willing and able collaborator who was playing a significant role in helping Phillip Bridgewater get away with murder. Again, his ignorance of the people inhabiting the small Gulf Coast community left him without a name or face to consider. The obvious could be staring him in the face, and he wouldn't see it.

Joe turned his attention to the blue-green waters of Lemon Bay as they motored along Beach Road. Approaching the final bridge leading to the roundabout at the intersection, he instinctively looked over at Flapjack's Bar.

Five vehicles sat in the parking lot, four cars and a pickup truck—a brown Dodge Ram. The bar being open surprised him, and he wondered if the truck had belonged to John Calloway.

Probst made the right turn onto North Beach Road as Joe pondered seeing the Dodge.

Why would Sammi be driving her father's truck? If that is John's truck. He paused to glance at the Lock N' Key. *Maybe her husband needed the car. Or maybe their car broke down.*

A late afternoon sun added a vibrant layer of color to an already beautiful landscaping on both sides of the road. Joe soaked in its allure as they neared the cottages, having decided to return to Flapjack's to enjoy a cold beer. Surely Sammi needed cheering up. If she didn't, then he would know that what she'd told him about her father was questionable, if not an outright lie. If she did, then perhaps he could coax a few answers out of her. A rotten scheme that he'd employed in the past. But all was fair when it came to murder—fair in his mind, anyway. Besides, Probst's mentioning that Sammi seemed a better fit for Phil than Olivia had struck him as curious.

Shells popping under tires on the narrow, sandy road pulled his attention away from his plan.

Joe made certain to get Probst's phone number before thanking him for lunch. He walked to the rear of the cottage, waiting for the detective to leave, and stood looking out over the Gulf. All he heard was the waves rolling and breaking on the shore. Ten minutes would be enough time—maybe fifteen—plenty of time for Probst to be far away from Manasota Key and from Flapjack's.

CHAPTER 12

Joe took a moment to let his eyes adjust as the front door to Flapjack's Bar closed behind him. He wanted his vision to be clear and sharp so he could see the expression on Sammi's face when she saw him—as much as the dim lighting in the room would allow, anyway.

Sammi was leaning against the counter, talking to a man wearing a black baseball cap. She didn't look at Joe right away, instead releasing subtle laughter at a remark made by the customer. It was only when Joe pulled out a bar chair and sat down that she gazed in his direction. The elation shaping her face vanished, replaced by a look somewhere between concern and caution.

"Hey, Joe."

"Hello, Sammi."

"What can I get you?"

"A draft."

"What kind?"

"Surprise me."

Sammi grabbed a glass and proceeded to fill it from the tap an arm's length away.

"There you go."

"Thanks. Speaking of surprises, I was surprised to see that you're open today."

"Dad didn't stay closed very often. One of the few times was

171

when Livie died. He gave me strict orders never to close except for certain holidays when I started workin' here full time. Even for...you know."

Not even out of respect for him? Joe thought. "I was sorry to hear about what happened to your father."

Sammi lowered her eyes. "Yeah...it sure knocked the wind outta me. The police think he caught somebody trying to rob his place."

Joe picked up the glass of beer. Probst hadn't mentioned anything about a possible robbery. "So I guess you're in charge now." He looked over one shoulder and then the other. "Is your husband going to help you run Flapjack's?"

"We haven't discussed it. Herb has a good job with the school system."

"Oh yeah? What does he do?"

"He maintains the football and baseball and softball fields for Lemon Bay High School."

Joe nodded and took another drink of beer.

"I'd hate to see him leave. Good jobs are hard to come by these days. I may wind up hiring someone."

"Is that your father's truck outside?"

"Yeah." Sammi picked up a bar towel and wiped the counter. "Herb got into a fender bender last night. He's out gettin' estimates on how much it's gonna cost."

"Was he hurt?"

"Just his pride." Sammi looked beyond him. "Excuse me, Joe. I need to check on Stuart and Gloria."

An odd feeling settled inside Joe as he took another drink. Could Herb have been the hit and run driver who killed Trish Nelson? Or were the two incidents coincidental? But what reason would Herb have for killing Trish? He was about to tip his glass once more when it hit him.

Not Herb! he thought. *Sammi! Of course. Sammi was jealous of Olivia because she wanted Phil for herself. She killed Trish because she knew that Trish overheard Phil and John arguing and...No, that can't be right. Trish told me that no one knew she was in John's house.*

Seeing Sammi walk behind the counter chased his thoughts away. She came to where he sat and picked up the bar towel.

"You seem to be holding up pretty well, Sammi. I mean, for someone who just lost her sister *and* her father."

"My stepsister," she corrected. "I don't know, Joe. Maybe I'm weird. I feel bad. Terrible, really. But I can't see cryin' and mopin' around for days on end. Yeah, I'm sorry that Dad and Livie are dead, but life goes on. Know what I mean?"

Joe turned up his glass and finished his beer. "Yes, Sammi, I know exactly what you mean."

"You want another?"

"I believe I do."

Small talk between them filled most of the next hour, and that was fine by Joe. If Sammi remained none the wiser as to the real reason he'd come to Flapjack's then his strategy had been successful. A couple of theories surrounding the deaths of Olivia Bridgewater, John Calloway, and Trish Nelson had begun to materialize in his mind. When he got back to the cottage, he would call Seth Probst. Once he'd finished relating the theories to him, he would know for certain whether the detective lived up to his claim of playing it straight.

CHAPTER 13

Joe sat on the screened-in porch facing the blackened waters of the Gulf. Only a smudge of blue, yellow, and orange painted the cloudless sky of the young evening. He'd decided against having supper, still full from his lunch with Seth Probst, and the glut of suspicion surrounding a person he hardly knew—Sammi. He'd thought about pouring himself a drink, but after three beers at Flapjack's, thought better of it. He wanted to be coherent when he made the call to the detective.

As the last bit of daylight disappeared beneath the darkened expanse, Joe picked up his phone.

"You caught me as I was about to leave the office," Probst said. "I'm really tired. Can this wait until tomorrow?"

"I think it's best you hear it now."

He heard Probst sigh.

"Go ahead."

"I don't think that Phillip Bridgewater killed his wife. I think Sammi killed Olivia."

The only response Joe heard were the cars passing from time to time on North Beach Road.

"How did you come up with that?" Probst asked.

"It was no secret that Bridgewater and Olivia were having problems—had been for a while, right?"

"I'm listening."

"John Calloway told me that Olivia had mentioned getting a

divorce more than once. Maybe she decided the time was right. I'm not up on Florida divorce laws, but I believe that she would have been entitled to half of everything."

"With no extenuating circumstances, that sounds about right."

"Now, knowing that Bridgewater could lose what little he had, Sammi kills Olivia, figuring that she can save him and make herself look good in his eyes. You told me that Sammi seemed a better fit for him anyway, and if it's true that she always wanted him, then what better time."

"For argument's sake, let's say you're right. How did Sammi get Olivia's body to Stump Pass Park?"

"She didn't. Bridgewater did. Maybe they discussed killing her beforehand. Sammi convinces him that by getting rid of Olivia he can keep his business. That wouldn't be too difficult. You admitted that Bridgewater is as dumb as a box of rocks."

"It certainly would explain his dumping her in the park and not somewhere out in the Gulf."

"Right. And maybe Sammi gave him too much credit, thinking he would take her body as far away as he could."

"I guess it's possible. Any ideas on the other murders?"

"Bridgewater didn't kill Olivia, but I do believe he killed John Calloway. Remember, Trish Nelson told me that when she was hiding in the bedroom, she overheard them arguing. And remember, during that argument, Bridgewater told John who *did* kill Olivia, but Trish didn't catch the name."

"Wait a minute! Why would Phil tell John that Sammi killed Livie?"

"After the way I saw him act toward you today, and the way he confronted me at Flapjack's, I believe he got tired of being accused and answering questions. Add to it a bad temper and booze, and I figure he'd had enough."

"But telling John doesn't make sense."

"Not to you or me."

Probst started to counter, then hesitated. "I see your point. So, naturally, John gets fighting mad when Phill tries to lay the blame on Sammi, and Phil ends up killing him."

"He didn't know that Trish was in the bedroom, because there was no other car outside. She told me that John preferred to pick her up at home when they had their trysts."

"John was screwing Trish?"

"That's what she told me in so many words."

"Mr. Hampton, you are certainly deserving of your reputation. So who killed Trish?"

"After you dropped me off, I went to Flapjack's. I noticed it was open when we passed by."

"Doesn't surprise me. John only closed for Thanksgiving and Christmas. No reason to break tradition."

"I saw his truck in the parking lot. When I asked Sammi if she was driving it, she said her husband had had an accident last night and was out getting estimates."

"They only have one car, so it won't be hard to verify. But you don't honestly think that Herb is involved in this conspiracy, do you?"

"No, I don't. I think Sammi is the hit-and-run driver you're looking for. She may have already known or found out about the meetings between Trish and John, and didn't want to take any chances. She probably told Herb that someone hit her in the Flapjack's parking lot and took off."

"So when all is said and done, Phil goes free because we can't prove that he killed Livie or John, and he gets to keep his house, his car, and his business."

"Then Sammi divorces Herb, and being the sole heir and owner of Flapjack's, sells it to him or buys him out, and lives happily ever after with Bridgewater."

"You know, Mr. Hampton, I'm starting to think I made a huge mistake."

"What do you mean?"

"When I fought to take on Livie's case, I thought I could separate myself from those I knew who were involved. Sammi being a part of all that's happened never crossed my mind. I want to thank you, and I'm going to follow up on your ideas right away."

Joe wanted to believe what Probst had said as he laid his phone in his lap, but how could he be sure? Maybe he should leave tomorrow. It would certainly be the safest thing to do. If he was right about everything, and wrong about the detective, then Bridgewater and Sammi would never be charged, and the deaths of three good people would go unpunished. Worse, Joe himself could die a mysterious death in the quaint little town of Englewood, and no one would be the wiser.

CHAPTER 14

The smell of salt air filled Joe's nostrils a minute before he heard the surf crash on the rocks. Now realizing he'd dozed off, he paused to gather himself, unaware of the time. Clicking bugs and whistling bird calls in the night were faint compared to the waves, but a pleasant complement. He knew he should get up and go climb into bed, but the will to do so was weak. After five or more minutes, he made himself stand up.

The streetlight next to the bend in the dirt road poured a wide band of light through the jalousie panes in the front door, enough for him to make his way across the living room. As he stepped into the bedroom, he thought he heard someone knock, the panes barely rattling. He hesitated, unsure whether he'd actually heard the knocking or was simply dreaming on his feet. When he heard it again, he left the bedroom and stuck his head around the corner. A blurry figure stood at the door, smaller and shorter than John Calloway and Seth Probst. Caution told him not to answer. Curiosity led him to discover the identity of the visitor.

"Who is it?"

"It's me...Sammi."

Joe unlatched the deadbolt and shoved the door open before the fuzzy feeling had left his brain.

Sammi took a step back, a silhouette set against the light.

"What's wrong?"

"I need your help, Joe. Someone's after me."

"Why did you come here? Why didn't you call the police?"

"He's going to kill me! Please, Joe!"

"Come inside and I'll..."

The minute he caught sight of Phil Bridgewater moving from behind the door, Joe knew that he'd been set up. Light glistening off the dark barrel of the automatic he held confirmed the man's intent.

"Get in the truck, old man."

"What's this all about, Sammi?" Joe asked.

"As if you didn't know."

"I ain't tellin' you again, old man."

"Easy with that automatic, Bridgewater, it's liable to go off. You already have three murders on your head."

"Huh? Whaddaya mean three?"

"Shut up, Phil!" Sammi whispered loudly. "Get in the truck, Joe!"

"Your wife, your father-in-law, and Trish Nelson," Joe said.

"I didn't kill Livie or Trish."

"But you did kill John."

Sammi drew back her right hand into a fist and punched Joe square in the mouth, then grabbed him by the arm and yanked him to the ground.

Stunned, Joe tasted blood, his legs unwilling to help him stand.

"Now get him in the truck, Phil, and let's get the hell outta here."

Joe felt two huge hands snatch him to his feet and drag him across the yard to the Dodge Ram. The creaking and popping of the passenger door opening reminded him of a frightful encounter with Mac McDougal. The thought of reliving that near-death experience in his past and shocked him out of his stupor. Sammi got behind the wheel as Bridgewater slid in beside Joe. He was trapped between them.

Sammi backed the truck onto the dirt road and eased away from the cottage.

Mild confusion filled Joe's head as he pondered what might become of him. When they turned left at the roundabout at Beach Road in the direction of the mainland, he figured a long ride into the country would be the next step. The right turn onto McCall Road didn't surprise him. Heading south by southeast would take them to any number of uninhabited wooded areas and, eventually, the Everglades. There, after being tied up and dumped in some leg of backwater, he would no doubt become a welcome feast for some alligator or python. After that, no one would ever know what happened to him. Carly and David wouldn't appear at the eleventh hour and save him this time. This time was truly the end.

How gruesome, he thought. *I hope they shoot me first.*

Sammi eased the truck into a right turn at Placida Road, then another right at Massachusetts Avenue.

Joe was surprised by the second right turn. *We're heading to Bridgewater's boat. They're going to take me miles away from shore and toss me overboard.*

The thought of being at the mercy of the sea didn't appeal to him any more than being eaten by an alligator. The minute he hit the water, every creature within a five-mile radius would become aware.

Great! I'm going to end up as chum for some underfed Bull shark. Now I really hope they shoot me.

His fear was confirmed when Sammi pulled up in front of the Bridgewater Charters building. Before he could take a breath, Bridgewater jammed the automatic into his ribs.

"No bullshit, old man. It doesn't matter to me where you die."

"Just get him outta the truck, Phil!" Sammi barked. "We need to get going."

Bridgewater unlocked the door and backed out with the automatic still leveled at Joe. When Joe cleared the door, Sammi popped open the glove box and pulled out a roll of duct tape. Bridgewater grabbed Joe by the collar of his shirt and slammed him face down across the hood.

Sammi came up behind them, took hold of Joe's arms, and taped his wrists together. Bridgewater then clamped his hand on Joe's shoulder, yanked him over onto his back, and Sammi slapped a strip of tape over his mouth.

"Now gimme the gun and hurry up," she said.

Bridgewater handed the automatic to her then broke into a sprint toward his boat.

Though the streetlight a few yards away provided some illumination, the prevailing darkness did little to hide the hatred in Sammi's eyes.

"Why did you have to come here, Joe? Why couldn't you have just stayed wherever the hell it is you came from?"

Knowing he was helpless to answer, she grasped his arm, the automatic planted firmly in his ribs.

When Joe heard the trio of Yamaha 300s fire up, his heart sank. His one-way trip would culminate in the deep, dark waters of the Gulf.

The path of white sand and crushed shell appeared to glow under Joe's feet as Sammi pulled him toward the dock. The stench of rotting fish or some other forms of marine life hung heavily in the air. The fear advancing through his body chilled Joe to the bone. When they drew even with Bridgewater standing at the center console, Sammi gave him a shove and sent him crashing into a rolled-up tarp on the deck. Pain from banging his kneecap shot up and down his right leg, and he let loose with a muffled moan. As he rolled over on his side, he saw that both ends of the tarp were bound with one-inch nylon line and weighted by two sixteen-pound fluke anchors. A pair of brushed leather work boots protruded from the end nearest the stern.

Who the hell is that? Joe wondered, his pain and discomfort magnified.

Sammi shoved the automatic into the waistband of her jeans and turned to go untie the bow line. Bridgewater was busy checking the gauges. Neither of them paid attention to Joe.

Rolling onto his back, he considered the odds of trying to escape. He noticed a ten-inch bone handle knife in a stained leather sheath hanging from Bridgewater's belt. Recalling the size of the incisions listed in Olivia's autopsy report, he guessed that it was not the knife that killed her. A much smaller knife had been used. A smaller knife wielded by a smaller person—like Sammi. Had his hands not been bound behind him, Joe would have been tempted to grab the big goon's knife and stab him before jumping out of the boat. He quickly dismissed the idea. The first of the two islands between them and Manasota Key wasn't that close, but if the current wasn't too strong, he figured he could get to it if he could maneuver his hands to his front, once he was in the water.

Better than doing nothing, he thought, and quietly got to his feet.

Sammi had just released the bow line when Joe employed a tactic he'd used once before.

Standing directly behind Bridgewater, he kicked him as hard as he could between the legs. Bridgewater let loose a deafening howl and crumpled to his knees. Joe stepped back and rolled over the starboard side. The water was deep enough, and he started kicking his legs, propelling himself into the channel. With the excitement of the moment, and never having been a good swimmer, he knew he would have to surface for air very soon. He kicked and kicked and tried to go deeper, blind in the unfriendly depths, his leg muscles tightening. Unable to kick anymore, he stopped and pulled his knees up to his chest. Struggling to swing his arms underneath his butt, he felt the current at his back, pushing him away from the dock. Slowly rising to the surface as he fought to pull his arms forward, the burning in his lungs grew stronger. About the time his head broke the surface, he yanked his arms to the front, tore the duct tape from his mouth, and began to gasp for air. Unsure of where he was, Joe jerked his head in all directions. Seeing the dock only ten yards behind gave him a jolt. He thought he'd drifted farther away.

A hand-held spotlight came on, first pointed at the shore, then began a deliberate trail over the water.

Joe turned over on his back and let the current take him, heaving to take in more air as he twisted and pulled his hands to loosen the tape around his wrists.

Back and forth the spotlight trolled until it lit up his face, reversing its track before finding him again.

"There he is!" Sammi yelled. "Get your ass up off the floor and let's go get him!"

Joe heard Bridgewater moan, then what sounded like scuffling. A minute later the boat started to ease backward into the channel.

Still on his back, Joe began kicking his legs, traveling faster with the current, using what little strength remained in an attempt to free his hands.

The spotlight found him again. The intensity of the beam increased as the boat drew nearer, now so close that Joe felt as if he might be run over. He rolled over onto his stomach and dove under, reversing his direction to against the current. Without the use of his arms his attempt to escape was futile, the current too strong an adversary.

When he surfaced this time, only five yards separated him from his captors. Sammi was leaning over the side, a landing gaff extending from her hands.

"Take a hold, Joe. Otherwise, I'll hook you and drag you aboard."

Joe grabbed the pole when it came within reach.

Sammi and Bridgewater pulled him over the side of the boat. Once on his feet, Sammi cracked him in the mouth again, knocking him against the tarp.

"You are *really* a pain in the ass, Joe."

CHAPTER 15

Exhausted from his failed escape attempt and sick of tasting blood, Joe lay back and tried to calculate how much time he had left to live. He had no idea how long it would take them to get out of Lemon Bay, but there had to be a land breach to the Gulf close by. Stump Pass Marina didn't get its name from being landlocked. And the passage had to be obvious enough for someone as dumb as Bridgewater to find it. Joe figured he had five minutes, tops, before they cruised into open water, then at least fifteen to twenty minutes before they threw him and the person wrapped in the tarp overboard. With Sammi standing next to Bridgewater at the console, the automatic pointed at him, the element of surprise was gone. Another attempted attack would get him shot. Not killed necessarily, but wounded, adding more pain to his aching body. They wanted him to suffer—before and while he was dying—punishment for being a nosy old goat. Carly's words rang truer than ever. Nothing about the situation presented an advantage, so he raised his eyes to the coal-black sky.

Countless stars glittered above, light years away and far removed. Far removed was where he wished to be at the moment—far from Englewood, anyway.

He felt the boat veer starboard, and thought he heard the faint sound of laughter and conversation.

Could be the marina, he thought. *Maybe they have a bar or restaurant on the water.*

He considered crying out for help, then decided against it, figuring that even the gunshot sure to follow wouldn't attract attention. And there would be more blood.

From where he lay he couldn't see over the side of the boat, but sensed by the continued veering that they were now heading west, close to entering the Gulf. His conclusions were verified when he heard the throaty roar of the three Yamahas and felt the rise of the bow before the boat planed out. Lying prone on the deck, he felt every bump and shudder as they sliced through the water, much faster than he had anticipated.

They're going to take me way out, probably beyond the sight of land.

An unexpected wallop, rougher than the scattering of others, nearly lifted him off the deck. One of the fluke anchors clanked and drew his attention to the boots sticking out of the tarp. The answer as to whose feet they were covering was quick in coming.

"Did you kill Herb, too, Sammi?" he said.

"Shut up, Joe!"

"Don't tell me you pawned him off on lover boy."

Bridgewater glanced over his shoulder.

"Did she? Did she talk you into doing it? Figured she'd let you take the fall for two murders instead of one?"

Sammi started toward Joe, her path erratic, jostled and unsteady.

"If you don't shut up, I'm gonna shoot you right now!"

"Why did you kill Olivia, Sammi? Couldn't you wait until after the divorce to sink your hooks into Dumbo?"

"Shoot him, Sammi!" Bridgewater yelled. "I'm tired of listenin' to his crap!"

"Olivia was going to leave him. But you couldn't wait, could you? I'll bet you two were already hopping into the sack."

"What do you know?" Sammi shouted. "You think you're so damn smart!"

"Herb found out, didn't he? You couldn't let him mess up

your plans. Better he disappeare than waste time getting a divorce."

"Stop the boat!"

"What?" Bridgewater said, and looked over his shoulder at her.

"Stop the damn boat!" She stepped back and snatched his knife from the sheath. "I'm gonna cut him good, and we'll throw him over the side. Let the damn sharks take care of him."

"But we ain't far enough from shore yet. Somebody's liable to see us."

"I don't care! I've had enough of this asshole!"

Bridgewater eased back on the throttles, the roar of the motors lowered to a rumble as the boat slowed to an idle.

Sammi handed Bridgewater the automatic and focused on Joe. "I should cut your balls off, you old son of a bitch." She took a step toward him.

"Hold on!" Bridgewater said, and grabbed her arm.

"What are you doing?"

"Shh!" He turned his head and stared south into the darkness. "Boat's comin'. Maybe two. Fast."

Sammi looked in the same direction. "I don't see any navigation lights."

"We got to go farther out."

Bridgewater thrust the automatic back at Sammi, spun around to the controls, and dropped the throttles. When the Grady-White lurched, she was thrown off-balance, the knife flying from her hand before she crashed into the deck. Joe lunged forward and grabbed it as she fired, hitting him in the shoulder. Struggling to her feet, she took aim to finish him off.

The Grady-White hadn't quite planed out when a spotlight lit up its stern and passengers.

"Dammit!" Bridgewater growled.

Sammi turned her back to Joe as they heard, "Charlotte County Sheriff's Office! Stop at once and prepare to be boarded!"

A second spotlight from a trailing boat found them—then a third.

Gritting his teeth, Joe clasped his shoulder and felt the blood oozing from between his fingers and down his arm.

"Grab the wheel, Sammi!" Bridgewater shouted.

Sammi turned and stumbled to the console. Once she had control of the boat, Bridgewater went after Joe.

Grabbing him by the leg and arm on his wounded shoulder, Bridgewater raised Joe chest high and flung him over the side. Joe cried out in pain before he hit the water. The impact knocked the wind out of him, but not the fear of being chopped to pieces by the propellers of the approaching boats. Dazed, but hearing the whine of their motors growing louder, he raised his good arm in an effort to signal them.

Two of the boats sailed by within ten feet of him and sent a large foamy wave rolling over his head. Coughing and gasping for air, he waited for the third boat to hit him, surprised when it didn't, then squinted in the blinding beam of a spotlight.

"There he is!" someone yelled.

The light grew brighter, and Joe heard the slapping of water against a hull. A heavy splash and the thrashing sound of some-one swimming drew closer. As he lay his head back, he felt an arm encircle his chest.

"Are you all right, mister?"

"I'm shot...in the shoulder."

"Hang on and we'll get you to the hospital as quick as we can."

Joe felt himself being pulled through the water then lifted up and over the side of another boat. A stabbing pain caused him to grit his teeth.

"He's gotta gunshot wound in the shoulder!" the man in the water yelled.

Now lying on the deck, Joe looked into the concerned eyes and weathered face of another man.

"Let me slap a bandage on that shoulder to control the

bleedin', then we'll get you back to shore."

Joe closed his eyes, feeling the boat list as the man who had saved him pulled himself aboard.

"We need to get goin', Charlie."

Before either of them could get to the wheel, a thundering explosion off in the distance shattered the night, shocking Joe's eyes open. He saw a massive ball of fire billow high in the air.

"Somebody done blowed up," one man said.

"Let's hope it was the bad guys," the other said.

"Thanks, fellas," Joe said. "Thanks for saving me."

"You just lay back and relax, mister. We're gonna get you some help real soon."

Joe did as his rescuer instructed, feeling the boat swing around and speed back toward the mainland.

CHAPTER 16

The trauma of being shot following the surge of adrenaline fueling his struggle to stay alive drained most of the energy out of Joe. Knowing that his rescuers were extending every effort to get him to shore was a mild comfort, though the pounding and jostling of the ride compounded his pain. The aftermath of what had happened filled him with questions as to who these people were. They weren't in uniform. No badges hung from their belts. Were they simply good Samaritans who were called upon in times of emergency? Joe closed his eyes, hoping the ordeal would not last much longer.

Be strong, my dear, he heard Joyce say.

I'm doing my best. Where have you been?

Right beside you, of course.

But you haven't...we haven't talked for some time.

I don't feel we need to talk anymore.

But how will I...you always know what is best for me.

You're going to be all right, Joe.

Her words echoed over and over until they faded into the drone of the outboard.

Joe opened his eyes and realized another man had joined the one kneeling beside him. Through the faint light of the moon, he recognized the uniform.

"I've radioed ahead, sir. An ambulance will be waiting for you."

"Thanks, Deputy," Joe croaked.

Several minutes passed, lost to the humming of the outboard. Then he heard a scattering of voices calling out as the boat slowed and bumped to a halt. Numerous hands lifted him onto a dock. Once he was moved onto a stretcher, the clacking of the casters rolling over the planks and the murmur of other voices filled his ears. He had no idea where they were—maybe Stump Pass Marina or a public pier. Where they'd landed didn't matter; there was no better feeling than being safe.

Joe closed his eyes as he felt himself being hoisted into the ambulance. The crisp, secure slamming of the doors rang hollow and gave way to the high, haunting wail of the siren.

CHAPTER 17

Whether he passed out or had been injected with a drug to help
ease his pain, Joe remembered very little of the ambulance ride
and had no recollection of being hauled into the emergency room.
What he did recall was an unsettling dream. John Calloway, Trish
Nelson, and a woman he assumed to be Olivia Bridgewater all
wore the friendliest of smiles and were urging him to remain in
Englewood. A struggle between his desire to stay in the quaint
little town and his unwillingness to desert Joyce, Carly, and David
raged inside him. His friends held him by the arms as his wife
implored him not to go. The smell of the salt-tinged air and the
crashing of the waves over the rocks on the shore were luring
him into submission, but his heart was breaking at the idea.
When it seemed he'd lost all hope of making the right decision,
Carly yanked on his arm as Joyce cried out, "Don't leave me,
Joe!" A pain like none he'd ever felt jabbed him in the shoulder
and jolted him awake.

The white and sterile hospital room smelled as clean as the
fresh linen covering him.

"Ohh! What have I done?" he moaned, reaching for his
shoulder. He stopped when he spied a length of plastic tubing
running from his good arm to an I.V. bottle.

A young nurse with short, brown hair that reminded him of
Carly breezed through the doorway and hurried to his side. She
studied him intently for a moment as he studied her green eyes.

191

"Where is the pain, Mr. Hampton?"

"My shoulder. I must have wrenched it in my sleep."

The nurse shifted her gaze to the bandage. "Everything appears to be okay. Is it still hurting?"

"Throbbing. I'll have to be more careful."

"I can get you something for it."

"Not right now. I've been out long enough."

She smiled and patted his hand.

"How long have I been out?"

"They brought you here last night and performed surgery to remove the bullet from your shoulder. You've been asleep most of the day."

"And where exactly is *here*?"

"Englewood Community Hospital."

"I see. Do you know...will there be any paralysis in my arm?"

"Let me go find the doctor."

Joe rolled his head over on the pillow. "That's just great. I come down here to relax, and wind up going home a cripple."

He wondered what Joyce would think of his predicament, remembering the pained expression on her face in his dream. Before he could sink deeper into self-pity, a tall doctor with black hair graying at the temples walked into the room, followed by the same nurse.

"Mr. Hampton, I'm Doctor Limroth. Nurse Oberon tells me that you're experiencing some discomfort."

"I was dreaming. I must have flinched or something."

"Yes, and I'm afraid that's going to be a problem for a while. You'll have to be careful and take it slow."

I've heard that before, Joe thought. *First it was my foot, and now it's my shoulder.* "Doctor, will I have full range of motion in my arm and shoulder once I'm fully healed?"

"I don't see why not. Your chart doesn't indicate any extensive damage. With the right amount of therapy, you should be fine." He paused as if waiting for Joe to say something. When Joe didn't respond, he smiled. "Getting shot is enough to ruin anyone's day."

"When can I get out of here?"

"We'd prefer you stay at least a week for observation. Is there a problem?"

A soft knocking interrupted their conversation.

"Detective Probst."

"Mr. Hampton."

"I'll stop by later this afternoon," Doctor Limroth said.

He nodded to Probst as he and Nurse Oberon passed by.

Probst moved to the foot of the bed. "How's the shoulder?"

"Could be better. Could be a lot better."

"At least you're still with us. We saw Phil toss you into the water and did our best not to run over you."

"*You* were chasing us?"

"I was with our marine unit in the lead boat."

"Who were the guys that stopped for me?"

"They're members of COPS, the marine unit of the Citizens Observation Patrol. An alert had been issued, and one of them spotted Phil's boat coming through Stump Pass. We don't normally allow them to get directly involved, but they volunteered. We put a marine patrol deputy on each boat."

"I'd like to personally thank those guys when I get out of here."

"I'm sure they'll appreciate it."

"So tell me, Detective, how did you know what Bridgewater and Sammi were up to?"

Probst lowered his head and ran a hand over the back of his neck. "To tell you the truth, Mr. Hampton, we didn't. I mentioned to you before that we'd been staking out his business since he claimed to be staying there. I got a call after Phil and Sammi drove you to the dock. I was en route when I got another call saying that they were aboard and pulling away from the dock, and there was some commotion going on."

"That was me trying to escape."

"Before Sammi punched you in the mouth?"

"The second time." Joe furrowed his brow. "How did you know that she hit me?"

"If Phil would've hit you, you'd be minus some teeth, and in no condition to attempt an escape." Probst looked him over. "Your bruises still look pretty nasty, though."

"Wonderful."

"I contacted the marine unit, put out an alert, and we went after them. The COPS volunteer radioed us, and we spotted them just outside the pass."

"I'm starting to like those COPS guys more and more. But tell me, where were your people staked out at Bridgewater Charters? I didn't see anybody anywhere."

"The fenced-in property abutting Phil's land is owned by the county. Two of our detectives were hiding in the bushes."

"Couldn't they have intervened before we left?"

"Being that you were in John Calloway's truck, I guess they thought you were Sammi's husband, Herb. They never really said. They didn't know what was happening at first. Not until they saw Phil and Sammi pull you out of the water."

"By the way, Herb is dead."

"What!"

"There was a rolled-up tarp on the deck. A pair of work boots was sticking out of one end. I figure they killed him to get him out of the way."

"Mr. Hampton, I spoke with Herb this morning, to tell him about Sammi being killed."

"Sammi's dead?"

"Both Sammi and Phil. They started shooting at us. We returned fire. We saw her go down, then the boat exploded. I guess a gas tank was hit."

The ball of fire I saw, Joe thought.

"We found Phil's body, but not Sammi's. Now I've got to figure out who the man in the tarp could be."

A short silence followed.

"Detective, when I talked to John Calloway, he mentioned

that there were rumors about Olivia screwing around. Maybe the fellow I saw was one of her lovers."

"Maybe. Or maybe he was the one who killed Trish Nelson. Herb confirmed what you suspected. Sammi told him someone at Flapjack's hit their car."

Again, silence lingered between them.

"Well, I've got to be going, Mr. Hampton."

"Detective, I'm in a bit of a quandary."

"I know, and I'm sorry you got hurt."

"That's not what I meant. I only rented the cottage at Sandpiper Shores for week. The doctor's going to keep me in this place long after my time is up."

Probst smiled. "I'll talk to Juanita and see what arrangements can be made. It's the least I can do for you."

"I need to make a call and see if my friends can come down here and drive me and my car back to Clearwater Beach. I guess my phone is done for since I went swimming twice."

Probst motioned with his head.

Joe looked to his left and saw a beige telephone sitting on a small table beside the bed.

"Don't worry about getting home, Mr. Hampton. After helping us solve two, and possibly three murders, the Charlotte County Sheriff's Office is going to escort you to the front door of your condo."

Joe lay back as a wave of relief rolled over him. When the nurse returned, he would ask her to help him with the phone. Carly would start to worry when she didn't hear from him, and, most likely, drive all the way to Englewood when he didn't return her calls. He didn't want to upset her, but he knew she would be when he told her what had happened.

Nurse Oberon came in to check on him, pleased that he appeared in better spirits. He told her he was hungry, and though supper time was more than an hour away, she promised to find him something to hold him over. Then she would help him get in touch with Carly.

The hour passed—slowly—and Joe was considering making a break for the hospital cafeteria when another visitor entered the room. Surprise wasn't a strong enough word to describe his reaction upon seeing the man's face.

"Herb!"

"Mr. Hampton, I..." He coughed and cleared his throat. "I'm sorry, Mr. Hampton. I'm sorry for what Sammi did to you. And I'm sorry for..." He coughed again.

"I'm sorry, too, Herb. Sorry for your loss."

"If there's anything I can do for ya, just let me know. I won't take up any more of your time, and again I'm sorry." He turned around and started to leave, then turned back to Joe. "Mr. Hampton, some time back, John told Sammi and me that he was leavin' Flapjack's to Livie and her in his will. With both of 'em gone, I don't know what's gonna happen. I guess I'll inherit the place. If that's the case, and you know somebody who'd like to buy it, get a hold of me. I'll see to it they get a square deal. I don't really care 'bout runnin' Flapjack's."

"Herb, why are you telling me this?"

"John was a good man. And Livie was a good woman. I liked 'em both. You're a good man, too, Mr. Hampton. Anybody with any sense can see that."

Saying no more, he disappeared through the doorway.

CHAPTER 18

After a week that seemed destined never to end, Joe felt relieved once he left Englewood Community Hospital. Seth Probst had his suitcase and all his belongings packed and was waiting to drive him home. He felt a little odd, sitting in the passenger seat of his own car and being chauffeured by the detective. Probst's partner following them in an unmarked sedan marked another first in his life.

Interstate 75 was teeming with vehicles as usual, but once they left the artery for Interstate 275, Joe relaxed a bit, anticipating the sight of the toll booths lining the entrance to the Skyway Bridge. Placing a hand on his injured shoulder, he adjusted his sling as he shifted in his seat.

"You all right, Mr. Hampton?"

"Yes. I'm just anxious to get home."

"Traffic is moving at a good pace. It shouldn't be too much longer."

"Are you familiar with the Tampa Bay area, Detective?"

"Some of it, but not where you live. I figured that you would know the best route to take."

"Stay on the interstate, and I'll show you where to get off." Joe glanced at a fenced-in tract of land filled with scrub brush and pine trees, their refreshing scent pouring in through the half-open window. The smell was more to his liking than the antiseptic odor of his hospital room. "Detective, if you don't mind my asking, did you ever find the body of the man I saw wrapped in the tarp on Phillip Bridgewater's boat?"

"Divers found him two days after I came to see you, still wrapped in the tarp and weighted down by the anchors. His name is Salvatore Carreras. Some of the people I talked to knew him as Sal. He was a regular at Flapjack's."

"Was he somehow involved in this mess?"

"It's looking that way. According to what I was told, he and Sammi were *real* friendly. We found his fingerprints on Herb and Sammi's car. He might have been the hit-and-run driver who killed Trish Nelson."

"Which would explain his being removed from the picture. The last time we spoke, I seem to recall your telling me that you'd found Bridgewater's body."

"Right, floating near the wreckage, but we still haven't found Sammi. We're close to calling off the search, though. I think she was either blown to bits or a shark got her."

As they neared the incline of the elevated span of the bridge, Joe stared at the shimmering blue waters of Tampa Bay.

So different from the woodsy countryside surrounding Englewood, he thought. "I don't know if I mentioned it, Detective, but Herb came to see me."

"What did he want?"

"He apologized for what Sammi did and offered to help me."

That's unusual. Herb's pretty much a loner, and as quiet a man as you'd ever want to meet."

"And he said that if I knew anyone who wanted to buy Flapjack's that he would make sure they got a good deal."

"He's a man of his word. I suppose with Livie and Sammi gone, there's no one else mentioned in John's will, so the bar will probably be sold."

Neither man said another word as they sailed along the strip of road leading into St. Petersburg. Joe was thinking he might point out a few sights in the downtown area when Probst surprised him.

"Ever thought of owning a bar, Mr. Hampton?"

Joe grinned at the notion. "My wife would have been dead set against it."

"Would have been?"

"I'm a widower."

"Oh, I'm sorry."

"For curiosity's sake, would Flapjack's be a good investment?"

"It wouldn't make you a millionaire, but the clientele is steady...and wouldn't stop coming if you didn't change the name, I believe. There hasn't been any trouble there in years."

"How about you, Detective? Is buying a bar something you would consider before you retire?"

"Maybe. I couldn't go it alone, though. I'd need a least one person to partner with. And he'd have to be the right person to make it work."

"Why do I get the feeling that this conversation is leading somewhere?"

"I don't know. I'm just speaking hypothetically."

Both men wore huge smiles as the dome of Tropicana Field appeared to the east.

Staying with the flow of traffic carried them to Roosevelt Boulevard where Joe motioned to Probst to get off the interstate. Intersecting with Ulmerton Road minutes later, they proceeded to U.S. 19 and turned north. Exiting at Gulf to Bay Boulevard brought them to Clearwater and closer to Joe's home near Clearwater Beach.

"Mr. Hampton, I have to admit that there's a lot going on between St. Petersburg and Clearwater. And I thought Tampa was a busy place."

"It's a very popular area. Makes you appreciate home, does it?"

"More than you know."

"Oh, I can understand your feelings for Englewood. I enjoyed staying there...for the most part."

"Enough to want to go back?"

"I believe so."

"I'm glad to hear you say that. I wouldn't want what happened to you in my town to leave a bad taste in your mouth."

Weaving through downtown Clearwater, Joe noticed his shoulder didn't hurt near as much. The relief of being home again was working wonders, so much so that he sat up straight at the sight of Memorial Causeway.

"This is beautiful," Probst said. "And the beach is straight ahead?"

"The causeway will take you right to it. You and your partner planning to take a little tour after you drop me off?"

"I don't see why not. I mean, it's not that far out of our way."

"Make a right at the next light. My condo is the Crimson Conch. I'll point you to my reserved parking spot."

Probst steered the Toyota onto Island Way and into the parking lot, commenting on the cleanliness of the area and the attractive landscape surrounding the building. The black sedan that had stayed with them the entire trip pulled up behind them as they got out.

"Let me give you a hand with your things," Probst said.

Joe was staring at the condo entrance. "Thanks, Detective, but I believe that help is on the way."

A woman with short brown hair and a welcoming smile approached them.

"Is that your daughter, Mr. Hampton?"

Joe didn't answer.

Carly walked up and carefully embraced him. "I'm glad you're home," she whispered.

"Good to be home."

"And is this the man I have to thank?"

"Detective Sergeant Carly Truffant, this is Detective Seth Probst, Charlotte County Sheriff's Office."

"Sergeant, a pleasure to make your acquaintance."

"The pleasure is all mine, Detective. Joe told me how you and your men came to his rescue."

"All in a day's work. Well, Mr. Hampton, it looks like you're in good hands, so I'll be on my way."

"Thank you again, Detective, and thanks for the escort."

"You're welcome, and Mr. Hampton, if you're so inclined, give me a call when you're feeling better. I'd like to talk more about Flapjack's."

"I just might do that...Seth."

Joe and Carly watched him climb into the sedan and drive away. Carly pulled Joe's suitcase out of the trunk, along with the rest of his belongings, and, together, they walked to the entrance.

The elevator ride to his floor helped Joe forget all about the maroon carpet and pink walls in the hallway. Nothing could upset him now that he was home.

Once Carly put away his clothes and suitcase, she headed straight for the balcony and stretched out on the matching blue chaise lounge beside him.

"It's really good to be home," Joe said.

"Is it?"

Joe leaned his head over. "Well, of course."

"Does that mean that you've decided to stay here?"

"I have to admit that Englewood was tempting. It's a nice little town."

"Even though you almost got killed there?"

"Carly, what happened could have—"

"Could have been the last thing that *ever* happened to you."

"You're right. At one point I thought I was finished."

"Then you should give up that silly notion of leaving."

Joe frowned. "It could just as easily have happened here. Why are you acting like this?"

"Because I..."

Carly looked in the direction of the Gulf.

"Well, put your mind at ease. I'm not going anywhere."

She jerked her head around, "Do you really mean that?"

"If I move away then who's going to help you and David with your cases?"

"Don't flatter yourself. We were doing just fine before you started getting in the way."

"Is that so?"

"Yeah, that's so."

Both of them burst into laughter a second later.

"You're really staying, Joe?"

"I'd have no problem moving to Englewood. You'll understand if you ever go down there. It's beautiful. But I've grown to like it here."

"I'm glad you changed your mind. When your shoulder gets better, I'm taking you out to dinner."

Joe reached up to adjust his sling and gave her an approving smile.

Sunshine, blue skies, and people going about their business occupied their minds for the next ten minutes. All seemed to have returned to normal until Carly rolled her head over.

"Joe, what did that detective mean when he said he wanted to talk more about flapjacks? Did you find some popular family restaurant in Englewood that makes good pancakes?"

Joe laughed. "One day I'll tell you all about it."

YESTERDAY RISING

CHAPTER 1

Joe was resting peacefully in the chaise lounge on his balcony, dozing off every so often, then catching himself. His condominium in Clearwater Beach finally felt like home. The light breezes drifting in from the Gulf with their salt-tinged scents had helped him decide to stay. A relaxed atmosphere of life on the beach was too satisfying to dismiss. The summer heat took some getting used to, but the other seasons made up for it. And then there was Carly and David, his closest friends, imploring him not to run off to Englewood or head back to Pennsylvania. How could he disappoint them? More importantly, he couldn't break his promise to Joyce.

Joe's chin dropped to his chest again. Everyday sounds of life from below serenaded him.

He'd decided to team with Seth Probst to become co-owner of Flapjack's Bar in Englewood. The Charlotte County Sheriff's Office detective had agreed to handle the necessary paperwork to obtain the establishment. And he would see to a few interior and exterior upgrades, as well as its operation. Joe would be the silent partner.

All in his life was good—for the moment.

The unexpected knocking on his front door sounded far off. The second round pulled him from his slumber. After a moment to exhale his disgust at being disturbed, he swung his feet to the balcony floor and stood up. Slowly opening the sliding glass door, he entered his condo and moved toward the front door. A momentary yawn delayed his peering through the peephole. When he did he saw no one standing in the hall.

"That's odd."

He unlocked the door and peered into the hallway, finding the stretch of hallway to his right empty and quiet. When he turned and gazed in the direction of the elevator, he spied a woman walking toward the elevator.

"Can I help you?"

The white-haired woman smiled as she turned around. He recognized her immediately.

"Christine."

"Hi, Joe." She moved to his door with little effort. "I went to the manager's office, but you weren't there, so I came here. When you didn't answer right away, I thought you'd gone out."

"I'm feeling lazy today. Why didn't you call me? I would have come down."

"It's not a problem. Besides, I needed the exercise."

Joe and the new tenant exchanged lingering smiles.

"Oh! Won't you come inside?"

Christine laughed. "I was starting to wonder."

He closed the door behind them and motioned to the sofa. "Have a seat. Can I get you something to drink?"

"I'm fine." She sat down at one end of the sofa. "I hate to bother you, but there's a situation in my unit that needs attention."

Joe eased into a , dark blue easy chair upholstered in dark blue. "What's wrong?"

"The kitchen faucet is dripping."

He grinned. "I thought it was something serious."

"It could be. Later on, I mean."

"I'll call the plumber right now. My phone is on the balcony."

"Could we sit out there for a while? It's such a lovely day."

They rose together and headed for the balcony.

Christine Orsay had moved into the Crimson Conch a month after his ordeal in Englewood. Her outgoing personality and lively brown eyes had attracted him from their very first meeting. Wary, though, after his near-death encounter with Victoria Combes and her daughter, Cecily Deamin, he'd decided to stick with platonic relationships. Maybe that would be best for both of them.

After Christine had stretched out on the blue chaise lounge, he lay down on the matching chair and picked up his phone. The conversation with the plumbing company was brief.

"Ten o'clock tomorrow morning."

"Fine," she said. A moment later, she released a sigh. "It's so beautiful here. What made you decide to come to Florida?"

"My wife chose Clearwater Beach for a vacation one year. She threatened to leave me if we didn't move here after I retired."

"She did not."

"I'm joking. She fell in love with the entire Tampa Bay area. And I knew she was looking to get away from the cold weather."

"I was told that your wife passed away some years ago. Were you living here then?"

"Yes. I'm glad that Joyce got to enjoy our new home." He grinned. "Been checking up on me, have you?"

"What can I say? I'm a curious person."

"Is that why you became an archeologist? Joe knew that she was world-renowned in her field.

"One reason. History is another. I enjoyed delving into the history of a person, a civilization, or a country. But what I found truly fascinating was prehistoric archeology."

"Dinosaur bones?"

Christine laughed. "Yes, but also the history of humans before written records were kept. To me, that was the greater mystery."

"And I guess you enjoyed traveling to different parts of the world."

"I love to travel. Or I did. I wouldn't have become an archeologist if I hadn't."

"So, why did you retire?"

"I'd done about all I could. And I figured it was time for the younger folks to take over."

"What persuaded you to settle in Clearwater Beach?"

"I researched the past for a long time, Joe. Then one day it hit me. I needed to start living in the present. A good friend who worked for the Mote Marine Laboratory and Aquarium suggested I move to Sarasota. On my way to visit, I stopped off to see a couple of friends who live in Palm Harbor. They gave me a tour of the area. That's when I decided on Clearwater Beach."

"And that's all it took?"

Christine paused, a puzzled expression on her face. "One vacation was all it took for your wife to decide."

"But she wanted a change of scenery. You could have lived anywhere in the world. What was the allure?"

"You certainly ask a lot of questions."

Joe shrugged. "What can I say. I'm a curious person."

Christine's expression became a crooked smile. "Well, Mr. Ex-Detective, I have a question for you."

"Uh-oh."

"Would you care to accompany me to Bingo tonight? I find it relaxing, but I hate going alone."

Joe lowered his head and turned away.

"Did I say something wrong?"

"No."

"Not a big Bingo fan?"

Joe was tempted to tell her about the last time he'd played the game, the time he'd discovered the body next to the seawall behind the Recreation Room.

"I don't really care for it."

"Then what *would* you like to do?"

Joe turned back to her. "Are you asking me on a date, Christine?"

"I am."

"That's nice of you, but maybe another night, okay?"

"Have other plans?"

"No, but I'm sure I'm going to have a headache." He laughed

when he saw her crooked smile again.

"That's it. I'm leaving."

"Now, Christine, I was only teasing you." He reached out and laid his hand on her forearm.

They gazed into one another's eyes. Searching. Wondering what the other was thinking. Silent seconds were interrupted by knocking.

Joe glanced through the sliding glass door. "Hmm."

"Expecting someone, Joe?"

"No. I recognize the knocking, though."

He followed Christine into the living room, and while she stood beside the sofa, he opened the door.

"Hi, Joe."

"Hi, Carly. Please come in."

His friend's somber green eyes told him that he was about to be recruited. She stopped short when she saw Christine.

"Sorry, Joe, I didn't know you were entertaining."

"Carly, you've met Christine."

"Yeah."

"I was just leaving," Christine said. She cut a sideward glance at Joe as she passed by him. "Maybe some other night."

Carly waited until he had closed the door behind her.

"I guess I don't need to ask you to put on your shoes."

"Another body?"

"Bones, actually."

"Bones!"

"Some kids were digging in the sand at the beach and uncovered an arm bone."

"Are you sure it's an arm bone? Maybe we should take Christine with us. She's an archeologist, you know."

Carly rolled her eyes. "Yes, Joe, you already told me. Criminal Analysis started digging around and found a skull. They were pulling out more bones when I left to get you."

"Give me a minute."

Joe hurried to his bedroom and slipped on his black running

shoes. Returning to the living room, he sat down in the easy chair and began to tie them.

"You could have called me and saved yourself a trip."

"I wasn't sure if you were cleared to drive yet. By the way, how's your arm?"

"Getting better all the time."

"*Has* the doctor given you permission to drive?"

"I don't need the doctor's permission to drive."

"Right. You always know best. Are you ready to go?"

Joe stood up. "Let me get my phone."

Carly huffed and nodded.

There was no denying that the young detective was wearing her game face. Joe had seen it before. Her expression rarely changed when she worked a case. This time, though, the lines in her furrowed brow ran deeper than usual. Something else was on her mind.

"Where are we going?" he asked.

"Sand Key Park."

Joe didn't react when the countless prickly spurs dug into his spine. The last time he'd gone to Sand Key Park was to view the body of his friend, Tony Dunham.

CHAPTER 2

The ride from the Crimson Conch Condominiums to Sand Key Park took fewer than ten minutes. Carly was unusually quiet. En route to other crime scenes, they had always tossed theories back and forth or talked over the possible involvement of suspects. Although the initial unearthing of human remains offered little in the way of discussion prior to further analysis, Joe had expected her to add to what she'd told him earlier. Her focusing on the road ahead struck him as odd.

"Everything okay with you, Carly?"

"Couldn't be better."

"You seem preoccupied."

"I'm thinking about this case."

"Nothing else you'd care to discuss?"

"Joe, once we get to the park, you'll understand what I'm..." She sighed and tightened her grip on the steering wheel. "Okay, there is something else, but now is not the time."

Joe looked down at the shimmering blue waters rolling into the mouth of Clearwater Harbor as they crossed over the bridge connecting Clearwater Beach and Sand Key. Uneasiness filled Joe as they drew closer to Sand Key Park. He shifted in his seat when they left Gulf Boulevard. He hadn't been back to the park since the last time Carly had summoned him, but he remembered every bend and bump in the winding asphalt road. An arm branching off to the right led to a small parking lot and dock. An indication that they were nearing the secluded spot where Tony's body had been found. He forced himself not to gape at that patch of ground as they drove by. The beach lay in the distance, but the road veered left before the entrance for parking. Three separate lots connected by small sandy accesses accommodated beach-going visitors. One quarter of the northernmost lot was occupied by police and Criminal Analysis Unit vehicles, as well as those belonging to curious gawkers. Folding plastic barricades and several patrolmen guarded this section. One of the patrolmen slid a barricade to the side so they might enter.

Carly's continued silence compounded Joe's apprehension as they left the car and strode across the lot before stepping onto a sandy trail leading to the tip of the beach.

A tent had been placed over the excavation pit with yellow and black barricade tape strung between the aluminum support poles on all four sides.

Carly and Joe dipped under the tape and joined a group of criminal analysis technicians standing next to the hole. A canvas tarp topped with skeletal remains covered the sand on the opposite side. Joe noticed the skull immediately. Most of the right rear quarter was missing. Only a small half-circle with jagged edges on either side of it remained. Numerous pieces of bone in a tight space next to the skull suggested the possibility of a bullet wound.

"Doesn't look like many pieces to this puzzle are missing," Carly said.

A technician turned to her. "We're being super careful, Sergeant Truffant, but we think they're all here," she said.

"Any idea of how old they are?"

"I wouldn't hazard a guess until we get back to the lab."

"Can you tell if it's a woman or a man?"

A woman, Joe thought.

"By the width of the pelvis, I'd say female."

Joe nodded.

"Have you uncovered any personal belongings?" Carly asked.

"Not so far. But, as I said, we're being super careful. Once we've got all the bones, or all we can find, we'll widen the pit."

She stopped talking when another technician lifted what appeared to be an ulna and started to clean it with a soft-bristle brush.

"May I have a word with you, Sergeant?"

Joe recognized the male voice.

David Sizemore stood a few feet outside of the tent. His fixed expression wasn't that much different form Carly's. They ducked under the tape and approached her partner.

"I just finished talking to the kids who made the initial discovery and their parents," he said. "Brittany and Connor Deegan were playing near the rocks and digging with their plastic shovels. Brittany uncovered what turned out to be a leg bone. She screamed when Connor picked it up and waved it in her face. That's when Mom and Dad intervened and called us."

"How are the kids doing?" Carly asked.

"Brittany's a little shaken. Connor thought it was cool. He wanted to watch Criminal Analysis while they were digging. Mrs. Deegan said no."

"Did the parents or anyone else look for bones?"

David shook his head. "The gawkers gathered after we showed up."

Carly looked out over the Gulf. "Guess we'll have to wait for the forensics report before we can start a missing-persons search."

Joe and David said nothing.

Carly turned back to them. "Anything to add? David, did you ask the kids how deep they had dug when the little girl saw the leg bone?" Joe said.

The detective held out his hands to indicate the depth. "Connor said about this deep. When Carly and I first looked at the hole, I'd say it was between eight and twelve inches."

Joe looked back at the tent and the area around it. "The tide line appears to support beach erosion, but it still seems awfully shallow. For a grave, I mean."

"It's wide open out here, Joe," Carly said. "Even at night a passing boat or people walking on the beach could spot someone digging."

"True, but would anyone give it a second thought?"

Neither Carly nor David answered.

"Anyway, I believe we can rule out the body washing ashore after a drowning."

"I think we'll have a better idea after we find out how old the bones are," David said.

"What does that have to do with the depth of the hole?" Joe said.

"Sand Key Park didn't always exist. Not like this, anyway."

"He's right, Joe," Carly said. "This spot and quite a bit of land to the south was nothing but Australian pines and scrub brush at one time. Dirt roads existed to get you from Gulf Boulevard to the beach, but nothing like this."

"It was known as *the* place for keg parties and making out, as they used to say," David said.

Joe and Carly stared at him.

"That's what my older cousin told me."

"How long ago was this?" Joe asked.

"Development began in the seventies. This park is all that's left."

"So the body could be fifty years old or more."

"And may have been buried deeper."

Joe was beginning to understand the glum expressions etched on their faces. Determining the identity of the victim would be hard enough. A local resident reported missing would allow them a more solid starting point. Relatives and acquaintances may be few by this time, but the person's history would be readily available. Or maybe not. When accumulating information, a victim who might have visited here from a different part of Florida would be easier to track than one from a different state. No matter who this victim turned out to be, solving a murder so many years old was going to be extremely difficult, if not impossible.

"This one is going to be a brain-buster," Joe muttered.

Carly and David agreed. Their silence spoke for them.

Glancing at the tent, Carly sighed. "I'm taking Joe home, David. I'll meet you back at the office."

She and Joe trudged through the sand to the parking lot. They could hear the gawkers murmuring as they made their way to the car. Once inside, Carly faced her friend.

"I don't like the feel of this one, Joe. I almost hope we come up empty as far as identifying the body. But I don't think that's going to happen. We're going to need all the experience we have among us. Luck, too."

"I'll help you as much as I can, Carly. You saw that the right rear part of the skull was missing, except for the collected pieces. It could be the result of a gunshot wound."

"An execution you mean. And the only thing that bothers me more is *why* she was executed." Carly reached out to start the car.

Joe wrapped his hand around her forearm. "What else is bothering you?"

Carly lowered her head and sat back. "You."

"Me?"

She looked up at him. "Joe, what the hell are you doing?"

"You'll have to give me more than that."

"Christine. You're making the same mistake with her that you did with Victoria."

"How can you say that? You don't anything about her."

"And you don't, either. You're moving way too fast."

"How do you know what I'm doing?"

"I'm a woman, Joe. I see the way she looks at you. And the way you look at her. You look like two puppies drooling over a bone."

"Really."

"Yes, really."

Joe paused. "You know, Carly, there was a time when I would have gotten mad at you for saying such a thing."

"And there was a time when I wouldn't have cared!"

Their eyes never left each other.

"You're really upset, aren't you?"

"I don't want to see you get hurt again."

"Christine is not like Victoria."

"What about what's-her-name? The one who took a nose-dive off her balcony."

"Anna Thewlis, A-K-A Leslie Symington?"

"She had you fooled."

Joe had forgotten about the woman who'd committed suicide to punish him. "Believe me, Carly, I'm being careful this time."

"Well, I hope so."

Joe smiled.

"It isn't funny."

"You love me, don't you?"

Carly growled, and started the car. "Of course I love you, you old fool."

Joe burst into laughter. "First I was a nosy old goat. Now I'm an old fool."

Carly laughed along with him as she drove them out of the parking lot and breezed along the road until it ended. Their amusement lasted until they turned onto Gulf Boulevard.

CHAPTER 3

Perched on his balcony once more but paying little attention to the late afternoon comings and goings below, Joe grappled with the apprehension gnawing at his insides. He knew it was more than Carly's opposition to his relationship with Christine. Something else had wrapped itself around her. Something she was not inclined to share. Her hope that they would be unable to put a name to the remains found on the beach had struck him all wrong. All detectives experienced gut feelings about their cases. Or should. The successful ones benefited from those instincts more often than not. But to express a desire for a case to be unsolvable at the beginning signaled an aversion to uncovering the truth. A bad sign, and not like Carly at all.

Perhaps it reminded her of an infamous cold case that had haunted the Clearwater Police Department. Maybe she was worried that it was some local celebrity or daughter from a wealthy family. He'd wanted to get to the heart of what had brought about Carly's misgivings, but didn't want to exacerbate the friction between them. Carly had exhibited similar behavior once when they'd first met. Trouble with her husband and their eventual divorce being the cause. She wasn't in a relationship now, and her objection to his interest in Christine appeared more in the vein of displaced aggression. Pushing her to open up was not a move he cared to make at this time. His phone ended his ruminations about his friend.

"Hi, Joe. Did I wake you from your nap?" Christine said.

"I wasn't napping, but I *was* lost in thought. More household problems?"

"I was just wondering if you'd gotten home yet."

"I'm sitting on the balcony."

"I wish my balcony faced the Gulf of Mexico."

"What can I do for you?"

"If you recall, I did ask you on a date. We were interrupted before you told me what you liked to do."

"I'm open to almost anything."

"Except Bingo."

"Except Bingo."

"How about the theatre?"

"Depends on the movie and who's in it."

Christine's laughter was warm. "I don't mean movies. I'm talking about the stage."

"I don't care for operas."

"What about musicals?"

"Some I like. Is there one in particular that interests you?"

"*Oklahoma.* There's a show tonight in St. Petersburg at a theatre called the Palladium. Want to go?"

"Sure, but it may be difficult to get tickets so late. Their shows are usually sold out."

"I can get tickets."

"Really?"

"I was talking to Alice Tonkin, my neighbor, and she has a pair for tonight. She and her husband were supposed to go, but he's not feeling well."

"Sounds good. What time does the show start?"

"Eight o'clock."

"Then we should probably leave no later than six-thirty."

"Shall we get something to eat on the way?"

"In that case, we should leave around five-thirty, which only gives us a little more than an hour to get ready. Is that enough time for you?"

"Very funny, Joe. I'll be ready."

Joe laughed to himself. "See you in a little while."

He laid his phone down on the folding table between the two chaise lounges, taking a moment to envision Christine. Besides her dark brown eyes, trim physique, and outdoorsy appearance, she was friendly and easy to engage in conversation. And her invitation couldn't have come at a better time. He needed to get away and be involved in something enjoyable. The last musical he'd seen was *South Pacific*. He and Joyce had sung some of the more memorable songs on their way home from the theatre. He smiled, picked up his phone, and went inside, humming "Oh, What A Beautiful Morning."

Joe and Christine began their trip a few minutes after five-thirty, stopping at Eddie's Eatery in Largo for supper. Eddie's was short on reputation, but the food was good, and the prices were reasonable. The traffic was heavier than Joe had anticipated after they left the restaurant, so they didn't arrive in downtown St. Petersburg until a half-hour before curtain time. Forced to park along 3rd Street, two blocks away from the theatre, they took a moment to gather themselves.

"I hope you don't mind walking," Joe said. "As you noticed when we swung by the parking lot, it's small and fills up fast."

"I don't mind. It will give me a chance to look around. I've never been to downtown St. Petersburg before." Christine gazed out the windshield. "That museum or art gallery we passed on Fourth Street looks interesting. We should go there sometime."

Joe smiled. "We need to get going."

As they strolled down the sidewalk, she was pleased by the sight of the oak trees lining both sides of the street and the mingling of small apartment buildings and houses adorned with gables and open-air porches. When they paused for the traffic light at 5th Avenue, Christine stared at the monstrous building on the other side.

"I can't get over how much it looks like a church, Joe. I feel like we're about to enter a sanctuary."

"I understand it used to be a church at one time. It housed other venues before becoming a theatre."

Two antiquated lamp posts sat on either side of the five-step entrance. Once they'd passed through the lobby, they were led up some stairs inside Hough Auditorium. Shown to their conventional movie theatre seats on the right aisle, they settled in for the evening's entertainment.

"This is so unbelievable, Joe. What an enchanting atmosphere. I feel like I've gone back in time."

"It brings back some delightful memories for me. How about you?"

"Makes me feel young again."

They chatted away the next few minutes until the house lights dimmed, and the orchestra began playing an overture of songs to come. Joe glanced at Christine from time to time, hoping that she was enjoying the event. Halfway through the first act, his focus started to slip back to the discovery in Sand Key Park.

Carly's behavior before and after their trip still clouded his mind. Not her protective attitude toward him. He appreciated her concern for his well-being. Like a daughter would care for her father. Reluctance to delve into a murder case was not part of her makeup. Not that he'd noticed, anyway. And he still couldn't rid himself of the notion that another incumbrance fed her longing to step away from responsibility. As much as he hated to admit it, her problem had become his problem.

Joe hadn't forgotten to silence the ring tone to vibrate on his phone. A wise move, he figured, when he felt it quiver and removed it from his coat pocket. The illuminated face showed the name Carly in bold black letters. Christine's frown was also revealed.

"I have to take this call," he whispered.

Christine's frown grew deeper.

He rose from his seat and moved to the rear of the auditorium.

An usher directed him to the nearest stairwell leading to the lobby. Finding an isolated corner, he raised the phone to return the call.

"Hi, Joe. Sorry to bother you."

Carly sounded glum.

"You're never a bother."

"I need to talk to you. Can I come over?"

"I'm not at home. I'm in St. Petersburg."

"Oh. What are you doing there?"

"Christine and I are taking in a play at the Palladium."

Carly's silence suggested a note of disapproval. "Can I talk to you after you get home? It's important."

"It may be late. The show just started."

"Call me, okay?

"Is this about your latest case?"

Again silence filled his ear.

"I may be involved."

Her answer surprised him. "How could you be involved?"

"Not directly. The victim might be... Look, just call me. I'll explain it to you then."

Joe slid the phone into his coat pocket. Now he was worried. He slowly entered the auditorium, nodded to the usher, and returned to his seat.

"You girlfriend need you to hold her hand?" Christine whispered.

Joe ignored her and tried to concentrate on the show. Act one was in full swing now, but his mind was on Carly and racing with possibilities. She knew something about the victim. Or thought she did. But how could she? No identity had been established. She must be guessing. Or an impropriety from her past had come back to haunt her. Joe shifted in his seat. More than ever, he wanted the evening to be over.

CHAPTER 4

Christine hadn't waited for another apology after they returned home. Upset at his being distracted by the call from Carly for the rest of the evening, she'd left Joe sitting in his car once he'd parked. Still stinging from her cold behavior, but not to the point of concern, he strode into the lobby and waited for the elevator. He would figure out a way to make it up to her later.

The ride to his floor was uninterrupted for a change, and the hallway was deserted.

Turning on the overhead light in the living room, he decided not to change out of his dress clothes and plopped down on the sofa. As he had promised, he called Carly.

"Joe, I apologize for ruining your evening. It's just..."

"Don't worry about it. I'll put on a pot of coffee. It should be ready by the time you get here."

"That's not necessary. I'm downstairs in the parking lot. I saw what happened between you and Christine."

Joe was surprised that he hadn't seen her. "She'll get over it. Come on up."

Five minutes later, Carly knocked on his door. Unlike the hardened expression she'd worn earlier, she now appeared lost and defeated. They took seats on the sofa, their place when personal talks were necessary.

"I, uh... You look very handsome, Joe."

"And you look beaten down, Carly. What's wrong?"

Carly sighed, pausing longer than usual. "My mother had two brothers and a sister. Carrie Anne was the oldest. I never knew her. She died before I was born. My mother never talked about her. I didn't even know I had an aunt on her side of the family until I was fourteen." She choked up and coughed.

Joe reached over and took her hand. "Take your time. Would you like something to drink?"

Carly shook her head. "One Thanksgiving, we were at my Uncle Leonard's house. We had dinner in the backyard, and when we had finished, the adults were talking while the children were playing. I always loved coming to my uncle's house, so I went inside to wander around. I came to the master bedroom, and when I looked inside, I saw him sitting on the edge of the bed. I asked if he was all right, and he told me to come sit next to him."

Joe noticed Carly's eyes were getting moist.

"He was holding a picture of Carrie Anne when she was in high school. Uncle Leonard drank a lot at our family gatherings and when he did, he started talking. It seems that a year after she graduated, Carrie Anne went to a party one Friday night. The boy she went with was the son of a prominent developer. She never came home. When he was questioned by the police, the boy admitted that he'd drunk too much and passed out. When his friends woke him hours later, Carrie Anne was gone. They never found her."

Carly went on to tell Joe that the boy figured her aunt had gotten mad at him and left with someone else. Everyone was drunk and having a good time. People were coming and going. No one remembered seeing her leave.

Joe patted her hand. "I'm sorry about your aunt, but I'm still confused as to why you were out of sorts this morning."

"The party she and the boy went to was on Sand Key. Bonfires, music, and booze was the theme of those parties. Uncle Leonard said that Carrie Anne was always looking for a good time and had a wild streak. She could have gone skinny-dipping with some of the others and drowned for all anyone knew. Or worse."

"But you don't know if those are the remains of your aunt."

"Remember I told you that I had a bad feeling after David and I were called to the park? When I was old enough to drive, I went to visit Uncle Leonard. I wanted to know more about her disappearance. He couldn't tell me much, but he did say that he never liked the boy she had gone with to the party. He told me he thought the boy was hiding something."

"Hiding what?"

"Uncle Leonard didn't know, but he thought Carrie Anne had been murdered."

"Then you should talk to him tomorrow."

"I can't. He died three years ago."

"Hmm." Joe exhaled. "Look, Carly, when you know the age of the remains, then you can start the process of identifying them. Until that time, you should try to relax. I know it'll be difficult, but you have to try."

Carly nodded, but he knew she wasn't convinced.

"Did Leonard tell you anything about the boy who took her to Sand Key?"

"Not much. His family was wealthy, and he made sure everyone knew it. He had a new car, wore nice clothes, and took his dates to fancy restaurants."

"But he and Carrie Anne went to a beer bash on the beach."

"I remember thinking the same thing. I should have asked Uncle Leonard."

"Did he tell you the boy's name?"

"He did, but I can't remember it."

"And he never told you what he thought this boy was hiding?"

"Joe, I was a curious girl even then. Some children called me a snoop. Guess that's why I became a cop." Carly attempted a smile. "I never mentioned it to my mom, but I talked to Uncle Randy, her other brother. He called Carrie Anne a slut. But she would only go out with boys whose parents had money."

"Could be she was looking for a wealthy husband."

"Uncle Randy didn't say. But he also thought that boy killed her, and money was the reason."

Joe paused. Money had long been a motivation for murder. History proved it. But if Carrie Anne had a reputation for being promiscuous, then most likely a lot of boys knew it. Her date may, in fact, have been telling the truth.

"Carly, have you talked this over with David?"

"Only what has been discovered so far. He knows something is bothering me, though."

"Did he question you?"

"He's worked with me long enough to know when to back off."

"You need to tell him. Everything. And as you come to know more, let him take the lead."

A pained expression covered her face. "I don't want him to know everything about my family."

"Not everything, but he needs to know what you told me."

"It's none of his business."

"It *is* his business. He's your partner. And if what you fear turns out to be true, he should be aware of what you two will be facing."

"And I should give up being lead detective on this case?"

"If it turns out that you're personally involved. And look at you. You're already getting emotional, and you don't even have all the facts. Your boss may yank you out of the game, anyway."

"I forgot about that."

Joe gave her a moment to let everything they'd discussed sink in.

"You know, Joe, sometimes I hate it when you're right."

"I forgive you."

"I'll talk to David in the morning." She exhaled long and slowly. "It's funny, but I don't feel as bad as I did."

"Sometimes it helps to let it all out."

"In fact, I'm exhausted."

"Not surprising with all that you've been keeping inside you today."

Carly leaned over and hugged him. "Thank you, Joe."

"My pleasure."

She released him and eased back, started to get up, then hesitated. "I'm really tired. Could I stay here tonight?"

"Mi sofa es su sofa."

"I'll take that to mean yes."

"Let me get you a pillow and a couple of sheets."

"A pillow will be fine. I'm comfortable."

After he'd seen to her needs, he went to his bedroom and closed the door. Once in bed, he shut his eyes and tried to rest. His brain was still processing their conversation.

First, he hoped the remains were not those of her aunt. Being free of that burden would allow her to focus on solving the case. If the skeleton did belong to Carrie Anne, then he would do everything possible to assist Carly and David in uncovering the truth.

The shattered pieces of skull he remembered seeing bothered him more than what he'd already learned. Almost certain to be made by a small caliber handgun, its location didn't suggest that the victim had refused to cooperate. Execution was the word that he couldn't release from his mind. An obvious act of hatred or the means to put an end to a person and the knowledge they might possess.

"The son of a prominent developer," Joe mumbled and rolled over on his right side.

What could this boy have known or done to necessitate the murder of a party girl? Had he uttered something incriminating while she was riding him? Or in the aftermath, whispered of some unethical dealings involving his father? And Sand Key. Was its future development a secret that had been leaked? Or were the names of those funding the projects and hoping to gain a foothold in the area tied to dirty money?

Like Carly, Joe had no idea who or what had brought about this killing. And worse, they might never know the answer.

CHAPTER 5

Joe barely heard the knocking but ignored it. A louder, second series of raps made him realize that he wasn't dreaming. He pulled off the covers, swung his feet to the floor, and waited a moment to clear his head. He stood up, headed for the chair where his jeans and a blue T-shirt lay draped over the arm, and put them on. A third volley of raps sounded as he left the hallway and entered the living room. The question of why Carly hadn't answered the door was apparent when he saw the pillow lying on the empty sofa. A glance through the peephole revealed the identity of the one responsible for his rousing. He smiled as he opened the door.

"Oh! I woke you, didn't I?"

"It's okay. Come in and sit down, Christine."

She stepped quietly past him and stopped next to the coffee table, staring at the sofa. "Why were you sleeping out here?"

"I wasn't."

As she sat down on the end opposite the pillow, an expression of understanding covered her face. "I ran into your girlfriend in the elevator."

"Is that what you stopped by to tell me?"

"No, I... I wanted to say I'm sorry for the way I acted last night."

"And I'm sorry that I was preoccupied and spoiled our evening."

Christine laid her hand on the armrest. "I'd like it if we could go out again sometime."

"Sounds good to me."

"I'm glad you agree. Now, maybe you can help me understand something. About your friend Charley."

"Her name is Carly, and I'm going to need some coffee first." Joe started for the kitchen.

"I'll make it. You have a seat."

Joe sat down in his blue easy chair and attempted to clear the cobwebs from his head. "The coffee and filters are in the cabinet above the coffeemaker."

As he yawned and contemplated the questions Christine might ask, he hoped that jealousy wasn't the motivation for this discussion. He decided the best position to take when answering was to be honest and straightforward. He closed his eyes and felt himself start to drift as the minutes slipped away.

"Here you go," Christine sang.

Joe sat up and took the mug of rich, brown liquid from her weathered hand. "Thank you."

"I left it black. Is that okay?"

"Just the way I like it." He was careful to sip the steaming rejuvenator. "Now, what's on your mind?"

Christine returned to her place on the sofa. "Joe, I think you know that I've grown fond of you in a very short time. I'm wondering how you feel about me."

"I like you, Christine."

A short and telling silence followed.

"Well, I'd like to get to know you better."

"Then let me explain my situation. It took me a while to get over the death of my wife, Joyce. And recently I've had a couple of unfortunate encounters. Seriously unfortunate encounters. I'm really not looking to jump into another relationship right away."

"I see. I know Carly works for the police department." Christine glanced at the pillow. "And it seems to me that you two are very close."

"We *are* very close, but not the way you think."

Joe proceeded to tell her how he and Carly had met and offered brief versions of her saving his life on two separate occasions.

"Because I was once a homicide detective, every so often she calls on me for advice or to help her. That's our relationship and nothing more."

"I've seen her around the condominium a few times. I've even spoken to her. She never answers. And this morning in the elevator she acted very distant and cold."

Joe grinned. "She's overly protective of me. Both of her parents are gone, so I guess she considers me a kind of surrogate father."

Christine paused, thinking. "So, she wasn't checking on you when she called last night?"

"After you left yesterday morning, she drove me to a crime scene to look it over. She wanted to talk about it when she called last night. She had no idea that I was out with you."

"Now I am *very* sorry for the way I acted. And curious. Can I ask you for some of the details?"

"I won't tell you everything, but the fact is we don't know that much. A human skeleton was discovered buried in the sand at a park a few miles south of here. We're pretty sure it was a woman and that's about it. The forensics report will hopefully give us a better idea of what happened to her."

"Am I right in thinking that will take a while? No offense, but coroners and forensics people usually aren't well-versed in reading skeletal remains."

"Dental records and DNA results will tell us a lot, but you're right about it taking time. The workload in forensics will be a factor, too."

Christine paused to do more thinking.

"Something I said bothering you?"

"I have an acquaintance who's a retired anthropologist. He's an expert at analyzing remains. He lives in Land O' Lakes. That's not far from here, is it?"

"Not at all."

"He might be willing to come take a look. At least you'll have some of the information you need much sooner."

"That would certainly help. I'll talk to Carly."

"Maybe then she'll stop hating me."

"She doesn't hate you, Christine. She just doesn't know you."

"I was very uncomfortable around her. I felt more at ease when I was confronted by government officials who resented me poking my nose into the graves of their ancestors."

Joe could see no point in dwelling upon the subject and went with the first idea that came to him. "Christine, have you had breakfast yet? I know a place with a beautiful view of Clearwater Harbor. I think you'd enjoy it."

"Why don't I cook you breakfast instead?"

"I don't want you to go to all that trouble. Let me take you there to make up for last night."

"Well, okay. Breakfast with a waterfront view does sound lovely. But one thing."

"What's that?"

"You will put on your shoes, right?"

They both looked down at his bare feet and laughed.

Maggie Mae's Sunrise Café was crowded, but Joe and Christine were able to get a table on the deck facing the harbor. Joe didn't bother to mention Sand Key Park when they passed by the entrance, glad their conversation was centered on Christine and her travels. Carly's name was never mentioned again. He found his new friend's recounting of her excavations in different parts of the world to be fascinating. Moreover, he came to appreciate what a unique person she was, quite unlike most others he'd met. When they'd finished eating and returned to the Crimson Conch, he was satisfied that all was right between them again.

Joe had finished washing the dishes left over from the day

before. His phone rang as he set the last glass in the dish rack. Drying his hands with a floral dish towel, one of Joyce's favorites, he flipped it on the kitchen counter and went into the living room.

"Joe, this is David. Do you have a moment to talk?"

"Sure, David. How have you been?"

"I'm fine."

"And how's Dani? Are you still seeing her?"

"Oh, yes. She's fine. We're spending a lot more time together. She is some woman. And quite a handful at times. Anyway, I hate to ask you this, but is anything bothering Carly? What I mean is...Is she having personal problems?"

"Not that I'm aware. Why do you ask?"

"She requested a leave of absence this morning."

"I don't believe it."

"It's not like her to do that at the start of a case. In fact, it's not like her to do it at all."

Joe sighed. "I can't say for certain, David, but I know the remains you found yesterday at Sand Key Park really bothered her. I don't know why."

An uneasy feeling filtered through Joe at the ensuing silence.

"If you know what's bothering her, then please tell me."

Joe struggled to pass along the story behind the disappearance of Carly's aunt. Although he felt like he was betraying a confidence, he understood that it was in David's best interest to understand the cause of Carly's unusual behavior.

"But, Joe, we have no idea whose bones they are. Not yet, anyway. And even if they do belong to her aunt, I would think that Carly would *want* to find out what really happened."

"I'm sure she does. But I mentioned that if your boss found out it's a family member, he might pull her off the case."

"You're probably right, but I'm not going to tell them. And I know Carly wouldn't."

"But if it came up down the road, it might work against you in getting a conviction."

"Joe, her aunt disappeared over fifty years ago. I doubt if

most of the people that knew her are still alive."

"Is that a fact?"

David paused. "I'm sorry, Joe, but you know what I mean. A lot could have happened between then and now."

"Well, here's the way I see it. If the remains turn out to be Carly's aunt, and Carly is pulled off the case, then you'll be working to find out who killed her. You saw the skull and the pieces beside it on the tarp. It reeks of an execution. Carly knows that, and she'll be looking for the killer, as well. Only in an unofficial capacity. No doubt she'll ask me to help her. We can all work together to solve this case."

This time David sighed. "Keep an eye on her. Please. I've seen her mad and I've seen her worried, but I've never seen her like this."

"I'll do my best. And I know that you'll do your best to solve this case as soon as you can."

"You can count on it. But, Joe, what if the bones turn out to be someone else?"

"Then I'd say you might be without your partner for a long time."

CHAPTER 6

Any information that had been accumulated over the past three days was unknown to Joe. He hadn't heard from Carly or David. Not that they were obligated to inform him. He was an advisor. Technically, an unofficial advisor since he'd resigned from the job offered him months ago. He felt no real need to inquire as to the current status of their latest case. Even the old itch that drove him all those years he'd been on the force had gone by the wayside.

On an odd note, Christine hadn't called or visited him, either. She'd spoken of wanting them to go out again with an eagerness he'd appreciated along with a pang of uncertainty. Stating his position in regard to relationships as clearly as possible, he'd sensed that his honesty had put off his new friend. He'd never been one for playing games with people's feelings, and hoped she possessed a similar conviction.

"I'll call her later," he whispered.

He sipped the remainder of his after-breakfast coffee then set the mug on the folding table beside his chaise lounge. The view from his balcony this morning was not unlike others he'd seen. Clouds tinted a pale tangerine were building over the Gulf, a harbinger of possible showers to come. Noises familiar to everyday life reached his ears as the usual throng of workers and visitors made their way to the beach. None of them was aware or cared about the lone observer sitting high above on a balcony. So much the better.

With both hands gripping the armrests, he smiled and lay back when he heard his phone ring and scooped it up from the table without looking at the caller I.D.

"Joe, it's David."

"How are you, David?"

"I need your help."

"Okay. What part of the case are we talking about?"

"Not the case. I need help with Carly."

"What's happened?"

"Her request for a leave of absence was denied and she's pissed. She's acting like… She's acting like she did when we first met you."

"When she was having problems with her husband?"

"Right. Only worse."

Joe recalled how abrasive Carly had been during their initial encounter. Since her husband Tim was no longer in the picture, something else must be feeding the cause of her emotional downturn.

"I guess she really wants to know what happened to her aunt," Joe said.

"Which is why I called you. Dani knows one of the guys in the coroner's office. The remains belong to a Morgan Gail Adcock. D-N-A and dental records verified the identification.

Carly ordered me to handle the case and keep her updated while she does her own personal investigation of her aunt's murder. If the brass find out, they'll burn her."

"And you, too, most likely, if you don't report her."

"You know I won't, Joe. But Carly's putting her career on the line. We can't let her do that."

David had made a valid point, but they were both aware of Carly's tenacity.

"What else do you know about this Morgan Gail Adcock?"

"She lived in Brandon, was single, and worked as an administrative assistant for the Suarez Data Corporation in Tampa."

"Do you know her age?

"She was twenty-three when she was reported missing five years ago."

"Missing?"

"She and some friends went to a nightclub in Ybor City. According to her friends' statements in the missing-persons report, she met some fellow named Chuck while they were there. None of them saw her or Chuck leave."

"Not telling any of her friends she was leaving seems strange."

"According to one friend, Morgan was a very independent woman."

"rBut, David, I still find it hard to believe that Carly would ignore her responsibility."

"I know, Joe. And I get that what happened to her aunt is important to her, but she could look into it during her off-hours. And I'd be willing to help."

"So, what do you want me to do?"

"Talk her into doing her job. I know I could handle this case by myself for a while, but the brass are sure to find out."

"Couldn't you ask some of the others to help you?"

"I'm sure they would, but Joe…"

The strain in David's voice was saying more than his words. Of course he was worried about his partner. The prospect of Carly's insubordination being uncovered had him shaken. Joe had met the other detectives in the homicide division. Rolling on one of their own seemed out of the question. He didn't know all of them, though. Only Dani. Had there been a change of command? A new higher-up who, under no circumstances, would tolerate defiance of orders?

"Okay, David. I'll talk to her."

"Thanks, Joe." The relief in his voice was clear.

"I don't know if it will do any good. You know how hard-headed your partner can be."

"She'll listen to you."

As he laid his phone on the table, Joe wished his optimism

was as lofty as that of his young friend. He remembered how defiant he himself had acted when others in his department had attempted to discourage him from traveling down a questionable road. In that way, he and Carly were no different. He smiled when he remembered her calling him a nosy old goat. A proven and undeniable fact.

But he couldn't slip into the shadows and watch her throw away an exemplary career, regardless of the reason. She had too much more to offer. Too much more to give.

He picked up his phone and searched the list of recent calls. He selected her number and waited. The voicemail message filled his ear after the fourth ring. He softly growled before it ended.

"Carly, please call me. It's important."

He hoped the serious tone of his voice might spark an urgent need in her to call him back right away. His anticipation of hearing from her in the ensuing minutes began to fade as his phone lay silent. Thirty minutes passed, so he got to his feet, picked up his phone and coffee mug, and walked inside his condo.

Carly was a smart woman. She would know that David would talk to him. So she would guess Joe's reason for calling her. A feeling that nothing or no one could change her mind gained a foothold in Joe. Rather than making an attempt to derail her current course of action, he would inquire as to why this family mystery was so important to her.

A bowl of vegetable soup had been the perfect solution to his stomach's calling at lunch, and Joe's hands were submerged in dishwater when the distraction sounded.

Wouldn't you know it, he thought. *The minute my hands are wet.*

Snatching the floral dish towel off the counter to dry them, he picked up his phone.

Silence answered his greeting, a sure sign the call was from Carly.

"I know it's you," he said. "We need to talk."

"There's nothing to talk about."

"You know those remains aren't your aunt's."

More silence.

"Carly, you're jeopardizing your career."

"I don't care about my career."

"Then tell me why this is so important."

"It's none of your business."

"It damn well is my business when one of my dearest friends is troubled."

Carly sighed. "Uncle Randy and I are the only ones in the family who still live around here. He has two daughters, but they're in Tennessee and Idaho. I don't see them very often. Leonard and his wife are gone, and their son lives in New Mexico. I haven't seen him in years." A few seconds of silence passed. "I spoke to Uncle Randy again. He said my grandparents never got over what happened to Carrie Anne. None of the family ever talked about her again, but all of them were affected."

Joe could hear the sadness in her voice and sensed what she was about to say next.

"I can't let go of this, Joe. Believe me, I've tried. I have to find out what happened to Carrie Anne."

"I understand, Carly. You love your family. But, please, hear me out. You're talking about a cold case more than fifty years old. Not only that, but you don't even know the name of the boy who was with her that night. Or his family's name. And who's to say that he's still alive?"

"I have to try, Joe. I won't be able to live with myself if I don't. And I promised Uncle Randy I would do everything possible."

Joe knew it was pointless to try to talk her out of it. His friend was determined, and she was willing to risk everything to find out the truth.

"Then let us help you."

"Us? Who is us?"

"David, Dani, me, anyone willing to put in the time. But

your job has to come first. It's a safe bet that Morgan Gail Adcock was murdered. You owe it to her family to find her killer and bring them closure."

This time Joe felt uncomfortable hearing her silence.

"I don't know if I can..."

"Carly, I'll do the research on your family while you're working. We can get together after hours and go over what I'm able to find. All of us."

"Okay. Thanks, Joe."

"And I think I know someone else who can help us."

CHAPTER 7

Informed that Carly's maiden name was Jernigan, Joe went down to the manager's office and set about doing a computer search of her parents.

Life after marriage for Floyd Andrew Jernigan and Sandra Jean Lawless became the prototypical stamp of Americana. An employee of a factory manufacturing optical lenses, Floyd had worked his way up from the loading docks to a floor supervisor's position. Sandra remained at home as a housewife—the customary occupation in the forties and fifties.

Jernigan's immediate family bore no signs of deviant or unlawful behavior. One of the many strong fibers woven into the framework of the blue-collar world. A similar résumé defined the Lawless clan. No scandalous acts tarnished their coat of arms. The only stain on the fabric of the family's lineage came with the disappearance of Carrie Anne.

With his focus on the computer monitor, Joe sat back and folded his arms over his chest. Nothing he'd read suggested that any misdeeds by Carrie Anne's parents or siblings might have triggered her vanishing. The question of something she'd done or someone she'd offended settled into his mind. Could her death have been accidental, and panic in the person responsible for her death the reason for the coverup?

Joe shook his head, his fingers moving to the keyboard as he leaned forward to log into another website. Having been granted access to Clearwater police files during his brief stint as an advisor, and access yet to be revoked, he searched the cold cases for the file on Carrie Anne. His search was successful, but unrewarding. Line after line of basic information filled the screen as he scrolled. Statements from those who knew her only succeeded in telling him what he didn't want or need to know. Others who'd been at Sand Key that evening spoke of her boisterous and flamboyant behavior. No altercation or dangerous intent on anyone's part appeared in the account.

Once again Joe leaned back, thinking. If the area at the time had been as wooded and overgrown as he'd been told, then a fight or disagreement may have taken place away from the rest of the partygoers. Or, given the inebriated condition of the attendees, Carrie Anne may have wandered off unnoticed to take a swim and drowned as Carly had speculated. But some partygoer would have found her clothes that night. Or the police when they had been notified and began their search. Joe stroked his chin. Carly never told him when the police got involved. A party on a Friday night was all she'd said. Could be she didn't know. Joe scrolled back to the top of the report to look for a date.

Neatly typed in the upper part of the first page was the date, August 4, 1968. Next, he searched for a calendar from that year. He didn't want to believe that even back then Clearwater P.D. subscribed to the "wait forty-eight hours before filing a missing-persons report" mentality. Only lazy law enforcement agencies and filmmakers held to that practice. When a calendar was located, he was relieved to find that the date on the report was a Saturday. The party must have taken place on Friday, August third, and Clearwater police had followed up less than twenty-four hours later.

The other positive coming from the report was that now he had the name of Carrie Anne's party-going friend. Boyd Alan Robinson Jr. had admitted taking her to Sand Key. As Carly's Uncle Leonard had told her, the boy confessed to passing out at some point. Thinking she'd gotten angry with him, he believed she had left with someone else. Joe held no doubt that with the information given them, the officers had done all they could to locate the missing girl. Now he needed to know more about the company owned by the boy's father.

Boca Bay Development Corporation had been a leader in the construction boom of the seventies. The building of condominiums gained a foothold and quickly spread along the coastlines of Florida. Boca Bay Development, led by its CEO, Boyd Alan Robinson Sr., landed the contracts for many of the concrete and steel structures in the Tampa Bay area. Now all Joe had to do was locate the residences of father and son, then he and Carly would look further into the disappearance of her aunt.

A quick search of the Robinsons brought good news and bad. Robinson Sr., retired and residing in the affluent community of Belleair, had died of a stroke in 2013. The good news was that Robinson Jr., retired CEO of Daddy's corporation, also lived in Belleair. Another point of interest was a daughter, Alicia Robinson Drayton, who lived in New York City. If need be, she might be inclined to offer a better understanding of her brother. Uncle Leonard had portrayed him as a narcissistic egotist. If that was true, then getting away with murder must have inflated his self-worth.

Joe noted the addresses of Junior and several others interviewed. An addition to the initial report was the on-scene findings of Officers Stanton and Porzingis. After going over the location of the gathering as described by several interviewees, they'd found the usual assortment of discarded trash and personal items: beach towels, blankets, and clothing. Nothing out of the ordinary was noted, and, to Joe, that meant the discovery of a freshly dug grave.

Stifling a yawn, Joe raised his arms above his head and stretched. In a moment he would search for the addresses of the two officers, hoping to find that at least one of them was still alive.

Joe understood the difficulty surrounding an investigation of this sort. He'd never worked a cold case during his time on the force in Philadelphia, but he knew a couple of detectives who had been assigned the task. They'd made it clear to him that encountering more roadblocks than leads was the norm. He hoped that Carly, with her insatiable desire to pursue the truth, knew what lay ahead of them. Especially when it came to being granted an interview with Boyd Alan Robinson Jr. The community of Belleair was foreign to Joe. Other residents at the Crimson Conch had described its spacious mansions, situated on sprawling acreage and surrounded by wrought-iron fences. Not every home was a mansion, but there were enough to give the town its monied reputation. And he knew that high-priced lawyers lined the avenue to dealing with the wealthy. Since no official permission had been granted to reopen the case, they might never be permitted to hear Robinson Jr.'s version of what had happened that night.

As he lay his fingers on the keyboard, Joe glanced at the lower right corner of the monitor. He was surprised to discover the time nearing seven o'clock. He'd spent a good portion of the day helping Carly. To avoid being confronted by angry residents for neglecting his responsibilities, Joe decided he'd better attend to condo business. He could get the addresses first thing in the morning.

A couple of messages had been left on the answering machine, minor problems of no urgency, so he called the residents to assure them their problems would be dealt with as soon as possible. Scooping up the paper on which he'd written the pertinent information, he folded it and got to his feet just as the office door swung open.

"I thought I might find you in here," Christine said.

Joe grinned and slipped the paper into his pants pocket. "Just looking after some official business."

"I was thinking about going for a walk. Care to join me?"

"Only if you're heading to the nearest restaurant. I haven't eaten yet."

"I haven't either." Christine's laughter was soft. "The weather today was so nice that I decided to sit on the balcony. I dozed off, and just woke up a few minutes ago."

"How about we order something and have it delivered. Does pizza by the pool sound good to you?"

"As long as it doesn't have anchovies on it."

"Medium or large?"

Christine didn't get the opportunity to answer. Joe's phone sounded and vibrated on top of the desk.

"Uh-oh. I bet I know who that is."

"Now don't you go running off," he said and picked it up.

"Joe, it's Carly. Just checking in. How's everything with you?"

"Good. Christine and I were about to get something for supper. I was able to gather some information for you. We can discuss it when you have the time."

"Then I'll make this quick. We caught a break in the Morgan Gail Adcock case. It seems she had a boyfriend, a guy named Carter Paul Fitzgibbons. He got popped for drug trafficking eighteen months after she disappeared. Not his first arrest. He's doing time at the Okeechobee Correctional Institution. David's going down there to talk to him tomorrow."

"You think he might have had something to do with her death?"

Christine's eyes grew large.

"That's what we're hoping to find out," Carly said.

"David mentioned that Morgan Adcock had met some fella named Chuck at a club the night she disappeared. Any news on him?"

"Nothing so far."

"I'm thinking there has to be a connection."

"It's possible. She might have seen something she shouldn't have when she was with him."

"Or it was a message to her boyfriend. Carly, are you sure it's this Adcock woman who was found at the park?"

"Yes, Joe. Look, I remember what you said about Christine's anthropologist friend, and I appreciate the offer, but we're good on this."

"Okay. Call me when you're ready to take a look at what I've got for you."

"I will. And tell Christine hello for me."

The surprised look on his face didn't escape his new friend.

"What's wrong, Joe?"

"Nothing. Carly says hello."

Christine's mouth dropped open. "You're kidding."

Joe grinned. "The woman never ceases to amaze me."

"So I'm starting to learn."

"Well, let me order that pizza. I'm starving."

CHAPTER 8

Joe sat at the desk in the manager's office, staring at the computer monitor. Bids were coming in from landscaping contractors for the job of maintaining the grounds of the Crimson Conch. He was attempting to scrutinize each offer carefully, but his mind lingered elsewhere. Since the call from Carly three days ago, he'd been dallying in limbo. He had thought that the information he'd gathered for her might pique her curiosity; that she might hurry over to see what he'd found. Instead, he had the feeling he'd been shuffled out of the scope of importance. Something had happened in the interim. Something significant enough to keep Carly occupied and away from him.

He pushed his chair back from the desk and focused on the far wall. Calling her was an option. And a risk. He didn't want to interfere if there had been a new development in the case. But he didn't like being ignored, either. He snapped out of the doldrums when Carly and David entered the office.

"Hey, Joe," Carly said. Her black blouse and slacks matched the dullness in her voice.

David nodded.

"I have to say that I've seen happier faces on cattle heading to the slaughter," Joe said.

"There's been another murder."

"Oh?"

"A body was found in the ditch next to the parking lot on

246

the southside of Memorial Causeway."

"That might clutter up your workdays for a while."

"Clutter is a polite way of saying it. Tell him, David."

"I went to the Okeechobee Correctional Institution a few days ago to talk to Carter Fitzgibbons about Morgan Adcock. Seeing as how she was his girlfriend, we figured he could tell us more about her. Well, he told us all right. They were 'fuck buddies,' as he put it, and nothing more. Free to go out with anyone and go wherever they wanted."

"That explains why she went to the club in Ybor City with her friends the night she disappeared," Joe said.

"When I asked him where he was that night, he said he was with a girl he'd met recently, who corroborated his alibi."

"We checked the report, Joe," Carly said. "He was telling the truth."

"Now for the good part," David continued. "He said he knows who killed Morgan Adcock."

"What?" Joe sat up straight. "Who killed her?"

"He said that if we got his sentence commuted, he would tell us."

"He's been talking to his lawyer. So, now you've got two cases to solve."

"And here's where things get really strange," Carly said. "The latest victim is Charles Phillip Robinson."

"Robinson?"

"Son of Boyd Robinson Jr."

Joe eyed Carly, then David. "Could he be Chuck? The same fella who picked up Morgan Adcock five years ago?"

"We don't know."

"And here's another problem," David said. "If the prosecutor agrees to cut a deal with Carter Fitzgibbons, and he tells us that Charles Robinson killed Morgan Adcock, all we have is his word."

"But that won't get him out of prison," Joe said.

"He also said he knows *why* Adcock was murdered."

Joe shook his head. "Wait a minute. If Robinson did kill Adcock, how did he know that she'd be at the club in Ybor City?"

Carly and David stared at him.

"You don't know."

"But here's what we *do* know," Carly said. "We ran a search on Fitzgibbons's father, Robert Carter Fitzgibbons, and his mother. Robert was employed by Florida United Construction. His position when he retired was construction manager. His company was often contracted by the Boca Bay Development Corporation."

"And that means he probably knew the Robinson family."

"Which may or may not have something to do with the disappearance of my aunt, Carrie Anne ."

"Carly, no offense, but that's stretching it a bit."

"There's one more little note of interest, Joe," David said. "Charles Robinson died from a gunshot wound behind his right ear."

"Am I to believe that *his* murder was a message to someone?"

"We consider it a possibility."

"But a message to who?"

"I believe it's *to whom*," Carly said.

Joe didn't catch on at first.

Carly answered with a tight smile.

"So, where do we go from here?"

"With Charles Robinson having been murdered, we can legally talk to Boyd Robinson Jr. now. Want to come along?"

Joe lifted himself from the chair. "Give me a minute to get my coat."

"What for?"

"If Boyd Robinson Jr. is as big a snob as he's rumored to be, I don't want to come off looking unprofessional."

CHAPTER 9

The home of the former development company CEO didn't resemble the O'Hara mansion from *Gone with the Wind*, but it was big enough. There was a good-size front yard and breathing room on both sides, so the place wasn't boxed in by the neighbors.

Carly brought the gray sedan to a halt. Like David and Joe, she paused a moment to look over the well-tended residence.

The two-story, tan and buff-brick house was fronted by six twelve-foot pillars. The porch was without furniture. Bougainvillea and hydrangea planted in brown ceramic urns and spaced perfectly were the only decoration. The one unusual ornamentation was a small fountain to the left of the front door, its narrow waterfall cascading from the mouth of a ceramic fish that was mounted on the wall three feet above the floor.

"So, this is what it's like to live in Belleair," Joe said.

"Damn, partner," David said. "We're in the wrong line of work."

Carly wasn't impressed. "Daddy probably bought it for him."

"You sound awfully bitter."

"Jerks who are spoon-fed and butt-wiped their whole lives make me sick."

"Maybe you should wait out here," Joe said.

"I'll be all right."

The three of them ambled along the travertine walkway,

cutting a path through a blanket of lush green St. Augustine grass. Standing in front of a pair of polished oak doors, they paused as Carly rang the doorbell.

"If a butler answers, I'm going to vomit," she said.

One of the doors opened, and a tall man with a full head of black hair painted with streaks of gray near his temples, stepped forward. His powder blue James Perse polo shirt and pressed navy slacks suggested he'd recently returned from the golf course.

Carly held up her badge. "Detective Sergeant Truffant, Clearwater Police Department. This is Detective Sizemore, and Special Advisor Hampton. Are you Mr. Robinson?"

The man sized up the trio before he spoke. "I'm Boyd's neighbor, Fudgie Fairbanks."

Joe was relieved when neither Carly nor David burst out laughing. Nevertheless, he couldn't help but wonder why the man had been saddled with such a humiliating nickname.

"We'd like to speak with Mr. Robinson."

"I'm not certain if Boyd is up to it at the moment. This terrible tragedy—"

"Where is he?"

"In the rear of the house, but—"

"Thank you."

Carly brushed past him with David right behind her. Joe lowered his eyes, feeling uneasy about their unsympathetic intrusion.

A room immediately to their left resembled a home-furnishing store's display window. Matching furniture, pairings of light fixtures, and perfectly mounted paintings on the walls appeared untouched since delivery.

At the end of an abbreviated, red-carpeted hallway, Carly stopped and gazed intently at a black walnut dining table surrounded by six chairs. A window behind it offered a partial view of a swimming pool and a spacious backyard. Looking to her left, Carly spied an over-sized kitchen. Wasting little time, she led the procession, with Fairbanks following, through the gleaming galley and on through a door with red satin curtains pulled to the sides of frosted glass panes.

Sitting alone at a white, glass-topped aluminum table on a large, screened-in patio deck was a man with thinning white hair and gaunt facial features. He was staring straight ahead.

The trio stopped next to the table as Fairbanks moved forward to approach the man.

"They insisted on seeing you, Boyd."

Robinson slowly turned and lifted his head. "Thank you, Fudgie. Would you mind looking in on Chelsea? Your Abigail took her to the bedroom to lie down."

Fairbanks glowered at Carly as he passed by her and disappeared through the kitchen door.

Robinson tilted his head back and eyed her. How he was able to look down his nose while seated fascinated Joe.

Carly raised her badge. "Mr. Robinson, I'm Detective Sergeant—"

"What do you want?"

"First, I'm sorry for your loss." She slipped her badge into the pocket of her slacks.

Robinson said nothing.

"Had your son mentioned having trouble with anyone lately?"

"Charles didn't discuss his personal life with Chelsea and me."

"Do you know of any reason why someone would do this to him?"

"Other than the fact that he's a member of a wealthy family, you mean?"

"You believe that robbery was the motive?"

"Don't you?"

"Can you give us the names of some of his friends?"

"Sergeant, I'm really not in the mood for this, so listen carefully. Charles was a miserable human being who cared for no one but himself. He had no friends, only acquaintances. And those people he bought. Now, if you will kindly see your way out."

"One more question, sir. Did Charles ever mention a man

named Carter Fitzgibbons?"

Robinson's jaw tightened. "Why he chose to associate with that pandering pustule I will never know."

David was the first to speak when they reached the car and were pulling away.

"Now we know that Carter Fitzgibbons and Charles Robinson knew each other. I wonder if they were partners in drug-trafficking? If they were, then Fitzgibbons's telling us why Morgan Adcock was murdered might lead us to some people who don't wish to be tied to them."

"That occurred to me, too," Carly said. "And now Fitzgibbons is willing to work with us because he got convicted, and Daddy kept Chuckie from going to prison."

"Did you find anything other than bones at Morgan Adcock's gravesite?" Joe asked from the back seat.

Carly looked in the rearview mirror at him, confused. "Nothing other than the bullet that killed her. They extended the pit three feet on all sides."

"So, it's possible that she was naked at the time she was buried."

"What are you getting at, Joe?"

"Had Charles Robinson been robbed when you searched his body?"

"We couldn't tell. His body had been stripped. That's why we initially had a problem identifying him."

"Then Carter Fitzgibbons's explanation as to why Morgan Adcock was murdered should be interesting."

CHAPTER 10

With no clouds in the sky, the mid-afternoon sun shone down on everything and everyone—including Joe. In an hour, the entire balcony would be sun-drenched. Until then he would remain stretched out on his chaise lounge. He'd been spending a good deal of time on the balcony during the past few weeks, having finally adjusted to the sub-tropical climate of central Florida. The open-ended cubicle was also a comfortable place to let his mind roam free or to focus on a responsibility or problem. At the moment, his focus was on the visit that he, Carly, and David had paid to Boyd Robinson Jr. Joe had elected not to accompany them to interview Robert Fitzgibbons, Carter's widower father. Though his request to be dropped off at home had left the two detectives noticeably curious, they didn't bother to ask the reason.

The off-hand remark Boyd Robinson Jr. had made about his son had struck Joe as insensitive. Regardless of whether the relationship between him and Charles had been strained, calling him a miserable, selfish human being suggested a total lack of paternal emotion. What had happened to fill this man with such disdain? If Charles had killed Morgan Adcock, had Boyd known it when he saved his son from going to prison? And why had Morgan been killed?. Was jealousy the cause? Had Charles resented the fact that she was Carter Fitzgibbons's girlfriend?

Joe shook his head.

Fitzgibbons had said that his relationship with Morgan

Adcock was purely sexual and nothing more. Maybe she'd spurned Charles's advances, and he couldn't handle the rejection. Disregarding any possibility was not a good practice, but a bruised ego didn't rank high on the list of motives for murder. Maybe both Robinson and Fitzgibbons had lied. There was no discounting what might drive a person to questionable acts.

Joe shifted his gaze to the folding table when he heard a familiar sound. He considered throwing the damn phone off the balcony. He picked it up, looked at the caller I.D., and was glad he hadn't.

"Hi, Joe. I hope I'm not disturbing you."

"Not at all, Christine. I was beginning to think that you'd moved away without telling me."

"What do you mean?"

"I haven't heard from you in quite a while."

"The last two times I came to see you, you weren't home. I guess you're spending a lot of time with Charley."

"Her name is Carly. And yes, there have been some new developments."

"Well, you could have called *me*, you know."

Her voice possessed an edge that Joe had never heard.

"Is everything okay?"

"Certainly. Why wouldn't it be?"

"You sound anxious."

"Well, I... It seems like you don't have time for me anymore."

"Christine, you know that isn't true."

"I'm not so sure. If you don't want me around, just say so."

Joe paused. "It's not that. I enjoy being with you. But when the police want my help, I feel obligated to assist them."

"You're retired, Joe. Your only obligation is to yourself."

"Christine, you don't understand. There's a bond between those of us in law enforcement. It's difficult for someone who has never worn a badge to comprehend our ongoing sense of dedication. It's a commitment that never goes away, no matter the time or place."

"I guess I don't understand. But tell me, who did they turn to before you moved here?"

Joe rolled his eyes. "I'm certain they managed quite well."

"Exactly. You told me you'd almost been killed twice. Is Charley going to be around when you get into trouble again?"

Joe's mind raced back to his recent trip to Englewood. He hadn't told her about his brush with death while vacationing there.

"Okay, I see your point. But I'm already involved in their latest cases. I really should see them through to the end."

An extended silence had Joe wondering if this would be their last conversation.

"Oh, dammit! I'm sorry, Joe."

"There's no need to apologize."

"Yes, there is. I'm doing it again."

"Doing what?"

"You made it very clear to me how you feel about relationships. And here I go pushing you again."

"Don't concern yourself. I'm flattered. Really."

"It's not right. And I promise I won't do it again."

Joe grinned. "Don't give it another thought."

"I really didn't call to argue. I'd like to talk something over with you."

"Shall I come down to your place then?"

"I'd rather come see you. The view from your balcony is prettier."

"Sounds good. The sun might be in our eyes, but it shouldn't be too bad."

"I won't mind. Thank you, Joe."

"And Christine."

"Yes?"

"Her name is Carly."

Minutes were few in passing before she arrived and greeted him with a surprise.

"What have you got there?" he asked. He swung the door

open wider.

"A pitcher of iced tea and a plate of fudge brownies I made myself."

"You didn't need to go to all that trouble."

"Consider it a peace offering."

"Well, come right in. I'll get some glasses."

"No, you go sit on the balcony. I'll take care of everything."

"You're spoiling me."

"All right, take these." She handed him the pitcher and plate.

Joe strode to the balcony and set the brownies on the folding table. Christine followed soon thereafter with a handful of napkins and a pair of glasses filled with ice. As she held the glasses steady, Joe filled them with tea. He waited until she was seated before stretching out on the other chaise lounge.

He tipped his glass toward her. "Cheers."

Christine mirrored the salute. "Cheers."

Both of them took a generous drink.

"Now, what's on your mind?" he said.

With sunlight laying over her tanned and weathered face, she lost the glow she'd worn earlier.

"I've been getting a lot of phone calls," she said. "Robo calls, I guess. I don't recognize the numbers, so I don't answer."

"Smart thinking. You've never gotten them before?"

"Not until I moved here. And only in the last month or two."

"It took them a while to locate your number. Those scum like to prey on retirees."

"They're really annoying. Is there any way I can stop them?"

"Most phones nowadays have call block. I'll look at yours in a few minutes."

"What a relief. I sometimes get three or four in a day. And the ones that wake me in the middle of the night are especially irritating."

Joe rolled his head over. "How many of these late-night calls have you received?"

"Oh, five or six, I guess."

"When did they start?"

"Last week, I believe. I answered once by mistake. I wasn't quite awake, and picked up my phone without thinking."

"What was the pitch?"

"I couldn't make out what he was saying at first. Before he hung up, though, he said something that sounded like 'Watch yourself, bitch' or 'Watch out, bitch.' It upset me so, I didn't fall back asleep for an hour."

"Sounds more like a crank call."

"I suppose. Anyway, it was disturbing."

Rolling his head back, Joe stared at the sun sitting low in the sky. Christine's phone was fairly new and equipped with the means to put an end to the harassing calls. But hackers today were smart, could pull up and use other phone numbers for their nefarious activities, and keep their identity unknown. Crank calls were a thing of the past. Sophisticated means of tracing a call, and the advent of call blocking, had brought an end to such foolishness. For someone to do it today would guarantee their getting caught. But not everyone was an internet genius. They didn't have to be. Burner phones protected a caller's name from being revealed. Too many avenues were available to those with devious intentions.

Joe sighed.

"Uh-oh. Are you bored with me already?"

"No, Christine. I was thinking of something else." Smiling, he turned to her. "And I shouldn't have been."

"Are you getting hungry, Joe?"

"Haven't heard any complaints from my stomach yet."

"I've got some ground beef in the fridge. I'm told I make a pretty good meatloaf. How does that sound?"

"Green beans to go with it?"

"Or corn if you like."

"Throw in mashed potatoes and you've talked me into it."

"Done. We'll save the brownies for dessert."

"Can I give you a hand?"

"Thanks, but I've got a handle on it. Besides, I owe it to you for acting so ornery."

"You don't owe me anything." Joe's smile widened. "But, honestly, I can't tell you the last time I had meatloaf."

"I'd better get started." Christine was on her feet with her hand on the sliding glass door handle when she stopped. "Joe, I just remembered. I don't have any potatoes. I'll have to run to the grocery store to get some."

"No need for that. I've got some spuds lying around in the pantry."

He got to his feet and escorted her inside.

Christine waited to hug him until he'd laid four good-sized Idaho beauties on the counter.

"I'll call you when it's ready." She picked up the potatoes. "And don't forget the brownies."

"I'll leave the plastic wrap on them for now. But I may have to sample one or two to see if they pass the tasty test."

Joe lingered in the doorway, watching her until she disappeared into the elevator. Then he lingered a bit longer. After he'd set up the call block on her phone, he would write down all the numbers unfamiliar to her. The Robo calls were a nuisance, but the late-night calls had set him to wondering. Perhaps he was being too protective of his new friend. And perhaps there was something she wasn't telling him.

CHAPTER 11

Supper with Christine and lounging by the pool with her for the rest of the evening allowed Joe to shed his chronic loneliness. Their interaction was relaxed and friendly, something he hadn't enjoyed in months. Not being interrupted by unexpected visitors or phone calls was the highlight of their time together. He especially noticed a brightness in her demeanor. He told himself that when he was ready to drive down to Englewood to check out Flapjack's Bar, he would ask Christine to go with him. She would marvel at the sunsets from the porch of the Sandpiper Shore cottages. His exhilaration from the evening kept him awake until well after midnight.

He didn't care that he'd forgotten to prepare the coffeemaker when he walked into the kitchen the next morning, still full from the meal Christine had cooked him. Two pieces of wheat toast was all he desired to eat. He was full of adoration for her. Laughing as he raised his mug drink his coffee, he remembered a similar feeling after a promising date when he was a teenager. Too many years had drifted down the river since that night. But he was glad that the memory remained.

His reverie was interrupted by the unexpected knocking at his front door. Rising from the dining table, he felt every soft step of the carpet against his bare feet. A glance through the peephole elevated his delighted state. Wearing a smile, he opened the door.

"Dani! What a surprise."

"I hope I'm not disturbing you, Joe."

"Not at all. Come in. Would you like some coffee?"

"No, thanks."

The relationship between Joe and Detective Dani McMasters had been prickly at first. Dani had blamed Joe for David Sizemore's getting shot until David had straightened her out. Then, during an investigation, Dani was taken hostage by a psychopath and Joe had been the one to risk his life to save her.

"Let's sit at the dining table. I'd like to finish my coffee."

Dani didn't speak as she moved to the table and pulled out a chair.

Joe sat down and took a quick pull from his mug. "Now, what brings you to the home of an old man on this fine morning?"

"I've gathered some information that... Has Carly or David spoken with you about their interview with Robert Fitzgibbons?"

"I haven't heard from either of them."

"Fitzgibbons told them that his son, Carter, and Charles Robinson were partners in drug dealing. He said he only found out about their collaboration when they got caught. He also told them that Robinson received a lesser sentence for testifying against his son."

"What was Robinson's testimony against Carter?"

"He pointed the finger at Carter Fitzgibbons, saying Carter was the leader, and provided the names of others they'd dealt with. And he also claimed that Carter was responsible for the disappearance of Morgan Adcock, but that was never proven."

"Did he give a reason why Carter supposedly killed Morgan?"

"Robinson claimed that Carter and Morgan had a falling out, and she threatened to tell the police everything. But Robert never believed that his son killed her."

"Of course not."

"David is going back to the Okeechobee Correctional Institution today because—"

"Because Carter says he knows who killed Morgan Adcock. I know that. And he, most likely, is going to say that Charles

Robinson did it."

"I agree."

"He thinks it will get his sentence reduced. But that deal is off the table now, because Charles Robinson is dead."

"But suppose Robinson did kill Adcock. Then who killed him?"

Joe could tell by her expression that she had more to tell him. "Did you uncover something?"

"My friend in the coroner's office gave me a copy of the preliminary report on the bullet they found in Robinson's skull. It doesn't match the one found in the grave of Morgan Adcock."

"Did you or someone else think it might?"

"I'm eliminating all the possibilities, Joe. Like Carly instructed me to do when I came to Homicide. I ran some background checks. No one named Robinson or Fitzgibbons owns a registered firearm."

"Of course, you've no way of knowing whether they own an unregistered gun."

"Right." Dani paused, her blue eyes searching his. "David told me about Carly's aunt. And about her...reputation."

Joe nodded, suggesting she continue.

"Both of Carrie Anne's brothers believed that Boyd Robinson Jr. killed her, but no one was able to prove it because they never found her body."

"How does that relate to what we were discussing?"

"A Smith and Wesson model ten is registered to a Leonard Jernigan. He's Carly's uncle."

"She mentioned him to me. Why is the revolver so important?"

"It's a thirty-eight caliber. The same caliber bullet that killed Charles Robinson."

"But, Dani, a thirty-eight is a popular handgun, even today. And Carly told me that Leonard died three years ago."

"Randall Jernigan is still alive."

"So, what are you thinking?"

"I'm thinking that Carly's Uncle Randall killed Charles

Robinson to take revenge on Boyd Robinson Jr. for killing Carrie Anne. The Jernigan's had to know Robinson when they were kids if their sister went out with him."

Joe sat back and thought a moment, taking another pull of coffee. "That's going to be difficult to prove without the murder weapon."

"I know. Joe, I don't know what to do. I know I should tell Carly what I discovered. But if we don't find the murder weapon, would it make that big a difference if I didn't tell her?"

"You have to tell her."

"But what if I'm wrong? I don't want to hurt her or make her angry. David told me how she can't shake loose of needing to know what happened to her aunt."

"Dani, think of how she'll feel if you don't tell her and you're right about her Uncle Randall."

Silence hung heavy between them for several long minutes.

"You're right. I have to tell her." Dani got to her feet. "I need to get back to work. Thanks, Joe."

As he had done with Christine, Joe walked with her to the door and waited as she ambled down the hall to the elevator. When she'd gone, he closed the door and returned to the dining table. Focusing on the placemat, he picked up his mug and drank the remainder of his coffee. The coffee was cold, but he didn't care.

The disappearance of a teenager many years ago teamed with the discovery of an executed young woman was obscuring the investigation of a more recent murder. Indiscretions from the past upending the lives of his dearest friends. And worse, he was unable to help them. Sure, they came to him for advice. Advice was free. Getting to the source of the enigmas, and exposing the truth hidden behind the walls of silence shielding the guilty was entirely different. Those were the pieces of the puzzle that he was not allowed to explore.

Joe gazed at the last drops of coffee in the bottom of his mug. He needed to do something to help his friends.

CHAPTER 12

Joe steered his white Toyota from Gulf Boulevard into the entrance of Sand Key Park, easily navigating the familiar bend in the road. He wanted to take another look at Morgan Adcock's gravesite. Technically, it was still a crime scene, off limits to the public, but he needed to check out the expanded pit. Since recently acquiring new facts about the events surrounding the woman's death, he hoped to gain a better understanding of why this patch of sand had become her final resting place.

Nearing the first of three parking lots running parallel to the beach, he slowed for a beige van and a pale green SUV traveling well below the posted speed limit. Joe figured they must be tourists. People from another part of the country in awe of beach life and the endless blue water stretching to the horizon. He smiled. A similar wave of wonderment had engulfed him and Joyce when they'd first visited Clearwater Beach. Remaining a comfortable distance behind the vehicles, he felt no sense of urgency in getting to the parking lot.

Leaving the small motorcade after the anticipated veering to the left, he wheeled into the lot between the rows of cars and searched for a vacant space. Mid-morning was the usual time for a number of people to flock to the beach. Almost to the cordoned-off section at the end, he spied the folding plastic barricades, as well as a police SUV creating a roadblock. He wondered if he would be permitted entry as he pulled into an opening facing the road, turned off the motor, and got out of his car. He'd already prepared an excuse as to why he should be allowed on the grounds. Once the patrolman standing by the SUV noticed his approach, Joe realized that an excuse wouldn't be necessary. He recognized the dark-haired young man.

"Mr. Hampton. How are you today, sir?"

"Doing fine, Officer Warner. And you?"

"Just another day in sunny F-L-A."

They both smiled and shook hands.

"Out to enjoy a day at the beach, Mr. Hampton?"

"Not really. Do you think I could have a look at the crime scene?"

Warner's face contorted into a grimace. "I'm not supposed to let anyone pass beyond this point. Will Sergeant Truffant and Detective Sizemore be along soon?"

"They don't know I'm here."

The young man glanced toward the Gulf. "I don't like to disobey orders. But you are assisting them with this investigation."

"Yes, I am."

"And I could go with you."

"I might have some questions you could answer."

Warner motioned with his head, then he and Joe started across the parking lot.

The same sandy path Carly had chosen on his first trip led them to the tent and the excavation site. Warner turned around to keep an eye on the parking lot. Joe took calculated steps around the tent poles strung with barricade tape, focusing on the pit, but periodically looking in different directions.

The open area on the end of this stretch of beach still bothered him. A gunshot could easily have been heard across the channel in Clearwater Beach or down the shoreline at the nearest resort. Why take the risk? Morgan Adcock's body still had to be buried. Even if she'd been shot somewhere else, why bring her to the park? He gazed at the rows of parked cars in the lot. Why would someone tote her body all the way from there, dig a hole, drop her inside, and cover her up? The amount of time and effort necessary to accomplish such a task would be too risky. Why not dump her body in the channel and let the current carry her away?

An odd sensation gripped Joe. A cold tightening of his insides that came with awareness. Morgan Adcock hadn't been killed by one man. Charles Robinson and Carter Fitzgibbons had worked in tandem. One or both of them brought her to this spot, distracted her, then proceeded with the execution. Quick, efficient, and less time-consuming. But one question kept gnawing at him: Why take the time to bury her? A reason too strong to ignore must have been behind the decision. Like the reason for the disappearance of Carrie Anne Jernigan. And with the killing of Charles Robinson, the answer might never be known.

Joe's focus drifted to the wooded section across the road. He'd been told that in the past, most of Sand Key had been covered in tropical foliage. Sandy roads no wider than a car or truck had snaked through the growth. Had Carly's aunt become a resident among the root systems? Or was she resting in the concrete foundation of one of the many resorts and condominiums that lined the coast to Belleair Beach. Regardless, the disappearance of two women, many years apart, held secrets known only to their abductors.

"Okay, Officer Warner, I've seen enough."

Joe and the young patrolman started in the direction of the parking lot.

"Find anything of interest, Mr. Hampton?"

"Not really. I was hoping to get an idea as to why the woman was buried here."

"I can't make any sense of it. Me, I'd take a boat and dump her fifty miles out in the Gulf."

Warner had covered close to three yards before he become aware that Joe had stopped walking.

"You remember something, Mr. Hampton?"

"Officer, were you born in Florida?"

"Yes, sir. Punta Gorda."

"That's close to the Gulf, right?"

"Yes, sir."

"When you were a teenager, what did you want more than anything?"

Warner's smile was wide. "You mean other than getting laid?"

Joe grinned. "Other than that."

"A nice car."

"Anything else?"

"I like to fish. I always wanted a boat so I could go fishing out there." He motioned with his head toward the water.

"Do you own a boat?"

"No. My wife and I can barely afford our cars."

"I take it you're not from a wealthy family."

"Hardly."

"If you had been a teenager from a wealthy family growing up in Punta Gorda, you *would* have had a beautiful boat, right?"

"And a Corvette."

"Officer Warner, I can't thank you enough for your help. I've got to go."

"Really? You'll have to explain it to me one day."

Joe thanked him again once they reached the parking lot, and climbing into his car, followed the road back to the entrance. Slowing to a stop, he shifted his gaze to the two-story building on the other side of Gulf Boulevard.

Next to Clearwater Harbor, the Clearwater Community Sailing Center, a parking lot, and a storage area for sailboats occupied a small but ideal parcel of land. Whether the facility had existed at the time when young people congregated on the Gulf side to party was unknown to Joe. But the land had been there for sure. A perfect location to beach a boat. And how simple it would have been for some rich boy to persuade an inebriated party girl to go for a ride. Once they were miles from shore, anything could have happened—including the disposal of a body. Was this the long, sought-after answer to Carrie Anne's disappearance? The search for her body would have included trolling the coastal waters for miles. Since her body was never found, one conclusion might be that she was never in or on the water. Another might have her becoming the evening meal for a school of sharks.

Joe pulled out of the park and headed north to the foot of the bridge, picking up speed as he approached the incline. He felt certain that he'd figured out what really happened to Carly's aunt. Still, the possibility existed that she lay in a sandy or concrete grave, and the chances of finding her remains were next to none. Passing along the information to Carly would serve no purpose at the present time. She needed to focus on her current cases.

Once Joe had stepped inside the lobby of his condominium complex, he stopped by the door to the building manager's office and pulled his phone out of his pants pocket. After hearing the third ring, he pondered the message he would leave. Christine answered before he'd thought it out.

"Did I wake you?" he asked.

"No, I'd just stepped out of the tub when you called."

"Now there's a pleasant vision."

"Joseph Hampton! You should be ashamed of yourself!"

Her laughter was sincere and warm.

"Would you be interested in going out to supper? I know a quiet little bar we could go to afterward."

"That sounds lovely, but I have other plans."

"Oh?"

"I'm going to a dance at the Sanders Senior Center."

"Dancing?"

"Don't sound so surprised. I've been taking lessons there, and twice a month they have a dance."

"I see."

"I'd ask you to go, but I'm meeting someone. And, quite frankly, you don't strike me as someone who enjoys dancing."

Truth was, Joe didn't care for dancing. It was one of the few activities in which he and Joyce agreed not to participate.

"Well, have a good time."

"Do you like to dance, Joe?"

"Not really."

"I didn't think so."

"So, who's your dance partner?"

"His name is Bobby, and he's a wonderful dancer. He's also my dance instructor."

"Bobby? How old is this *Bobby*?"

Christine laughed again. "Our age. He's taught me a lot of new moves."

"How nice for you."

"And he's handsome."

"Sounds like you're in for quite an evening. I take it he's not married."

"He's a widower. You're not jealous, are you, Joe?"

"Why should I be jealous?"

Her laughter was louder and longer this time. "I'm sorry. I really shouldn't tease you."

"No, you shouldn't, but I do enjoy hearing you laugh. Well, I'd better let you go."

Joe went into the office and sat down at the desk. Calling Christine had reminded him that he needed to check on the numbers of the suspected nuisance callers he'd copied down from her phone. He didn't expect many positive results. The cyberspace pirates were clever when it came to covering their tracks.

CHAPTER 13

As expected, Joe found the majority of phone numbers to be untraceable. A couple had been pegged many times: an expired automobile warranty scam and a bogus call from the IRS threatening to take legal action. Predatory activities of those who chose to abuse today's technology by preying upon trusting and unsuspecting senior citizens. What the lowlifes behind the rest of the calls were up to was anyone's guess.

He then listened to complaints and pleas for help from three of the residents, and made certain the problems would be resolved the following day. When he'd finished with the necessary paperwork, he sat back in his chair and tried to relax.

A distraction had kept sneaking into his mind while he'd been working. He'd managed to get past it each time only to have it return again and again. Odd in that the persistent invader had nothing to do with police work. Christine was the source of the diversion. In the past when he'd found himself attracted to a woman, he'd been able to put aside his sentiments when necessary. Faltering discipline dogged him today.

Never had he been more thankful to hear his phone ring.

"Hi, Joe."

"Well, hello, Carly."

"Are you in the middle of something or entertaining?"

"You have my complete attention."

"I'd like to meet you for dinner."

"My goodness. This is so sudden."

His humor failed to reach her.

"Are you familiar with Roody's Restaurant on North Fort Harrison?"

"I can find it."

"Is six o'clock good for you?"

"Fine."

"We'll see you then."

"Carly, is this business or pleasure? I want to make sure that I'm properly dressed."

Again, he was unsuccessful in getting her to laugh.

"We need to go over a few things," she said. "And I..."

"If you need to discuss something now, I have time."

"I'd rather not. See you at Roody's."

Joe laid his phone on the desk and leaned back. Meeting with Carly to discuss various elements of a case or cases had never been an issue. This time she was the issue. She didn't sound right. He understood that wanting to solve the mystery of her aunt's disappearance was weighing on her. David's pointing out her uncharacteristic behavior had deepened his concern.

But her absence bothered him most. Her calling or dropping by was occurring less and less. Christine coming into his life could be the reason. Or possibly his brushes with death had been a warning for her to cut back on the amount of time they worked together. Sad, he felt, if that were true. Understandable, nonetheless. They'd grown close in a short amount of time. Neither wanted to lose the friendship of the other.

Slowly rising from the chair, Joe stretched then picked up his phone. He had plenty of time to get ready. Though he'd wanted to spend the evening with Christine, any time alone with Carly brightened his mood.

Roody's Restaurant presented the perfect venue for those preferring an unpretentious atmosphere with an uncomplicated menu and reasonable prices. Simple and straightforward.

Carly was seated in a red-padded booth along the wall near the back of the room. Two others were sitting across the table from her. Joe wasn't able to see their faces as he moved to the side of the group of tables assembled on the floor. Curiosity turned to delight when he reached the booth.

"Well, David and Dani. If I'd known you were going to be here, I would have worn a nicer shirt."

Their smiles were half-hearted at best. He was familiar with Carly's no-nonsense expression.

Their server, a pretty brunette with lively blue eyes, walked up as he sat down. "You folks ready to order?"

"I need to look at a menu," Joe said.

Carly slid hers over to him.

"What can I get you to drink?"

"Iced tea."

"I'll be right back."

"I thought it best that we meet here," Carly said. "I'll let you know why after we're through talking." She paused a number of seconds. "Joe, we think Robert Fitzgibbons killed Charles Robinson."

Joe glanced at Dani. "Because Robinson set up his son?"

"That's part of it. And before we go any further, Dani told me about her meeting with you. While I don't agree with her theory that my uncle is the killer, I'm good with it."

The server came back with Joe's tea.

"What can I get you folks?"

The group gave her their orders. Carly waited until the server was gone to continue.

"When David and I talked to Fitzgibbons, he confirmed that Charles Robinson had testified against his son. Robinson swore that Carter Fitzgibbons was the brains behind their drug trafficking operation. Of course, Carter told his father it wasn't true."

"To be expected," Joe said.

"Carter may not have been lying, though, since Charles Robinson came from money and had a college education. He probably had all the connections, as well. Carter was working class like his old man."

"And when you asked Carter's father who he thought killed Charles Robinson?"

"He said it could have been any number of people. According to him, the kid was disliked as much as his father."

"Robert Fitzgibbons said that about Boyd Robinson Jr.? And how would he know about Charles, anyway?"

"Maybe Carter told him that Charles was like his father."

"Carter also lied about his association with Charles. He claimed they weren't friends." Joe turned to David. "The second time you went to see Carter, who did he say killed Morgan Adcock?"

"Charles Robinson," David said. "And he recanted his original story about his relationship with Adcock being strictly sexual. He said he really loved her, but downplayed it because he knew that Charles was jealous."

"How did he react when you told him that Charles was dead?"

"He smiled."

Joe took the opportunity to tell them about his trip to Sand Key Park, and his multiple-killers theory regarding the disposal of Morgan Adcock's body. He kept his belief of how Carrie Anne had vanished to himself.

"That's interesting, Joe," Carly said, "but it further complicates the matter. We won't ever know Charles Robinson's side of the story, and we can't rely on Carter Fitzgibbons. He's been lying to us from the start."

"True...about the Adcock murder anyway. And since Robert Fitzgibbons doesn't legally own a gun, nailing him for Charles Robinson's murder will be just as difficult to prove."

Silence hung over them until their server brought their meals. She carefully set down each plate, then paused to observe the group.

"I sure hope y'all don't look this sad after you've eaten," she said.

Her words failed to lighten their disposition. She shrugged, turned around, and walked away.

Joe was removing the silverware from inside the napkin when he sensed the others staring at him.

"Is there something else I should know?"

"I got a call from Boyd Robinson Jr. this morning," Carly said. "He questioned me as to why we hadn't arrested Robert Fitzgibbons for murdering his son."

Joe set down his silverware. "But he told us that he believed robbery to be the motive."

"I asked him why he thought Fitzgibbons had done it. In his usual snobbish manner, he suggested the motive was obvious, and if I was incapable of proving it then I should turn in my badge."

David looked over his shoulder as the couple seated in the booth behind them got up to leave.

"Was he talking about revenge for his son being a rat?" Joe said.

"I'm guessing that's what he meant. He then said that he might hire a private investigator to do my job for me."

"Typical behavior from someone so high and mighty."

"He added that he'd been in touch with the chief."

"It figures. And now you're concerned that you might get yanked off the case if you don't make an arrest soon."

"The chief hasn't called me into his office yet, which is a good sign, but..."

"But what?"

"I don't want to believe it, Joe, but someone in the department might be reporting back to him."

"Has something happened to make you suspect that?"

David leaned forward. "When I came into the office this morning, I noticed some things about my desk were different."

"What things?" Joe asked.

"My chair was pushed in. I never push my chair in."

"I'll vouch for that," Dani said and nestled against him.

"And my computer keyboard was up against the monitor stand. I've never put it that close."

"You don't think the janitor might have moved them after you went home?"

"The cleaning crew understands that they are never to move or rearrange anything," Carly said. "I don't feel like I can trust anyone but David and Dani. And you. That's why I suggested we meet here."

Joe looked down at his plate of food. A spy within their tight circle made for a guarded atmosphere. Trusting your fellow detectives was important. Without trust, the stress and tension associated with everyday life on the job only worsened. And if his friends didn't have enough to worry about, now some pompous pinhead was issuing threats. The pointed accusation leveled at Robert Fitzgibbons by Boyd Robinson Jr. indicated an immense dislike of one man toward the other—or worse. A question of whether Carrie Anne Jernigan had been the initial cause of that loathing loomed over him.

CHAPTER 14

Meeting Carly for supper hadn't gone as well as Joe had wanted. The possibility of an informer hidden within the Homicide department had had a noticeable effect on David and Dani. They kept glancing at each other and hardly touched their food. Carly's hardened expression remained intact, though she was able to finish her meal. They left Roody's Restaurant with the understanding that all future findings in regard to both cases would be kept among them unless requested from higher up. Carly made it a point to impress upon her colleagues that under no circumstances were they to jeopardize their careers in an effort to protect her.

Once he'd gotten home, Joe went to the kitchen and filled a glass with ice and poured himself a healthy amount of Evan Williams. He hadn't tasted a drop of whiskey since he'd returned from Englewood. Tonight, he felt as though he needed it.

Settled into his comfortable perch on the balcony, he stared at the slate-gray clouds hovering over the Gulf, broken in places to allow a select number of stars to shine through. After taking a sip of the whiskey, he set his glass on the folding table beside him.

More and more he was beginning to believe that a feud existed between Boyd Robinson Jr. and Robert Fitzgibbons. Perhaps it wasn't a feud as much as an immense dislike for each other. Social standing aside, buying one's son out of a felony conviction, or at least getting the sentence reduced, was enough to destroy a relationship. Particularly when the other son had had to bear the brunt of the punishment. Mulling over this paradox on his ride home had opened the door to an additional possibility. Bad blood between them may have begun much earlier in their lives. A disagreement over a girl they both wanted.

Joe stuck by his newly adopted belief that Carrie Anne Jernigan had agreed to a boat ride, but not with Robert Fitzgibbons. The offer had come from Boyd Robinson Jr. It made more sense that he would own a boat. And he'd admitted taking her to the party. What hadn't been confirmed in the police report was how they had traveled to Sand Key. Carrie Anne's alleged promiscuity opened an easy avenue for him to coerce her into taking a ride after they'd had a few beers. And his friend Robert? He'd been invited along so they both could take advantage of her.

Picking up his glass, Joe took a longer drink.

The only people who knew what happened to her the night she disappeared were Carrie Anne and the person who'd killed her. And those who'd covered for Robinson Jr. by saying that he'd passed out before Carrie Anne went missing were either lying or had been bribed. That had to be the truth behind the story.

"And I could be full of shit," Joe whispered.

The party girl could have easily hopped into a car with someone unknown to the rest of the teenage revelers and whisked off to some nearby community where she was killed. Or even taken to some other part of the county, away from the coast.

Joe felt his eyelids getting heavy, and he lost the will to resist. Opening them a short time later, he saw the lights in the distance and needed a minute to get his bearings. He finished his drink and got up from the chaise lounge. Closing the sliding glass door behind him, he walked into the kitchen and set his glass in the sink. As he walked past the dining table, he picked up his phone and checked the time. 10:15 p.m. He stepped out the front door after making certain he had his keys.

He'd learned to tolerate the annoyance he'd once felt at seeing the maroon carpet and pink walls that stretched the length of the hallway. Tonight, the sight of the bilious combination created a repulsive feeling deep inside that quickened his pace to the elevator.

Not a single resident roamed about downstairs this time of night. Silence filled the lobby due to the Rec room not being use.

Joe went straight from the elevator to the back door and strode across the grass to the dock. Standing by the seawall, he stared at the shimmering lights reflected in the dark water from a condominium on the opposite side of the channel. Laughter from those languishing on a balcony high above filled his ears. He suddenly felt tired. Not from exhaustion. From the drain that came from living. The longing to get away from this place was tugging at him again. The same kind of restlessness that had him running off to Englewood. He'd promised Carly that he would stay in Clearwater Beach. And promised Joyce, too. At this particular moment he wondered how he would feel if he broke those promises.

The face of Christine became a vibrant picture in his mind. He knew she wanted a relationship. She'd made that clear. In the way her eyes brightened when they talked, along with little clues, like the brownies and other tidbits she'd given him. His own stubbornness had held him back. And fear she might turn out to be a closet predator like Shirley Lyon and Victoria Combes. But the need for companionship was aching to free him from inside the walls of denial he'd erected around himself. He wanted to love and be loved again. Releasing a long, slow sigh, he took one last look at the dark channel then turned and headed back in the direction of the building.

He was nearing the elevator when he heard the automatic doors to the main entrance open. Laughter preceded their closing. A man and a woman engaged in conversation. He recognized the woman's voice. A pressing need to head back outside came over him. He started to leave but didn't.

"Joe, what are you doing here at this hour?" Christine said.

"I was in the office finishing up some paperwork."

The man standing beside her was tall with graying brown hair, a bit overweight, and not especially good looking. His deep acorn tan was indicative of someone who'd spent most of his life in the Florida sunshine.

"Joe, I'd like you to meet Bobby," she said.

"Nice to meet you, Joe."

"You, too, Bobby."

They shook hands.

Bobby's palm was soft, but his grip was strong.

"Bobby and I are going to a nightclub on the beach," Christine said. "We stopped off on the way so I could change into something more comfortable."

Joe looked over her floral-print midi dress and evergreen jacket. "You look very nice."

"Prettiest girl at the dance," Bobby said.

Christine gave him an easy shove. "Oh, Bobby."

"Chrissie speaks highly of you, Joe. She told me you work for the police department."

"I work *with* the police department. More of a consultant than anything else."

"Sounds fascinating. I understand you're working a case at Sand Key Park."

"I guess it's all over the news by now."

"Yeah, they found a skeleton or something like that. Do you know if it's a man or a woman?"

"Bobby, I'm not permitted to discuss the details of a case that's currently being investigated."

"Oh! Right. Pardon me for being so nosy. I enjoy watching police shows on T-V and sometimes I get...well, you understand, I'm sure."

Joe smiled and nodded.

"We'd better get moving. Bobby," Christine said. "We have more dancing to do."

"Enjoy yourselves." Joe did his best to hold his smile.

"Were you going up/"

"I was, but now I think I'll sit by the pool for a while. It's a beautiful night."

Joe watched them enter the elevator then headed back to the door. Once he'd reached the aluminum fence surrounding the pool deck, he stopped and leaned against it.

"Bobby," he said and snorted. "Bet he was a jock in high school. Had to be someone special. A face like that wouldn't charm the girls. And he calls her *Chrissie*."

He set his gaze on the far side of the darkened pool deck. A timer had shut off the lights at ten o'clock. He felt as though he'd been shut off from Christine. A sense of responsibility had pulled him away from her. Reluctance had played a part as well. Time for a decision, he decided.

One that he must stick with. The difficult choice of whether to devote himself to her or spend the rest of his life alone. Too much emotional back and forth was wearing him out. But when it came to matters of the heart, choices were always difficult. He allowed himself a final look at the darkened channel beyond the pool and turned to go inside.

CHAPTER 15

Up early the next morning, Joe showered and shaved before his first cup of coffee. A decision had been made the very moment he opened his eyes. Breakfast at Maggie Mae's Sunrise Café had charmed and delighted Christine when he had taken her there before. Today he would suggest they go there again so he could tell her what she longed to hear. His desire to be with her more often, to get to know her better, to put an end to the loneliness they both had endured. No doubts about his decision puzzled or exasperated him today. He felt good, in fact.

The coffee tasted better than usual as he set his mug on the dining table, laughing at the excitement that filled him. The antic-ipation calling her, hoping that she would accept his invitation, barely corralling his eagerness to pour his heart out. One step at a time would be the way to approach her, so as not to come off as a blathering idiot. He'd fallen into that trap with Joyce. To his relief, she'd thought his bumbling and fumbling cute. Young people in love acted silly anyway. He and Christine weren't young anymore, but he did experience a resurgence of vitality when around her. Feelings more in line with those of a twenty-year-old. The brightening of her deep brown eyes had betrayed the secrets of her thoughts, as well.

Joe picked up his phone to check the time. Eight-thirty was too early to call after her night of dancing with Bobby. He shook his head. *Bobby.* Talk about someone trying to hold on to the past. Thinking himself a stud in his youth, he was still playing the part for all it was worth.

And by the way Christine had been acting around him, she had fallen for his charade.

"I'd better call her," he said, scrolling the contacts list until he located her number. "It'll take her an hour to get ready."

His elation began to fade when he heard the third ring, thinking she'd turned off her phone. He sighed as he waited for the recording. "Good morning, Christine, it's Joe. I'd like to take you to breakfast. I have something I want to tell you."

He picked up his coffee mug after he'd ended the call and rose from the chair. The balcony was inviting him outside to enjoy the onset of morning. A trace of disappointment poured into him as he closed the sliding glass door. Assuming a relaxed position on his chaise lounge, he set his mug on the folding table. Noticing banks of slate-gray clouds building in the west, he hoped that Christine would get back to him soon. The chance of rain reaching the coast before they arrived at the café further dampened his spirits. An alternative plan might be necessary. Not as appealing, but necessary. He'd do a search for another eatery after he'd heard from her.

The morning became noon, then mid-afternoon, and he still hadn't heard from her. Mounting protests in his stomach finally forced him from the balcony.

A turkey sandwich seemed in order. He removed the fixings from the refrigerator once he'd folded two paper towels and placed two thick slices of wheat bread on them. Lathering the bread with mayonnaise, he covered one slice with a piece of Swiss cheese between two portions of turkey. Rolling separate slices of turkey and cheese into a cylinder, he dipped them into the mayonnaise and shoved the appetizer into his mouth. Six whole baby Gherkins came next, followed by more turkey and cheese and the remaining slice of bread. Savoring the huge bite of his masterpiece, he thought about making another sandwich. His phone decided a second bite was enough for the time being.

"Joe, are you busy?"

"I'm enjoying a gourmet gobbler sandwich. What can I do for you, Carly?"

"This morning Dani and her partner arrested a guy for attempted armed robbery. No one was hurt, but the guy said he wanted to make a deal. We went ahead and booked him and held him until he had a chance to meet with his lawyer."

Joe took another bite of his sandwich, licking a dollop of mayonnaise off the end of his finger.

"Through his lawyer, the guy said he was an acquaintance of Charles Robinson and sold him an automatic five years ago."

"Like the one used on Morgan Adcock? Sounds like a load of crapola to me. How does he intend to prove it?"

"He says he knows where Robinson keeps it hidden in his house."

"Now I know he's full of it. Robinson wouldn't be dumb enough to hang onto it after committing murder."

"That's what I told Dani, but we're working on getting a search warrant anyway."

"Good luck, but it's going to be difficult matching the bullet to the gun after all this time."

"Yeah, I know. Do you want to come with us when we go through Robinson's house?"

"I would, but I have other plans today."

"I'll let you know what we find. Tell Christine I said hello."

Joe grinned. "I will."

He laid down his sandwich on the paper towels and went to the refrigerator for a bottle of water, cracking the cap open and taking a long drink.

Sometimes a detective can catch a break during an investigation. Joe considered the odds of the gun being the same weapon used to kill Morgan Adcock. He came to the conclusion that he was unable to count that high. And what if it was the same gun? The robber could have sold it to Charles Robinson after the murder since they were alleged to be acquaintances. Once again, too many possibilities clouded the picture of what had actually happened. And the biggest detriment to discovering the truth? The robber could be lying like Carter Fitzgibbons. Charles Robinson was dead, leaving no one to offer a rebuttal.

Joe finished his sandwich, passed on making another, and left the building to go for a walk. He would ask Christine out to supper instead.

A stroll down Island Way was something he'd never considered. He began to notice things he'd taken for granted. The road was divided, and the medians were covered with grass and palm trees.

A bright yellow sun with its fiery tendrils was painted on the front wall of the condominium complex next door. The landscaping of other buildings held a similar theme: lush green grass, palm trees, and podocarp hedges. Carports and tennis courts set back off the road popped up here and there, but the scenery remained consistent. A surprising number of people his age were out walking, acknowledging him with friendly greetings as they passed by. Guessing that Christine would enjoy accompanying him, Joe decided he should get out more often. Thinking of her got him to wondering why she hadn't called him back. Was she ignoring him out of spite? Or was she so enamored with Bobby that Joe was no longer the object of her affection. He continued his walk and berated himself for being so cautious.

The final stretch of Island Way was thick with fine, well-tended homes. A surprising sight after viewing so many condominiums. He navigated the loop at the end of the road and headed back.

Joe took a time-out for a breather as he stepped into the lobby of the Crimson Conch. His walk had lasted longer than expected, the sky now glowing late afternoon. He debated whether to call Christine again or forget the whole matter, not wanting to come off like a love-starved moron. He could ask her out the next time he saw her.

Deciding to rest a bit more before heading upstairs, he went into the manager's office and sat down at the desk. In the time it took for him to close his eyes, he heard a familiar sound. He smiled when he saw Christine's name across the face of his phone.

"Well, I was wondering when you were going to call," he said.

"Were you, now?"

Joe didn't recognize the male voice. "Who is this?"

"Shut up and listen closely. You have until midnight to do what I tell you or you'll never see Chrissie again."

"Bobby? Is this you? What are you talking about?"

"I want you to kill Boyd Robinson Jr."

"Are you crazy? How do you know Boyd Robinson Jr.?"

"If you don't kill him by midnight, she dies."

"I can't do that! Where's Christine?"

"Suit yourself."

"Why do you want me to kill him? What have you done with Christine?"

Silence filled his ear.

"Hello? Hello?"

Stunned, Joe dropped his phone on the desk. He had a little more than six hours to save Christine—if she wasn't dead already. How did Bobby know Boyd Robinson Jr.? Why did he want him dead? And where was Christine?

Joe's mind raced to make the connection between the men. What could possibly tie a smooth-talking dance instructor to a snobbish land developer? The hand of stupidity slapped him hard with the answer.

"Oh, my god! Bobby is Robert Fitzgibbons!"

Whether Fitzgibbons had killed Charles Robinson no longer mattered. Joe had to figure out a way to save Christine. He had no weapon and finding a gun shop wasn't an option. The law required a waiting period with every purchase. Finagling a revolver from a pawn shop was a longshot anyway. Joe shook his head. What was he thinking? He picked up his phone and called Carly.

"Hey, Joe, what's on your mind?"

"What are you doing right now?"

"I'm heading home. The judge is taking his time in getting us the warrant, so we're hoping for tomorrow."

"I need your help. If I don't kill Boyd Robinson Jr. by midnight tonight, Christine is going to die." Joe gave her a brief account of everything that had happened the previous night, leading up to the call from Robert Fitzgibbons. "I don't know where he's holding her, Carly."

"We need to work out a plan and fast. I'll call David and Dani. They can help us."

"We'll have to be careful. I'm pretty sure he's going to be watching me."

"I'll get back to you as soon as I've spoken to them."

"I won't let her die, Carly."

"I know, Joe. I know."

CHAPTER 16

To Joe, agony was knowing something terrible is about to happen and being helpless to stop it. Standing by Joyce during her final hours had been a torment Joe never wanted to experience again. And yet, here he was being subjected to another dire situation with no foreseeable remedy at hand.

Agreeing to wait for Carly's call had been done without thinking. Even if Robert Fitzgibbons was watching him, he had to know that Joe would contact the police. He hadn't insisted on keeping them out of it. Joe wanted to be part of the team that was piecing together the plan to save Christine. Being excluded from the decision-making group made the fleeting moments unbearable.

Joe still had his hand wrapped around his phone an hour later. Battling the mounting urge to call Carly, he'd held off for a long as he could. He would allow her five more minutes. Thinking of nothing or no one but Christine, he jumped when it rang.

"Okay, Joe, this is the best idea we could come up with," Carly said.

"I'm listening."

"You're going to shoot Boyd Robinson Jr."

"Carly, if that's supposed to be a joke, I'm not laughing."

"I'm not joking. Dani is on her way to your place. She's going to leave a brown paper bag at your door. Inside the bag is a revolver filled with blanks. She'll knock twice to signal you."

"What if Fitzgibbons is watching the parking lot? He'll recognize the car she's driving, even if it's unmarked."

"She's using her own car. Fitzgibbons has never met her. She'll look like she's dropping off food to someone. Give her a few minutes to get back to the stairwell before you pick up the bag."

"Why doesn't she use the elevator? It'll be quicker."

"She's going to get off two floors below yours. I'm not taking any chances with this guy. He's got your phone number, so he knows where you live."

"Okay, what do you want me to do next?"

"Drive to Robinson's house. He's agreed to work with us. When he answers the door, stick the gun in his face. Go inside, fire a couple of rounds, then get out of there as fast as you can. I doubt if any of the neighbors will hear the shots, so make your escape look obvious."

"Why don't you tip off his neighbor, Fudgie Fairbanks? He can call Belleair P-D and say he heard gunfire."

"We've already contacted them. They're working with us and will be stationed close by. Joe, David ran a search on Robert Fitzgibbons and found out that he co-owns a house on Belleview Island. We're sending a team to check it out."

"Where is Belleview Island?"

"Near the Belleair Country Club. He may be holding Christine in the house."

"Should I wait for your call, so I'll know when to leave?"

"Wait thirty minutes after Dani drops off the package. If he's watching, it may look suspicious if you leave right away. I'll let you know the minute I hear something."

"Then I guess all I can do is wait for Dani."

He ended the call feeling that Carly didn't sound very optimistic about the plan. The reason had already crossed his mind. In hostage situations similar to this one, the demanding of results by the abductors before the release of a hostage didn't always ensure a favorable ending. Christine may already be dead. With all that had transpired to this point, what would Fitzgibbons have to lose except his freedom or his life? In his mind, the price of an assassination may not be that high.

Among other questions nagging at Joe was why did Robert Fitzgibbons want Boyd Robinson Jr. killed? The fact that Charles Robinson was the cause of Carter Fitzgibbons's imprisonment was a given. But there had to be an underlying motive. One that might go back to when the two men were teenagers. And that motive might bear the name of Carrie Anne Jernigan.

Joe snapped his head around when he heard a soft knocking. He glanced at his phone.

The next thirty minutes would be the longest and most excruciating of his life.

Throwing on a coat over his dark blue T-shirt, Joe dropped the snub-nosed revolver into his pocket. Considering the quickest way to Belleair was foremost on his mind. Watching for a familiar face while in route ran a close second.

Uninterrupted on his elevator ride to the first floor, Joe was nearing the front entrance when a man's voice called out.

"Excuse me. Aren't you the building manager?"

Joe spun around.

A squatty bald-headed man approached him, wearing a yellow short-sleeve shirt covered in palm trees, baggy green cargo shorts, and sandals covering his yellow socks. The uniform of a recent Florida transplant.

"Yes, I am," Joe said.

"I'm having a problem with the curtain covering the balcony door. It gets hung up sometimes. My wife and I moved in here a month ago and—"

"Excuse me, sir, but I'm running late for an appointment. Could this wait until tomorrow?"

The man narrowed his bushy gray-black eyebrows.

"Okay, come with me," Joe said. "I'll see to it when I get back."

He led the man into the office and noted the necessary information while enduring the resident's incessant babbling.

When they finally parted company, Joe hurried through the parking lot and climbed into his car. Checking the clock after firing up the engine, he realized that he'd lost twenty minutes. Slamming his Toyota into reverse, he squealed tires out of his parking space and sped out of the lot. He'd decided to travel South on Fort Harrison and look for the turnoff to Belleair. Fewer traffic lights on Gulf Boulevard would be less frustrating, but the closest exit would put him below the community. He never liked having to backtrack.

Luck was with him as the number of red lights was minimal. He recognized Belleview Boulevard and turned right until he came to Indian Rocks Road. Making a left turn, he ran alongside the grounds of the Belleair Country Club and turned right onto Ponce de Leon Boulevard. From there he weaved through various neighborhoods until slowing to a halt in front of the Robinson home.

Taking a deep breath, he paused a moment to prepare himself. The sound of his phone didn't help matters.

"Joe, where are you?" Carly asked.

"In front of Robinson's house."

"The house on Belleview Island was empty. There was a cabin cruiser docked out back, but no luck."

"Then I guess all that's left for me to do is shoot Boyd Robinson Jr."

Although his assassination of the former land development CEO would only be a ruse, Joe couldn't help but feel that in no way was it going to help Christine. Not after what Carly told him. Another thorn had been digging into his side during the trip. How would Robert Fitzgibbons know if he'd actually killed Robinson Jr.? He'd never told Joe where to confront the man. Or if he would be watching. A cold notion began to strangle him. Fitzgibbons had to be inside the house with Christine. It was the only explanation as to why Robinson Jr. had agreed to go along with the plan. Joe punched redial to call Carly back. His heart began to pound when he heard her voicemail message.

"Carly, I think Fitzgibbons is already in the house! Get Belleair P-D over here fast! I'm going in!"

He threw open the door and rolled out of the seat. Hustling up the walkway that split the enormous front lawn offered scant seconds to concoct a new plan. If he was confronted by Fitzgibbons, he would attempt to bluff him with the revolver, hoping for a standoff, until help arrived. Steps from the front door, he eased the revolver from inside his coat pocket. As he stood on the porch, he glanced in both directions, noticing something he'd overlooked during the first visit. Security cameras were mounted on either end. He stared at the one to his right and held the gun so it was easily seen. The more witnesses, the better his chances of help arriving sooner. Returning his gaze to the polished oak doors, he pounded long and hard. One door opened immediately, and an apathetic Boyd Robinson Jr. appeared. His eyes grew wide at the sight of the revolver pointed at his face.

"Is Fitzgibbons inside?" Joe whispered.

"Not while there is breath left in me. And would you kindly lower your weapon."

"Back up slowly."

Robinson Jr. did as he was ordered. Joe closed the door behind him.

"Where is your wife?" Joe asked.

"Away visiting relatives. She is still quite grief-stricken. Otherwise, I would not have agreed to this cockamamie scheme."

"Why didn't you go with her?"

"I had to see to the funeral arrangements for Charles. Would you please lower your weapon?"

Joe obliged. "Let's go to the rear of the house."

"And the reasoning behind your decision?"

"If I was actually going to shoot you I would do it in the most discreet location. Anyone looking through the front windows wouldn't see your body lying there."

"Very logical, I must say. Did you derive this idea on your drive over?"

"No, I watch a lot of movies."

As they moved together down the hall, the contemptuous expression on Robinson Jr.'s face made it clear that Joe's sarcastic remark was not appreciated.

"How come Fitzgibbons wants you dead? Other than Charles ratting out his son, I mean."

"Charles did not *rat out* Carter, as you put it. He simply told the truth. He was naïve enough to trust that excuse for a human being."

"How long had they known each other?"

"Since childhood. They never associated though. Why they became close in later years I'll never understand."

They reached the end of the hall and stood in front of the dining table.

"I guess the trouble between them started with Morgan Adcock," Joe said.

"Charles had nothing to do with that trollop."

"But it was my understanding that—"

"I don't wish to discuss it further. Now instruct me as to how I should proceed."

Joe looked to his right. "What's in there?"

"It is our study."

"That'll work."

He and Robinson Jr. walked into the den. When they reached the middle of the room, Joe turned and faced him.

"Where shall I stand, Mr. Hampton?"

"Right where you are."

Joe raised the revolver above his head and popped off two rounds.

"Jesus Christ that was loud!" Robinson yelled and slapped his hands over his ears.

Lowering his arm, Joe remained calm and studied the man.

"Are you okay? Other than losing your pretentiousness?"

Robinson removed his hands and glowered at him.

"I'd love to stay and chat a while longer, but I have to make my getaway."

"Don't feel you must linger further on my account. And lock the door on your way out."

Joe turned to leave and instinctively raised the revolver.

The man had an automatic trained on Joe and Robinson Jr. "No one is going anywhere," he said.

Robinson Jr.'s mouth dropped open. "Robert!"

Fitzgibbons wore an uncaring smirk. "Drop the gun, Joe. Chrissie's life depends on it."

CHAPTER 17

In all his years of police work, and in all those since, Joe couldn't recall ever being in this kind of situation. Regardless, one thing was certain. He wasn't about to give up the revolver.

"What about *your* life?" Joe said. "I can end you before you have time to think."

"You don't know where I've got her hidden. Kill me, and I guarantee she'll die before you find her."

"How did you get inside?" Robinson Jr. asked.

Fitzgibbons let go throaty laughter. "You left the front door unlocked. You've been forgetful your whole life."

"So you say, but I know one experience I'll never forget."

"Shut up, Boyd!"

Fitzgibbons tensed and aimed the automatic at him.

Joe kept his weapon leveled, his finger slipping down to the trigger. "Why risk losing everything by killing this man?"

"My life ended when my wife died. I lost everything when this snooty scum and his punk son sent Carter to prison."

"And you killed Charles!" Robinson Jr. yelled.

"Why did you kill him?" Joe asked. "Because Charles killed Morgan Adcock?"

"Carter loved Morgan. Then Boyd's useless boy killed her because she wanted nothing to do with him!"

"Liar!" Robinson Jr. screamed.

"And now I'm going to kill him!"

Just then, someone began pounding on the front door.

"Belleair Police! Open up!" a man shouted.

None of the three men moved. More pounding followed.

"Open up!"

"Drop the gun, Robert," Joe said. "He's not worth it."

"They take what they want!" Fitzgibbons yelled.

"Drop the gun, Robert."

"They take what they want! They always have!"

His gun hand started to tremble. His murderous expression softened, his arm slowly wavering before dropping to his side.

"They take what they want. No one else matters."

He lowered his head and flipped the automatic onto the carpet. Joe kept the revolver pointed at him.

Robinson Jr. lurched forward before Joe could move, scooped up the gun, and got off three rounds.

Hit in the chest, Fitzgibbons staggered backward and crumpled in the doorway.

"No!" Joe yelled, then cracked Robinson Jr. in the back of the head with his revolver.

A loud crashing and splintering of wood caused Joe to step away from the men and raise his hands high over his head. Seconds later, a member of the Clearwater Police SWAT team leapt over Fitzgibbons with his Colt M4 carbine aimed at him.

"Don't shoot!" Joe hollered.

"Drop it!" the SWAT team member shouted.

Four more of the SWAT team poured into the room.

Joe let the revolver fall from his hand.

Carly hurried in next, followed by David and Dani.

"Hold on, fellas!" Carly ordered. "He's one of us."

Everyone in the room relaxed, including Joe. Two of the team separated to allow Carly to pass by them. She glanced at Fitzgibbons and Robinson Jr. before facing Joe. "Are you all right?"

"Yeah."

"What happened?"

"I'd convinced Fitzgibbons into giving up, and he tossed his gun on the floor. Robinson Jr. grabbed it and shot Fitzgibbons before I could stop him." Joe stared down at Fitzgibbons. "Then I knocked the rich bastard out."

"Where's Christine?"

"I don't know."

"Detective Sizemore, cuff Robinson and get him the hell out of here." Carly then faced the SWAT team. "Do a thorough search of the house."

The team dispersed.

Carly took Joe by the arm and led him outside. They stopped a short distance from the front porch. Joe nodded to each member of the SWAT team as they left the house. Carly was facing the street as the last team member stopped and said something to her.

"No luck, Joe. We'll check Fitzgibbons' house. If she's not there... We'll do the best we can."

"That son of a bitch," he said.

"Yeah, kidnapping her was a real shitty thing to do."

"I don't mean Fitzgibbons. I'm talking about Robinson Jr. Fitzgibbons had lost his nerve. He wasn't going to shoot either of us. Then that jackass shot him before I could find out where Christine was being held."

Silence enveloped them. Carly broke it first. "Looks like the vultures are gathering in the street."

Joe turned and looked in the direction she was staring. A small crowd was gathered, whispering, and gawking at them. He turned back to her as a peculiar thought settled in his head. "I wonder why Fudgie isn't out here."

"Who?"

"The neighbor, Fudgie Fairbanks. The one who answered the door the first time we came here."

David and Dani emerged from the house clutching the arms of Boyd Robinson Jr. His face was drawn up in pain.

"Dani, take him in and charge him with murder," Carly said.

Robinson's face lost its color as horror set in. "You can't be serious."

"Watch me."

"I'll have your badge!"

Dani grabbed hold of his arm and snatched him away.

"David, where does Fudgie Fairbanks live?" Carly asked.

"Over there."

David nodded toward a house sitting in the distance to the east.

"Let's go."

Cutting across yards of green St. Augustine grass, Carly lifted her automatic out of her holster.

David mirrored his partner. "You think Fairbanks is a part of this?"

"I don't know. There might be someone else, though."

Only one mahogany door graced the front of the Fairbanks's house. Joe waited several yards to the right of it while Carly and David positioned themselves on either side. Carly nodded to David before reaching out and knocking on the door.

No one answered.

She knocked a second time.

Still no answer.

She gave the doorknob a twist. The door opened. Nodding to David again, she shoved it open wider and they scrambled inside.

Joe waited as long as his nerves would allow then hustled to the doorway, pausing to make certain it was safe to enter. Carly and David were nowhere to be seen.

A maroon velvet sofa with matching chairs were teamed with a black oak coffee table, etched in an old Victorian style. Tiffany floor lamps sat on either side of a bookcase loaded with leather-bound volumes against a far wall.

Cautious footsteps guided him toward a room on his left.

Moving to enter the room, he was surprised when David appeared in the hall.

"She's in here, Joe."

Joe followed the stoic detective halfway down the hall to a bedroom.

Christine was sitting on the edge of a king-size bed, crying, her legs still bound with a rope. Carly was untying the handkerchief used to gag her mouth. Joe sat down beside her, and when she was free of the gag, she threw her arms around him.

"Oh, Joe, it was horrible. Just horrible."

"It's over now. You're safe."

After she'd unbound the rope from Christine's legs, Carly got to her feet.

Joe looked up at her. "Fudgie and his wife?"

Carly glanced at Christine before she answered, then looked back at him and shook her head.

Christine released him and eased away with tears rolling down her face. "He shot them. I heard him do it." She broke down and hugged him again.

"There's an ambulance team outside, Joe," Carly said. "Why don't you have them take a look at her."

Joe helped Christine up off the bed and held her close as they walked out of the bedroom.

CHAPTER 18

A Sun Tracker 22DLX cleared the mouth of Clearwater Harbor, heading for the open waters of the Gulf. Six passengers and the captain of the pontoon boat looked into a sun burning low in the western sky.

Joe sat on a padded seat on the starboard stern with his arm around Christine. He gave her arm a squeeze. She smiled at him and placed her hand on his knee. In the three weeks since being held hostage, she had overcome her fears and driven off her nightmares. A strong woman to be admired. He was proud of her.

David and Dani sat opposite them, and like them, were still finding their way through the beginning of a relationship. So much to learn about each other. And themselves.

Joe smiled at the young couple. Memories of his first and only love filled his heart, not with sadness, but with contentment. Joyce would be happy that he'd found Christine.

The two passengers seated in the front of the pontoon boat wore somber faces.

Carly and her uncle, Randall Jernigan, would soon bring an end to the suffering endured by their family for years over the loss of a loved one.

"Christine, I need to speak with David," Joe said.

"Okay, but not too long. Otherwise I'll get jealous."

"I'll ask Dani to keep you company. You two have something

298

in common."

"Really? What is it?"

Joe grinned. "Ask her."

He got up slowly and stepped across the deck on unsteady feet as the boat plowed through the shimmering water.

"Dani, I'd like to speak with David. Do you mind?"

"Maybe you should ask him if he minds."

David nudged her with his elbow. "Ha. Ha."

"Sure, Joe." Dani leaned over and kissed David on the cheek.

"Christine has something she wants to ask you," Joe said.

"Oh?"

Joe settled in beside David after she'd left. "It was nice of you to get your buddy to do this."

"Carly's a good woman and an even better friend. Helping her and her family was the least I could do."

"I haven't spoken with either of you since you arrested Boyd Robinson Jr. What came of it?"

"Oh, he was most cooperative once his hotshot lawyer convinced him that he was facing a murder charge. He wasn't going to buy his way out of this one."

"What did he have to say?"

"He admitted that he'd known his son killed Morgan Adcock, yet he helped him shift the blame to Carter Fitzgibbons."

"Why?"

"He said Carter led Charles to believe that she would hop in the sack with anyone. When she refused Charles, he killed her. Then he ran crying to Daddy."

"Did he say how they disposed of her body?"

"Charles called two guys that were part of his drug trafficking operation with Carter. Real bottom feeders. They dug the hole on the beach and helped Charles bury her. They confirmed it after we arrested them."

"Was there a reason they chose Sand Key Park?"

"Robinson Jr. said it was his idea. He wanted to send a message to Robert Fitzgibbons."

"I'm guessing this message had something to do with Carly's aunt?"

"The story, as Robinson Jr. explained it, is that he talked Carrie Anne into having sex with both of them the night of the party. They were all drunk, according to him. He'd brought her to Sand Key by boat to impress her, and the three of them climbed aboard to go out in the Gulf. Once they lost sight of land and stopped, Carrie Anne decided she wanted nothing to do with Fitzgibbons, so he got mad and killed her."

"Why didn't Robinson Jr. try to stop him?"

"He said he did, but Fitzgibbons hit him so hard that he was unable to recover right away."

"How convenient."

"Fitzgibbons then struggled with Carrie Anne, punched her, and she hit her head on the starboard gunwale. When they determined she was dead, they panicked. They wrapped a nylon rope around her, weighted her down with two fluke anchors, and tossed her overboard."

Joe shook his head. "But the kids at the party swore Robinson Jr. had passed out. I read the report."

"That's what he told them, and they believed him. Everyone was drunk, remember? Then Robinson Jr. got this smug look on his face and said, 'She was a party girl with an unsavory reputation. No one was going to miss her.' I thought Carly was going to kill him. I had to grab her before she went over the table after him."

"What an incredible story."

David didn't say anything for a few seconds. "If it isn't a fabrication. We don't know what really happened in either case. Boyd Robinson Jr. could be as big a liar as Carter Fitzgibbons."

Joe paused, still mulling over all he'd heard. "David, did you ever find out if there was a snitch in your office?"

"Yeah. It was Cliff Parton. A janitor caught him at my desk one night. Carly got him to admit that he was paid off by Robinson Jr."

"Cliff?" Joe shook his head. "I would never have suspected him."

"We didn't, either."

"Guess that's the end of his career."

David shrugged. "He should have thought about that sooner."

Joe thanked him and got up.

He and Dani exchanged smiles as they passed each other.

Christine leaned into him as soon as he sat down. "You're my hero."

"I am?"

"Dani told me how you saved her life. You just can't help yourself, can you?"

"I guess not."

The captain gradually backed off on the throttle, shut down the engine, and brought the boat about. The foursome stood up. Along with the captain, they moved toward the bow.

Carly and Randall were standing port side. Carly was holding a lei of pink, yellow, and white plumeria. She set her gaze on the sun kissing the horizon. Then she looked down at the lei.

"I never knew my aunt Carrie Anne Jernigan, but I wish I'd had the chance. Regardless of who she was or how she chose to live her life, she didn't deserve to die so young. Though Uncle Randy and I are the only immediate family members present, I know the rest of our family and friends are happy that we are finally able to know the truth. Rest in peace, Carrie Anne."

She tossed the lei into the water. The others solemnly looked on as the ring of flowers drifted off toward the sun.

ACKNOWLEDGMENTS

Thanks to George Salter, Claire Kemp, Theresa R. Richardson, D.T. Bush, Sue Lloyd-Davies, Patricia Grayson, Heloise Jones, Tom Horrigan, Joyce Wagner, the Gulfport Fiction Writers, David Mather and the Gulfport Public Library, Technical Advisors Rod Steckel and Ken Beaudoin, Alex Cameron, Dia and the wonderful folks at the Neptune Bar and Grill, and Gini and Mike of the Beach Bazaar. Special thanks to Lynn Taylor, Steph Post, Jeffery Hess, and Johnnie M. Clark for their guidance, support, and friendship. Many thanks to my dear friends Mike O'Malley, John and Nancy Lamson, Al and Nancy Karnavicius, Rim Karnavicius and Michelle Rego, Charles Lyon, and Jim and Debby Herden. And most of all, I wish to express my grateful appreciation for my family.

Photo credit Sue Lloyd-Davies

STEPHEN BURDICK was born and raised in Florida. He is a retired civil servant currently living in the Tampa Bay area. He enjoys getting together with friends and attending various events.

On the following pages are a few
more great titles from the
Down & Out Books publishing family.

For a complete list of books and to
sign up for our newsletter,
go to DownAndOutBooks.com.

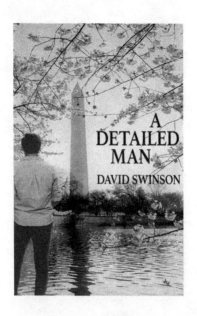

A Detailed Man
David Swinson

Down & Out Books
January 2023
978-1-64396-297-9

Half of DC Police Detective Ezra Simeon's face is immobilized from a persistent case of Bell's Palsy—he must drink through a straw and eat carefully to avoid chewing through his own cheek. He has been detailed from robbery to the cold case squad while he heals.

Detective Simeon's half-frozen world begins to heat up when a friend from his Academy days drops dead of a heart attack, and Sim is tapped to replace him, detailed now to homicide, where he inherits the high-profile case of a murdered escort he alone thinks may be the victim of a serial killer.

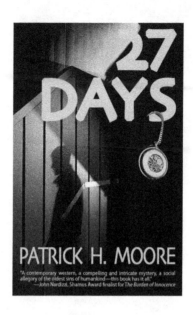

27 Days
A Nick Crane Thriller
Patrick H. Moore

Down & Out Books
February 2023
978-1-64396-298-6

27 Days is a topical political thriller in which veteran Los Angeles PI Nick Crane races against time to save his partner Bobby Moore, who has been abducted by a powerful right wing domestic terrorist named Marguerite Ferguson.

If Nick doesn't surrender to Marguerite within twenty-seven days, Bobby Moore will be sent to Scorpion Prison in Egypt where he will be tortured and killed.

Quietly Into the Night
Vincent Zandri

Down & Out Books
February 2023
978-1-64396-299-3

A bestselling author wakes up on a train and has no idea how he got there. When he finds himself accused of throwing a fellow author off the balcony of a New York City high-rise apartment building, he now must battle not only memory loss, but he must also fight for his very life.

From *New York Times* and *USA Today* bestselling Thriller and Shamus Award-winning author Vincent Zandri comes a novel of deception, murder, and double-crosses that only Alfred Hitchcock could concoct.

Right Between the Eyes
Scott Loring Sanders

Down & Out Books
February 2023
978-1-64396-300-6

When a young girl is abducted in an historic New England town in 1981, a family seeks full and total revenge.

Decades later, when two boys skip school to go fishing at Thoreau's iconic Walden Pond, instead of catching a trophy bass, they reel in a human skull which once again brings to the forefront a litany of wicked lies and murderous betrayal.